Flashes of Life

by

DeDe Ramey

Dalton Skies Series

Flashes of Life

Cover Art by *Kristian Norris*

The Wild Rose Press, Inc.
PO Box 708
Adams Basin, NY 14410-0708
Visit us at www.thewildrosepress.com

Publishing History
First Edition, 2023
Trade Paperback ISBN 978-1-5092-4716-5
Digital ISBN 978-1-5092-4717-2

Dalton Skies Series
Published in the United States of America

The tirade Mitch was on ripped at Jessi's heart like a wild animal. His hardened voice left no room for question and his eyes told her he was seconds from blowing up. She quickly stepped back and turned away; fear taking hold. Her arms wrapped her body and her voice quieted as she said, "Whether you believe I've been traumatized by this whole situation or not, I have. And you questioning my feelings isn't helping. I'm sorry if my feelings don't line up with how you think I should feel. The truth is, I do still have feelings for him. I care about him. We were together in a committed relationship for a long time. Those feelings don't just die overnight because he screwed up. And I realize it seems wrong, but I can't help it. My emotions are all over the place right now. My whole life was flipped upside down. And honestly, I am just trying to hang on to any strand of sanity I have." She wiped her cheek that was now wet from tears. The anger was gone from Mitch's eyes when her gaze returned to his and he reached for her, but she stepped back. She was overwhelmed as every memory from the last month seemed to hit all at once. All the pain. All the happiness. Everything was sending her into an emotional tailspin, and she was about to break. "I'm sorry Mitch. I can't."

"Jessi—"

"No. I need you to go. I'm done."

Praise for DeDe Ramey

Sleuths' Ink Author Award Winner

"This was one of the best suspenseful romances I have read in a very long time. I have a strong feeling that DeDe Ramey is going to make a name for herself with this book and the rest of the series."

~ *Confessions of Bookaholics*

Dedication

A huge thank you to the authors who have helped me in my journey, and those who helped bring this story to life. You are cherished friends.

Chapter One

Jessi Maddox stood at the window and searched the darkness for the fifth time since she got the call that they were on their way. Her tongue brushed against her swollen busted lip, and it sent a shooting pain through her cheek. The metal taste still lingered.

Beyond the streetlamp, at the edge of the small yard of the townhouse, the night sky twinkled with a scattering of stars. She had shared the place with her boyfriend of four years. Tonight though, was where it would end.

Her fingers lightly touched the bandage above her eye as she replayed the events of the evening. When she pulled them away, she realized her hands were still shaking. Curling them around her waist, she watched as the gauzy curtains billowed with the light breeze coming from the open window. *Please hurry.*

A pair of bright lights broke through the darkness, and then another, and then a third. Her heart thumped in a fevered pitch, and it took everything within her not to burst into tears. *Oh, thank God. Finally.* Jessi tugged opened the door and watched as the final truck backed a large flatbed trailer in front of her porch. She carefully stepped out onto the cold concrete not sure if her legs would hold her up.

A woman in her fifties with copper, shoulder length hair, exited the pickup with the flatbed, along with a tall burly man with a short beard. Jessi's throat thickened and she tightened her arms around herself trying to stop shaking. She told herself she wouldn't cry.

The older woman closed the space between them gently putting her hands up to Jessi's face. "Hey girl," was all her mom, Tess, had to say before tears pooled in Jessi's lashes and she collapsed into her. "It's going to be okay," Tess whispered, stroking her hand through Jessi's hair.

She had held it together for hours when the police arrived and escorted her boyfriend away. And later when she was at the hospital. But now that her parents had arrived, she couldn't fight off the sobs that stole her breath.

Jessi backed away, finally composing herself enough to give her mom a sad, crooked smile. Carefully wiping away her tears, she glanced up to see her dad, Tom Maddox, along with four twenty-something guys lined up behind him. "We got Rod's boys, and they brought two of their buddies to help."

"Hey, Daddy," Jessi said. Her voice sounded raspy, so she tried clearing her throat and realized how much it hurt. She was in so much pain.

Stepping closer, Tom narrowed his eyes as he studied her swollen and bruised face. "He better hope like hell he never crosses my path ever again." Gently grabbing her chin, he moved her head from side to side. "What did the doctor say?"

She stepped back, becoming uncomfortable with his scrutiny, and ushered the crew into the house. "Nothing's broken. They put some dissolvable stitches inside my lip."

Tom scoped out the room. "You've taken care of

everything with the police?"

"Yeah. He's there for the night at least."

"Then let's get this stuff loaded and get on the road." Tom walked through the living room into the kitchen. "Where do you want us to start?"

"There's not a whole lot that has to go right now. The place I am renting is partially furnished. I put pink sticky notes on all the furniture that goes, and I think I have everything else boxed up other than some clothes."

Walking through the rest of the house, Tom scanned the items then gave directions to the four boys, and they started loading the back of the trucks and trailer.

Jessi took a deep breath then winced in pain from her bruised ribs. She never would have dreamed anything like this would happen. When they met, Dante was sweet and caring. He treated her like she was his princess. His everything. It was like a fairy tale. She loved the way he doted on her, and wrote her sweet notes, sometimes hiding them where she would find them. And it hadn't been that long ago that she'd hoped he would ask her to marry him. And if he had, she would have said yes in a heartbeat. Now though, he barely resembled the man she met at the restaurant four years ago.

She glanced at the clock. It was well after midnight and would take a while to get all her belongings loaded. The trip to Dalton was going to be at least two full days pulling the trailer. She was still unsure about moving so far away. Nevertheless, she needed to disappear. Not only to get away from Dante, but also from his family. This move across the country would allow her to get away at least until she could figure something else out.

When things started to unravel between her and Dante, Jessi had confided to her mom. Her advice was to get out before she got hurt and asked her to consider moving to Arkansas after a friend said her sister had a job opportunity. At first, she said no. She enjoyed being close enough to visit family on the weekends and had hoped it would all blow over.

She knew things would be stressful when she found out Dante had lost his job. However, she figured it was only a matter of time before he found something. When the job didn't transpire after months of searching, he became desperate. He told her many times about how much he hated his uncle and would never work for him. But reluctantly, he accepted a position at his commercial construction company. She thought, maybe, he would work for him just long enough to find another job and then things would return to normal, although she should have known once he was in, there was no getting out, and things spiraled from bad to worse. She finally gave in and got the information for the job from her mom.

After calling the lady to discuss flying down to interview for the job, it became apparent that wouldn't be necessary when the woman offered her the job over the phone.

Still unsure, Jessi asked for some time to consider it. A couple of days later, the woman called unexpectedly, upping the ante. She had spoken to the owner of a new upscale restaurant in the area who jumped at the chance of having such a highly acclaimed sommelier on the premises. With both opportunities dropped in her lap, and knowing her situation was spinning out of control in Philadelphia, Jessi decided to delve further into the possibility of relocating. She made some phone calls on places to rent and found a nice one-bedroom cottage. It was time to relent to the idea of relocating. She needed to get away from the situation before it got worse. Unfortunately, it got worse before she could leave.

Jessi scanned the almost empty room as memories flashed like lightening through her mind. Some were sweet. Unfortunately, though, the bad ones, she feared, would leave lasting scars that she doubted would ever heal.

Tess passed by her carrying a couple of boxes. "Those have wine glasses in them. Let me get my keys so you can put them in my car." She quickly searched the room and located them on the end table. Walking to the open door, she hit the fob on the keyring and lights flashed on a deep blue sports car. "It's unlocked." Working as a sommelier at Austere Nouveau, one of the most exclusive restaurants in Philadelphia, had afforded her some of the finer things in life. The townhouse was hers as well as most of the stuff inside. Not that Dante had been living off her income. He did well for himself before the layoff. They had decided to live together in her townhouse because of its location. It wasn't quite downtown, although the community she was in allowed her all the creature comforts of living in the city without the traffic. It was within walking distance to coffee shops, restaurants, and grocery stores.

Moving to Dalton would be a huge change. The pay wouldn't be anything close to what she was making in Philadelphia. However, the cost of living wouldn't be as much either. The biggest change would be living in a rural community. She had gotten used to being able to walk to her favorite coffee shop and pick up ingredients she needed at the grocery store around the corner.

Being raised in a small town in Delaware, she moved to the city the first chance she got and loved it.

Now, she would have to reacclimate. Her new landlord did tell her the cottage was not far from town though.

Everything was happening so fast. Even though she knew she was leaving, her plans were to do it in a couple of weeks which would have given her time to talk to Dante and tell him when the time was right. Now, she was running for her life.

Voices from outside drifted through the open front door. She could hear her dad giving the boys instructions. A couple of smaller boxes sat on the dining room table that she thought would fit in the backseat of her car. She reached to pick them up and pain shot through her body causing her to drop them, and immediately reminded her of why she was leaving.

Visions from earlier in the evening rushed in. Dante had come home early, already drunk and upset. When she asked him what was wrong, he didn't answer. Jessi knew not to push him, so she walked away hoping he would pass out and sleep it off.

Busying herself cleaning the kitchen and doing the laundry, she returned to the living room with a basket of clothes, to put away upstairs, and brushed against a small end table at the end of the sofa, tipping it over. The lamp that was sitting on it fell to the floor. Jessi jumped at the noise then noticed a black pistol lying at the base of the lamp. Dante had a gun in the house. So did she. This one wasn't his. At least not the one she knew about. He'd obviously hidden it. His glassy hollow eyes cut to her, and she stopped. Her breath stalled in her lungs as her thoughts whipped like the wind wondering if he was protecting himself or using it for something much more nefarious. The storm brewing in his gaze had her pulse thumping in her ears. His jaw ticked and in a flash, he leaped over the back of the sofa and grabbed the gun off the floor. His eyes flicked back to her and the demon staring into her soul bore no resemblance to the man she'd loved.

Dropping the basket between them, she ran, hoping to make it to the bathroom where she could lock the door, but he quickly caught her by the ankle. She fought to get away, kicking at him and twisting. He was too strong. Little by little he dragged her to him. The first time he backhanded her, it was like something snapped inside him and he couldn't stop.

Tom's voice pulled her from her thoughts. "Go through and see if we missed anything. I'm going to go strap everything down."

Jessi headed upstairs checking each room, each closet, each drawer, then did the same on the lower level. "I think we have everything I need for now," she said stepping into the open doorway. The coolness of the breeze had her wrapping her arms around herself as she watched her dad cinch the tie-down straps.

Tom eyed her in the doorway. "Okay. Lock it up and let's get rolling." His focus moved across the parking lot. "I think you need to let Tyler drive." Before the words were out of his mouth her head was shaking. No one drove her car. Well, no one except Dante, and her. Tom softened his voice, obviously seeing the pain in her eyes, adding, "We need to get as far as we can before we stop, Jessi. Tyler slept on the way over so he should be able to handle it."

Her gaze tracked to the young man leaning against his truck talking to his brother and the two other boys. He had been a hired hand on her family's small farm since he was barely a teenager. He was like a little brother. Now, in his twenties, he still looked like a boy to her, even though there was only six years difference in their ages. Could she trust him to drive her baby? She knew if she told her dad no, he would try to convince her, and she really didn't have the strength or the desire to argue. "Okay."

Tom glanced over at Tyler and jerked his head when he caught Tyler's attention. The slender young man with spikey blond hair immediately headed their way. "You good driving her car? It's manual transmission."

Tyler nodded. "Yeah, my truck is manual."

Jessi broke in. "It's kind of finicky."

Tyler smirked. "Don't worry. I will be gentle."

She hesitantly handed over her keys.

Tom walked away. "Let's get going. It's already breaking daylight," he called back over his shoulder.

Jessi scanned the townhouse one last time then shut the door. A rock settled in her gut as she walked away. Tears filled her eyes and Tyler quickly turned to Tom. "We are taking fifty-five south, right?"

"Yeah. Tanner will be behind you. Mike and Wayne will be behind him, and I will bring up the rear. You have everyone's number in your phone?"

"Yep."

"Great." Tom turned and hopped into his truck.

Jessi wiped her cheeks and glanced at Tyler, then they both pulled open the doors of the Jaguar. Tyler started the car and revved the engine. Jessi cut her eyes to him, giving him a warning. A cocky grin spread across his face before he slowly drove away. Her stomach tightened and cheeks puffed before she let out a long sigh realizing what they had just set in motion.

****

Raindrops splattered against the windshield outside of Rolla Missouri. The musty scent penetrated the interior of the car. It had been a long drive, at least the portion that she was awake. She had no idea where they were when they stopped for the night, and she didn't care. Nor did she care when her parents made her sleep in their room so they could keep an eye on her. Everything going on around her seemed surreal, almost like she was in a dream, although this one was more of a nightmare that she couldn't seem to wake up from.

The next day they had gotten up early and continued the journey. Tyler had been a good travel partner, letting her rest, and talking only when she had started the conversation. And they had had some good conversations. He even had her laughing at some of his crazy stories. Although, she could tell, he was a bit lost for what to do when she woke to his panicked voice after falling asleep. He'd pulled over when he said she started screaming. Once she'd reassured him it was a bad dream and she was okay, he hesitantly got back on the road.

When they stopped at the rest stop to eat, he moved to his pickup to give her some space. Or maybe it was to give him some. She wasn't sure. Either way, it was a sweet gesture and immediately made her sad. She remembered when Dante was thoughtful like that. When he would do anything to make her smile. She closed her eyes hoping to get a short nap, but she couldn't keep the tears from falling. Like every other time she thought of him.

It was one in the afternoon when they hit the road again. They expected to be in Dalton around five. Her landlord said he would be around when she called him.

The closer they got to Dalton the more isolated it

seemed. However, taking in the scenery calmed her broken spirit. Tall pine trees and rolling hills dotted the landscape. It was breathtaking. As the sun drifted lower on the horizon, it cast a mix of pinks and purples and blues across the sky. It was so different from the cityscape she was used to.

Tyler swerved hard, and Jessi was thrown up against the side window.

"Sorry. Are you okay? The truck ahead of us lost a bucket." His eyes darted to the rearview mirror. "Damn. I think Tom hit it." Jessi spun in her seat and watched as her dad fought to regain control of the truck and trailer.

Tyler slowed as more and more buildings appeared along the side of the road and the car rolled to a stop at a light. Jessi took in all the old buildings with antique streetlamps holding baskets of flowers and pink blossomed bushes lining the sidewalks. Cars were parked at an angle and people sat in front of the stores talking. Jessi was surprised when a spark of excitement shot through her. *This is kind of a quaint little town.*

"What's the address?" Tyler asked.

Confused, Jessi asked, "Is this Dalton?" Her voice came out more enthusiastic than she expected.

"Yep."

Retrieving her phone and tapping the screen a couple of times, she responded. "It's 209 Spruce."

The light changed to green, and he pulled away. "Would you mind giving me directions?"

"Oh, duh. Sure." She tapped the address into the map app on her phone, then paused. "Okay, at the next light take a right." He did as she instructed. "The next street should be tenth and take a left, then Spruce is the next right, and the house is on the left."

Within minutes they arrived at a red brick, two-story colonial with a long driveway that angled up in the back. The truck with the trailer pulled up halfway into the driveway. Jessi's eyes met Tyler's. "How bad do I look?"

"Um…do you want the truth?"

"I just don't want to scare the guy."

"What did you tell him on the phone?"

"My plans had changed, and I needed the place now?"

"I would go with the truth and see what happens."

"Yeah, I'm sure, since he knows where I'm from, and the urgency of the move, once he sees my face, he will probably figure it out. Anything else I could tell him would sound like a lie. And it would be."

She eased out of the car and slowly stood, groaning from the pain shooting through her body. Heading up the sidewalk, she saw an older, gray-headed man push open the door.

"Hello," he said cheerily, though his voice faded quickly as she approached. He studied her face. "Are you Jessica?"

"I am." Heat rushed to her face. "I'm sorry for my appearance. It's kind of the reason I needed to move so quickly. I hope it doesn't change anything."

The older gentleman was silent, and Jessi began to worry.

"I'm so sorry that happened to you. I'm Dale Adkins. Come on in."

She glanced back at the trucks and held up a finger, then entered the house. Within a few minutes she had the keys to the small cottage that sat on the other side of the driveway. As she crossed the grass, she directed the truck with the trailer to pull up closer to the cottage. When it started to move, a box slid off the back, onto the concrete followed by a second. Tyler picked them up on his way to the cottage. Studying the empty straps, he hesitantly commented, "Uh. Jessi? I think we might have a problem." She came around the front of the truck and saw the uneasiness on his face.

"What is it?"

He held up the empty straps. "I think you might have lost some of your stuff."

"Dammit. Are you sure?"

"Well, there was something here, or there wouldn't be a strap. So, yeah."

Tom hopped out of the truck and Jessi's eyes darted to him. "Dad, do you remember what was on the end of the trailer?"

His mouth pulled to one side as he thought. "No. Why?"

"Because a couple of boxes fell out when you drove up the driveway and Tyler thinks something might have slipped the strap."

Tom searched the items on the trailer. "I want to say we had a good-sized box on the end. Check and see if it is in the back of the trucks." Jessi skimmed the loads in the trucks and didn't see a large box. It didn't mean it wasn't there. The boys had packed her stuff so tightly she couldn't really tell where anything was.

"Let's get this stuff unpacked and maybe I can see what is missing." She spun around and unlocked the heavy wooden door to the cottage and pushed it open. Windows were everywhere covered in white muslin drapes with sheer teal insets. The floors were scraped hardwood in a mix of dark and light stains. Thick beams adorned the ceiling. There was an off-white overstuffed sectional facing a fireplace that had a sturdy slate mantel. A small wooden end table sat on one end of the sectional with two teal barrel chairs on the other side.

Set off to one side, behind the living room, was the kitchen. The bar had pendent lights hanging above it and two small rectangular skylights inset in the ceiling. It wasn't a huge kitchen, although it was larger than she expected.

Between the living room and kitchen, was a small dining area with a whitewashed wooden table and two rattan chairs. Above it hung a teal chandelier. It was so different than what she had imagined. It felt peaceful. Tom walked in followed by Tess and the boys.

"This used to be a garden shed," a voice behind her said. She turned to see her landlord, Dale. "When we bought the house, it was filled to the brim with old junk. We dug everything out and thought maybe we would use it, but neither of us had green thumbs. So after it sat here for a while, we decided to remodel it and use it as a guesthouse. My granddaughter lived in it for a few years. She moved out a few weeks ago. Most of this stuff is hers, so if you don't need it let me know. I can have her, or her husband come and get it."

"It's beautiful. I love all the windows."

"My granddaughter said it was a bit drafty, so I had new windows put in. Hopefully that will help."

"I'm sure it will be fine. I really appreciate you letting me move in on such short notice."

"Oh, it wasn't a problem at all. It was sitting empty." Silence fell between them. Dale watched as Tom and two of the boys filed by with their hands full of boxes. "Well, I better let you get to unpacking. Let me know if you need anything."

Tom set his boxes down and held out his hand. "Tom Maddox."

"Dale Adkins. I'm guessing this is your daughter." Tom nodded. "I was telling her my granddaughter just moved out of here a few weeks ago. Most of the furniture is hers, so if you guys find you don't need something, let me know and we can move it out."

With a quick scan of the room, Tom's attention fell back on Dale. "This place is really nice."

"Thank you. We decided it was crazy to use it for storage since we already had a barn out back, and knew we weren't going to be using it for what it was intended to be, so we figured we'd turn it into a guest house. At some point we discussed renting it out to have a little added income." Dale smiled at Jessi. "You, young lady, are my first renter."

Tess walked up next to Tom. "You wouldn't by chance know of a hotel nearby, would you? We had a long drive and once we get her settled, we will need to find a place to stay."

"We only have one hotel in town now, and honestly, I wouldn't recommend it. There's plenty in Fayetteville of course if you're willing to drive the thirty miles. We had an old historic hotel that was nice, but it's going to be converted into a senior complex. They shot a movie in it recently." He paused for a moment. "You're welcome to stay at my house. I have plenty of bedrooms."

"Oh no. We couldn't ask you to do that. You have already been too kind letting Jessi come in early."

"I'm in the process of making it into a bed and breakfast, so it's perfectly fine. My wife and I live a couple of miles away. The beds and baths have clean linens and towels. I'll make you some sandwiches while you unpack. Betty, my wife, can come over in the morning and make you breakfast."

"Are you sure?"

"Absolutely." Dale's eyes fixed on Jessi as he spoke. "You guys seem like good people and I'm sure, under the circumstances, she would like to have you close for as long as possible." His focus swung back to Tess. "I'll leave the back door open. There are two bedrooms and baths downstairs. Three bedrooms and baths upstairs. Make sure to lock up when you are in for the night."

Tess lifted a brow, questioning Tom, who shrugged, and her attention returned to Dale. "That sounds perfect."

"Good." Dale walked out the door. "I will be back in a few minutes with sandwiches for you."

"Oh, you don't—" Tess stopped mid-sentence when she noticed he had already disappeared.

Jessi headed up the hallway by the kitchen and opened each door finding a large linen closet, a bathroom, and at the end of the hallway a large bedroom. A smile spread across her face. She wasn't expecting much out of the place, so she was pleasantly surprised at how warm and cozy it felt. And she loved how secluded it was. When she returned to the living room the guys had already unloaded several boxes. Tyler came through with a large box. "Where do you want this? It says paperwork?"

"Oh, that's my office stuff." She spun her head around then pointed beside the sectional. "Put it down there. I will have to figure out where I want my desk to go later.

Boxes piled up in every corner of the cottage. Jessi and her mom were already unpacking items when Dale returned with the sandwiches. They thanked him again and divvied up the sandwiches. By the time all the trucks and the trailer were unloaded it was nearly eleven and exhaustion had set in. Jessi took in her new home. It looked like a bomb had gone off. There wasn't a flat surface visible. Pieces of newspaper filled the kitchen floor and counters. Luckily her mom had insisted that they put her bed together and she made it up so she would have a place to sleep.

When everyone finally left for the night, she dug through her clothes and found a pair of flannel pajama pants and a T-shirt and put them on. Crawling into bed, she snuggled into her favorite pillow ready to fall asleep. Inhaling a deep breath, she felt her heart twinge. The pillow smelled like Dante.

Chapter Two

"All units, all units we have a report of debris in the road, southbound highway fifty-one, mile marker thirty-six."

Mitch Gallagher's eyes scanned the area as he keyed his mic. "Four twenty-nine responding." His hand palmed the steering wheel, and he whipped the car around, heading up the road, away from the streetlights surrounding Dalton's downtown. It had been a quiet night. Mitch was ready for it to be over. His mind played through the events that were about to turn his life upside down.

He had joint custody of his two kids after divorcing his wife Lorrie four years ago. Tomorrow, he would officially have them full time. His gut tightened at the thought. It had been months of planning and preparing. He had hired his buddy, Joe, to do a little light remodeling of his house just to make sure their rooms were exactly how they wanted them. He'd also found a teacher living a few streets over from him, with five kids, two similar in age to his, who agreed to watch his son and daughter while he was at work, since they were on summer break. The only thing he had left to do before heading to the airport to pick them up, was stock up on groceries. He would do that in the morning.

Mile marker thirty-two flew by and he slowed his speed. As he approached the area, he flipped his strobes on and shined his spotlight. Near the shoulder of the road was a large cardboard box, plus a couple of smaller ones off in the grass. Mitch eased off into the gravel shoulder leaving the car running. His headlights shined on the objects. The larger box had busted, spilling some papers, so he figured he would retrieve the smaller ones first.

Stacking one on top of the other, he carried them to the car, setting them on the trunk before heading back to the larger one. Several papers had blown into the median and out onto the road. He grabbed his flashlight to get a better idea of how many and how far they had blown. His eyes darted to the road as a paper flew up when a car passed by. Collecting the first few papers, he quickly realized they were photos, so he intensified his search, gathering as many as he could find. Carefully shining his flashlight over the area one last time, he trekked back over to the box. The bottom was busted through, so he had to man handle it to get it back to the car.

Tossing the loose photos into the front seat through the window, Mitch then opened the back passenger door and shoved the box in, setting the two other boxes on top. Once he was back in the car, his eyes drifted to one of the photos in the seat, and he picked it up to study it. The woman in the photo had a swollen eye, bloodied nose and lip, and the start of bruising along her jaw and neck. Mitch knew what those injuries usually stemmed from. Reaching for the rest of the photos, he thumbed through them and found several showing different areas of her body where she had red marks, scratches and bruises. His jaw clenched as anger roiled in his gut.

Other photos appeared to be fun snapshots with friends. He stopped on one that might have been taken when she was a bit younger. She wore a scoop neck, tightly fitted, T-shirt with a pi sign on it, tied at the waist. Her hair was the color of dark brown sugar, and her bright smile was surrounded by a pair of blush pink lips. She held a tray with a large pizza out to the side. He swallowed hard. Who in their right mind would hurt her? He set the photos back in the seat.

Throwing the car in drive, he pulled out slowly leaving his high beams on to try to spot any wayward photos he might have missed. After a mile or so, he flipped around and checked the other side of the road in case some blew that direction. He needed to make sure none of the photos were left behind in case the injuries to her were man made, which he was certain they were. Sweeping the area a couple more times, he deemed it clear and headed back to the station.

Once he had the boxes safely in his office, he retrieved the loose photos and sifted through them again trying to find any clue as to the identity of the woman. The photos of the injuries were taken from a non-descript bedroom. There was nothing in the background that gave him any clues. The photos of her with her friends were at a restaurant although there was nothing, he could make out, to give him a name. The older photo of her holding the pizza looked like one of the popular chains. Even if he found the name it would take forever to find out which one she worked at.

He ripped open the top of the busted box and found several photo albums along with some framed photos on top of more loose photos. One of the framed photos was of her holding a cream-colored cocker spaniel puppy, and the other, more of a shadow box of the cocker spaniel only older. At the base of the frame was a collar with a tag. "Layla." "Who is your mommy, Layla?" he said out loud.

Digging through the box, he found several photo albums and began flipping through pages of baby photos and photos of a cherub faced brown headed toddler. There were family photos with her and two other girls, maybe a bit older, with lighter colored hair, a man with a beard and a woman with fiery red hair. As he flipped from page to page, he watched as the toddler grew into a little girl then grew into a teenager.

The second album was more of a scrapbook filled with memorabilia, patches from contests, playbills, and programs from productions and concerts. He picked up one of the programs. It appeared to be a concert program from Dover, Delaware. Checking others, he noticed many from around the same area. Still, nothing to tell him who she was.

The last album was filled with photos and memorabilia from around the world. "Well, she traveled. That's for sure." Still, nothing that gave him her name or got him any closer to finding out where she might have been going. *If she was from somewhere in Delaware, how did her stuff get here. Is she here? Is she running?*

The noise of a heavy door shutting, and steps drawing closer, had him shifting his focus to his open door. "Hey, Mitch, are you planning on going home?" Garrett Cleveland, a patrol officer stood in Mitch's doorway.

Mitch dug for his phone and checked the time. It was nearly one in the morning. His shift ended at midnight. "Yeah. I got distracted trying to solve a mystery." He motioned with his hand over the items strewn across his desk.

"What is it?"

"I'm trying to find out who this stuff belongs to. It was dumped on the side of fifty-one."

Garrett scanned the photos, and his brows drew together as his eyes landed on a photo showing the woman with a swollen eye. He picked it up and studied it shaking his head. "Have you checked with the hospitals?"

"Not yet." Mitch stood from his desk and walked around it. Garrett dropped the photo back into the rest of the pile and followed him out the door. "I'm done for the night. I'll pick up where I left off when I get back."

He found himself thinking about the photos on his way home and decided to drive by the spot once more in case the woman in the photos realized her things were missing and came to search for them. There were no cars stopped on the side of the road, so he headed home.

****

The light penetrated the crack between the slats in the blinds over the window, shooting a beam across Mitch's face. He barely peeled his eyes open then snapped them shut. His fingers and thumb rubbed the sleep from his eyes, and he slowly blinked them open again. Picking his phone up from the nightstand, he noticed it was already after eight. His thoughts went back to the night before and the haunting images of the woman in the photos. He needed to find her and give her back her stuff. And also make sure she wasn't in danger, and she was okay. He was very familiar with domestic assault and had dealt with more cases than he cared to remember. Most were cut and dried cases. There was a victim and an assailant. This was different. All he had was the evidence. He wanted to go into the office to search for more clues and maybe come up with a plan to find her, but his day was already full.

Reaching for his sweatpants at the end of the bed, he sat up, letting his head clear, before putting one foot in each hole and dragging them to his hips and tying a knot.

A yawn escaped as he strolled into the kitchen and pulled open the refrigerator. On the center shelf was a half empty container of milk and a carton with three eggs. He glanced at the rest of the offerings. A bottle of ketchup, a small bag of Colby cheese, two apples and a container of leftovers from his favorite Mexican food restaurant. It wasn't good anymore, but garbage pickup wasn't for two more days. Grabbing the milk, he opened the jug and drained it, then stared into the refrigerator hoping, by some bit of magic, it would be filled with something to satisfy his hunger. No such luck. He needed to get groceries. An irritated groan escaped. He despised shopping and had no idea what the kids liked other than mac 'n' cheese and chicken nuggets.

It was still a few hours before he needed to be at the airport, so he figured he could spend an hour at the office searching through the boxes, and calling the hospital, then hit the grocery store. It would still leave him enough time to run the groceries home and make it to the airport in time to pick up the kids. *Sounds like a plan.* He threw the carton of milk in the trash and headed for the bathroom.

Once he'd showered and dressed, he picked up his keys, perched his sunglasses on his damp hair, and punched the button to the garage door.

The air was filled with the smell of fresh mowed grass as the door slowly rose. Cranking the engine to his bright blue Camaro, he settled in the seat listening to the low growl. He never got tired of the sound. It was part of his buddy, Cody's, late father's estate. The car was in mint condition, and Cody let him have it for a steal.

Rolling through the downtown area, he parked in front of a small storefront with a large sign shaped like a sombrero above the door with Tia Luna scrolled in bright red letters. It was his favorite place to get breakfast tacos. Minutes later, with a bag of tacos in his hand, he headed to the office. His fingers tapped the steering wheel to the Brantley Gilbert song "Bullet in a Bonfire" and his thoughts returned to the photos. He wanted to kick the ass of whoever left those injuries on the woman. Sure, she might have gotten them in a car accident, or some other accident. But his money was on an assault. Why would there be pictures of it otherwise? And the fear in her eyes was unmistakable. It was strange having such a visceral reaction, since he had no idea who she was. But no one deserved to be beaten like that.

When he came to the stop sign where he needed to turn, he instead went straight, taking the road out to the highway to check the area in the daylight. As he approached the location, he noticed a dark blue Jaguar slowly leaving the shoulder, heading the other direction. Jaguars were not a common car in the small town, and his heart skipped with the thought that it might be the owner of the photos. He sped up to get to the turnaround before he lost the car. Making a U turn, he increased his speed hoping to catch up. He tried to keep his speed in check realizing he was not in his police cruiser, except the car was starting to get away. As he entered the downtown area again, he prayed the stoplight would be on his side and stop the car. Seeing the red light in view, there was a glimmer of hope. The light turned green, and it looked like the car turned right, so once he got to the intersection he did too. Each street he passed he searched for the car, but it had vanished. Slowly, he cruised to the downtown area and let out a disappointed sigh. "Dammit."

Glancing at his dashboard, he checked the time. His fingers dug though his hair, and he realized he had wasted the time he was planning to use to search through the stuff at his office. At least he might have a possible lead. It was a long shot, but better than nothing. Making a left on Pecan, he headed for the grocery store which was a couple of blocks away. As he drove into the parking lot, his phone buzzed.

—*We are getting ready to board the plane*—

He had thought long and hard about giving his ten-year-old son Brandon a phone for Christmas. Although he had always been responsible, he was still only ten. In the end though, he was glad he chose to, for moments like this. He walked toward the entrance to the grocery store trying to text him back.

— *That's great. I will be there when you land. I'm at the store getting some groceries so let me know what you and your sister want to eat*—

He shoved the phone back in his pocket, pushed his sunglasses on top of his head and grabbed a buggy. His eyes darted around the store as he tried to find the best place to start. Seldom cooking for himself since he lived alone, he had to admit, when the kids were there, he cooked stuff that was easy. Pizza, hot dogs, chicken nuggets, and fries. Now though, he was going to have them full time and he wanted to step up his game and do it right. He had a nice grill that had barely been used, so he headed for the meat section first.

He grabbed some steaks and chicken thighs and then

noticed the pork ribs and threw them in the buggy too. For the summer, he figured, it would be easy to throw something on the grill. His phone buzzed again.

— *Pizza and spaghetti for Georgia...and chicken nuggets. I like pizza and hamburgers, mac n cheese, ice cream, hotdogs, and be sure and get some root beer. Gotta go they said we have to turn our devices off—*

Lord. Lorrie must not be feeding them any better than me. Either that, or they are taking advantage of living with Dad. He found some noodles for spaghetti, and sauce, some rice, baked beans, lunch meat for sandwiches. Anything that caught his eye went into the buggy. He strolled back up to the produce, realizing most of what he had in the buggy was meat or starches, and picked up some celery, carrots, broccoli, cucumbers, tomatoes, and onions, then moved on to the fruit. Lost for a moment, staring at the different types of apples, he was drawn from his daze when he heard someone clear their throat.

A woman, wearing sunglasses and a ballcap, was pointing at the apples he was standing in front of. Her chestnut brown hair was in a ponytail draped through the back of the cap. She wore skin-tight jeans with a white V-necked T-shirt that read, "Wine. Because adulting is hard." Everything hugged her in the right spots and when Mitch's eyes finally locked onto her face, he winced, realizing from the scowl, he probably took a little longer than he should have staring at her.

With heat crawling up his neck, Mitch pushed his buggy out of the way and responded with an apologetic, "Sorry," adding a slight smile that she didn't return. "There are so many to choose from," he continued. Still nothing. Deciding to cut his losses, he moved away to the bananas, finding a nice bunch that were slightly green on the edges. He added a large carton of red grapes to the buggy, while catching a glimpse of the woman who was still picking out apples. Now *she* was hogging the apple stand. The more he focused on her, the more something didn't sit right with him. She loaded a few apples in a plastic bag and pushed away with her cart. He returned to the apples to get a few, and as she disappeared around the corner, it hit him. Sunglasses. Why was she wearing sunglasses inside the store?

His eyes scanned the area to see if she was still around. Pushing his cart down the aisles, he searched each one to see if he could find her. Out of the corner of his eye he spotted her standing at the self-checkout. Racing up the aisle, he noticed all the self-check machines were full, so he found a cashier open a few rows down. His attention remained on her while the cashier scanned his groceries. She moved out of the lane, headed for the door, and his eyes darted to the peppered haired cashier in front of him trying to will her to speed up. With the last bag loaded, he walked quickly out of the lane and nearly took out a small boy who had escaped from his mom.

Racing out the door he scanned the parking lot. Two cars down from his he saw her loading groceries in the back of her dark blue Jaguar. *Bingo! It's her. It has to be.* He pushed his cart quickly up the row of cars and saw her gaze in his direction. She moved around the car keeping her focus on him as she climbed in and slammed the door. The reverse lights flicked on, and he broke into a jog hoping he wouldn't lose her again. Stopping the cart behind her car he prayed she wouldn't run over him and the food. She glared at him through the rear window and waved her hand signaling him to move.

"Mind moving your cart?" she yelled.

He put his hands on his knees trying to catch his breath and slowly stood. "I need to ask you if you—"

"Move it or I'll run it over," she growled.

Something about her sass had him biting back a smile as he walked to the driver's side window. "No. I don't think you will. Not in this car. I just need to find out—"

"Move your shit dammit, or I'll call the cops." This time he did smile.

"I am the cops. Could you please just roll your window down, I need to—"

"Sure, you are."

He had to admit, she did take her safety seriously. He figured whoever gave her the bruises, that he now saw through the window, had something to do with it.

He sighed. "Look. I found a box—"

He was so focused on trying to talk to her he didn't notice the car ahead of her start to move. As it did, so did she. With a crooked smirk and wave, she quickly drove out of the space and through the parking lot.

His hands flew up in frustration. "Well, shit." He tugged the cart to his car and loaded his groceries as quickly as possible trying to keep an eye on where she was going. Once everything was loaded, he raced through the lot and out the exit she took, but she was nowhere in sight. His fingers dug into his hair then his hand slammed against the steering wheel. "I nearly had her."

Once the groceries were dropped off and put away, he took off up the highway toward Fayetteville. It had been nearly two months since he had seen his kids.

27

During a previous visit, his ex-wife informed him that she was getting remarried. It didn't come as a shock since she had been dating the guy for over a year. He seemed like a good guy and the kids liked him. What did shock him was when she told him they were planning on moving to Poland where his company had bought a plastics plant that they wanted him to manage. Mitch was ready to put up a fight for the kids. However, Lorrie quickly suggested it would be best if the kids stayed in America to go to school. She said the company paid for trips to the U.S. every three months so she would be able to fly back to see them.

Even though they had worked out a plan where he normally got to see the kids when his days off fell on the weekend, he agreed to let her have more time with them since she was going to be leaving. They sat down together with the kids to tell them about the move, and he was pleasantly surprised that they were excited about coming to live with him full time, which made it even harder for him to be without them for so long.

Pulling into short-term parking at the airport, he had twenty minutes to spare before their flight arrived. After clearing security, he was allowed to go to the gate where their plane had just landed. His hands shoved deep in his pockets, and he waited. Soon, voices could be heard coming from the jetway. People carrying bags filed out into the terminal. Mitch kept scanning the crowd hoping to see familiar faces. Minutes passed and anxiety took over when the groups of people leaving the plane became a trickle. Finally, he saw a woman in a blue uniform walking up the jetway talking to two very happy kids with backpacks, appearing like they just left school. Brandon saw Mitch first. "Dad! We got to sit in the cockpit and talk to the pilots."

Mitch's eyes locked on him. "I bet that was cool." A knot immediately lodged in his throat as Georgia, his six-year-old daughter, ran to him with her arms spread wide. Mitch opened his arms as she leaped and wrapped herself around him like a koala bear.

"Mr. Harvey even let me steer."

"And you still made it here safely."

"I guess these two troublemakers are yours?" The flight attendant teased.

"Uh. Depends. How much trouble are they in?"

Georgia smiled at the flight attendant. "We were good. Weren't we Miss Arlene?"

She winked at Georgia who was still clinging to Mitch and smiled. "The best."

"See, Daddy. We were good." Mitch heard a distinct lisp when she spoke and noticed her two front teeth missing.

"You lost your teeth." She smiled, happily revealing the space in the front of her mouth. Mitch opened his eyes wide and dropped his jaw in animated fashion which made Georgia giggle. Then his attention returned to the flight attendant. "Thank you for taking care of them," Mitch said as they walked up the corridor.

"Oh, I was happy to do it. The kids were great."

"Did you get the root beer?" Brandon broke in.

"Shoot. No, I didn't." His thoughts flashed to the woman who distracted him at the store, and he wondered how he was going to solve the mystery. Glancing back at Brandon who had a discouraged expression, he said, "I guess we will have to make a trip to the grocery store later."

The flight attendant leaned in and cupped her hand

against her face. "He had two on the flight," she said in a loud whisper. Brandon glared at her as his mouth formed a straight line.

"Ah. Maybe we can wait on the trip to the store then," Mitch said squeezing Brandon's shoulder. "I was thinking maybe we could run and get some burgers at 'All the Fixins' grill though."

"Okay," Brandon responded with a smile.

"Well, I think you guys are in good hands." The flight attendant said and stopped. "I need to go get my luggage, so I will need for you to sign off on their claim sheets."

Mitch stopped and lowered Georgia to the ground. "I'm sorry. This is the first—"

"Oh, no. Don't apologize." She reached into the plastic pouch hanging around Brandon's neck then the one hanging around Georgia's. "I need to see your I.D. and then you will sign the sheet showing you picked them up." Mitch retrieved his wallet and showed her his I.D. while she reached in her pocket and retrieved a pen. Studying the I.D. and the papers, her face reflected a satisfied expression, and she handed him the pen and the two papers. He scribbled his name and handed them back to her.

"Thanks again for taking care of them."

She folded the papers and stuffed them into her pocket with the pen. "Oh, it was my pleasure. I hope you guys fly with us again soon." Waving goodbye, she stepped on the escalator and smiled back at them.

Mitch turned to Brandon. "You guys don't have luggage, do you?"

Brandon shook his head. "Mom said she was sending a couple of boxes."

"Yeah. They're supposed to arrive Tuesday. I think everything else you have is already here." They exited the terminal and waited for the crossing guard to wave them through before they stepped out onto the street. Mitch reached for Georgia's hand, glanced down at her, and watched her honey-colored curls bounce. Her hair was longer than the last time he saw her. Brandon seemed like he had grown a foot. It was good to have them back. He missed them and quietly hoped he could figure out the single dad thing without too many hiccups. When they got to the car, he loaded their backpacks into the trunk. Brandon crawled in the passenger seat while Mitch strapped Georgia into her car seat. As he drove out of the lot, he noticed a black Jaguar that was the same model of sportscar as the one the woman was driving, and it brought his thoughts back to her. He was becoming obsessed with the mystery. "Guys I am going to make a stop at the station to pick up some things before we get the burgers."

"Can we come in?" Brandon asked excitedly.

"Sure, if you stay with me. You can't run all over the place."

"Yay!" Georgia exclaimed from the backseat, clapping her hands.

Chapter Three

Jessi's heart pounded so hard she could barely breathe. Seeing the blue Camaro slow down as it passed her on the highway only to flip around and follow her, made her wonder if Dante's family had tailed them from Philadelphia and knew where she was. And then to see the same blue Camaro two cars down from her in the parking lot at the grocery store, was almost enough to throw her into a major panic attack. Not to mention the crazy guy cornering her. It wasn't that he looked like a vagrant. He was clean cut. Nice looking, with short-cropped silver hair and aviators. It still didn't dampen the fact that he creeped her out walking up to her window. Thank goodness the other car moved. He couldn't have been sent by the Angenelli family, otherwise he would have made a move. The thought crossed her mind when he mentioned the box, that he found her lost stuff. But how would he have known it was hers? Questions swirled through her head ramping up her pulse by the minute.

After unloading her belongings the night before, she was too exhausted to even remember that something might have fallen off the trailer. She went straight to bed when the others left. The next morning her dad asked about the box. She went through every room and didn't see it anywhere. Tyler suggested driving back out where the truck lost the bucket on the highway. That was the most logical place it would have gotten lost. They all drove out there on their way out of town. When nothing was found, her dad suggested she check with the police to see if anyone turned it in. She didn't want to mess with it since it was Sunday, however with the car that followed her, and the run-in at the grocery store, she thought maybe it would be a good idea to get acquainted with the local law enforcement.

Once the groceries were put away, she surveyed the mess in her new house. With the help of her mom, they had gotten quite a bit done. Still, there was a ton to unpack, and she really didn't feel like it right now. She needed to get picture hangers and a few other things at the hardware store anyway, so she snatched her keys off the small side table and headed for the door.

The hardware store wasn't far away. She picked up the items she needed then decided to drive around the downtown to get more familiar with her new surroundings. It really was quite quaint.

Still not ready to return to her empty house, she headed out of town to search for her missing stuff one last time. She hopped up on the highway to see if maybe the box fell off a little farther down the road. Stopping at an area with a steep embankment, she searched in the grass, but still found nothing. As she slowly headed back to her car, Jessi noticed the blue Camaro drive by once again. This time though it didn't slow down. It still rattled her enough to find the address of the police station on her phone. She climbed back in her car and headed back into town wondering if anyone would be in the office since it was Sunday.

Her heart sank as she observed the empty lot when she slowed to park. *Might as well try the door since I'm here.* She tugged on the heavy glass door, and, to her surprise, it opened. Securing her sunglasses on her cap, she walked in. No one was at the front welcome area, so she pressed the button that was at the window. She could hear a buzz in the back followed by the faint sound of voices. Within moments a loud buzz sounded at a heavy metal door off to her left. When it opened the silver haired man she saw in the grocery store parking lot, was standing before her along with a young girl with strawberry blonde hair, and a boy with darker hair and freckles. The man's sunglasses were pushed on top of his silver hair and damn he filled out that T-shirt and jeans perfectly.

Her breath caught as she tried to speak. "You," was all her brain could put together.

A smile crossed his face. "I told you I was a cop."

Holy moly. His smile practically knocked her to the floor. "I—"

He shoved the door all the way open, planted a door stop under it, then raised both hands in surrender. "Look. I realize I scared you. I'm sorry. I picked your stuff up last night while I was on patrol, and I was simply trying to get it back to you. I saw you on the side of the road this morning and decided to try to follow you, but you got away. Then when I made the connection at the grocery store I—

"You're the blue Camaro?" A wave of relief washed over her.

He lowered his head and sheepishly gazed at her through his lashes. "Guilty." *Lord. And those eyes. This man is seriously dangerous.*

Her eyes darted to the front door, and she gestured over her shoulder. "I didn't see it in the parking—"

He tipped his head. "I park out back."

"Ah." She pressed her lips together trying to keep her smile at bay, but a sharp pain quickly reminded her of what brought her to Dalton and succeeded in stifling her smile. But only partially. "You did have me pretty freaked out."

"Again, I'm really sor—"

She waved her hand, "It's okay. It was a misunderstanding, I'm just a little…" the words died as embarrassment sent a surge of heat through her.

The little girl walked up to her and tilted her head, studying her. "What happened to your face?"

Jessi's hand flew to her face, and she realized her sunglasses were on top of her head and the damage Dante inflicted was on full display. She must have put them there from force of habit. The heat that was making its way up her body consumed her cheeks and she glanced up to see the man's tan complexion becoming crimson.

"Georgia Denise," he said, exasperated, as he spun the little girl around to face him, "that was not a nice thing to say. Apologize."

She quickly escaped his grasp and hid behind him, burying her head in his legs. He grabbed ahold of her arm pulling her back in front of him, where she went limp and crumbled to the ground. His eyes went back to Jessi filled with humiliation.

Her insides clenched as she watched him gently wrestle the little girl.

Slowly squatting, he lifted Georgia, bringing her eye level with him but she quickly put her arm over her eyes and sniffled, then whimpered. Jessi's heart was breaking for the little girl, who didn't understand.

"It's okay. She was just curious," Jessi said quietly.

The man glanced up at her. "No. She doesn't get a pass on this."

"She just wants to know what happened."

His lips thinned. "I know. But she needs to know it hurts others when she says things like that. She has to learn."

Georgia dropped her arm and wailed. "I didn't mean to hurt her, Daddy."

Jessi put her hand over her mouth trying to hold back her own tears. Brandon leaned up against the doorframe and rolled his eyes. The man's face softened as he focused on his daughter who was now in a full-blown meltdown. "Georgia baby, you need to tell her you are sorry."

Georgia turned to Jessi, sobbing. "I-I'm sorry."

Jessi dropped to her knees and Georgia wrapped her arms around her. Her body flinched from the pain of the sudden contact. However, the little girl's hug had a calming effect, and Jessi rubbed her hand up and down the child's back.

The man stood up, let out a long sigh and tried to pull his daughter off Jessi but it made her tighten her grip and caused Jessi to lose her balance and fall over. He lunged forward and caught Georgia while his sunglasses slid down his neck and onto the floor. Georgia whacked him in the nose when she spun around to wrap her arms around him. He winced and rubbed his nose then his eyes drifted to Jessi's. She met his gaze and started giggling which made him chuckle. "God. I am so sorry." He held out his hand and helped her up. "Seems I keep having to apologize to you." She picked up his glasses and handed them to him. "Maybe we should start over. I'm Sergeant Mitch Gallagher. You can call me Mitch."

She dusted her pants off and debated whether to give him her name or not. She planned on using an alias until she knew she was safe, although she might need his help later. "Jessica Maddox. My friends call me Jessi." Her hand reached up and rubbed Georgia's back who now had her face pressed into in Mitch's shoulder.

"This is Georgia as you may have heard, and my silent son over there," he tipped his head, "is Brandon."

"Just don't want to cause any trouble." Brandon mumbled.

Mitch glanced at Jessi who smirked, and they both cracked up laughing again at his offhanded comment.

"Come on back." Mitch kicked the door stop out and held the door until she walked through, then walked up a dark hallway. He pushed open the door to his office and Jessi saw the busted box sitting on the chair in front of his desk. Her eyes glanced around the dated bland office. File boxes were piled in the corner against dusty, orange-tinged paneling.

Her gaze landed on the photo albums that sat in the middle of his desk. On top were several photos that her neighbor had taken of her injuries. The smile that had been planted firmly on her face quickly evaporated.

Mitch cleared his throat. "There were several photos that had fallen out of the box when I found it. I think I got them all, but I can't guarantee it." He lowered Georgia to the ground and walked around the edge of his desk. Gathering up the photo albums, he rounded the desk again and put them in the box. She picked up some of the photos, thumbed through them and swallowed. Even with makeup to cover the bruises on her face, she knew it only did so much. The swelling and cuts were still there and the bruises on the rest of her body were now even more visible than when the photos were taken. It made her tremble thinking about it.

A darkness filled Mitch's eyes as he dug in his pocket. "Brandon, take your sister to the break room and get a root beer." Brandon stepped up to the desk and took the change then pushed his sister out the door. As soon as they were gone Jessi closed her eyes trying to dispel the memories the photos snuck into her mind, then lifted her gaze to Mitch. She could see the concern sparking in the gray hues of his eyes. She knew what was coming.

"My boyfriend," she huffed, "*ex*-boyfriend…hurt me." The words thickened in her mouth as she tried to speak while fighting off the impending tears. The idea that he wasn't going to be in her life from now on, because of what he'd done, felt like she spoke it into existence with the utterance of the words.

Until now she hadn't addressed it. The neighbor called the police. Even when she was asked to give her statement, she said he attacked her, never acknowledging that he'd hurt her. That one simple word seemed to speak volumes because it wasn't merely physical pain he'd inflicted. With each passing day, her emotions seemed to change from sadness to anger to fear, leaving her completely disoriented and overwhelmed.

"When?" Mitch's voice dropped to a low growl and the line between his brows deepened.

"Thursday," she said on a breath and scanned the photos again. Her stomach soured from the memories of the night. Every bruise displayed in the photos now sent a twinge of pain through her. She could almost feel his hands on her again. Grabbing at her. Striking her. The acid crawled up her throat to the point her words came out barely audible. Hot tears leaked out of the corner of her eyes. "My neighbor heard me scream and pulled him off me. His wife took the photos. She said the police would need them, but they took their own."

"Any broken bones?"

"No. I have cuts and bruises and some stitches. That's all."

"That's all?" he questioned sarcastically with a grunt. "You pressed charges." It was not a question.

"Yes. He's probably out by now though." She sat down in the empty chair. "He comes from a pretty influential family."

"In Philadelphia?" Mitch sat down behind his desk.

"How did you know?" Her eyes again focused on the photos wondering how he got that much information from them.

"License plate."

Jessi nodded.

"Noticed it in the grocery store parking lot. Some of the photos looked like you were in some pretty high dollar establishments, and I figured from the Pennsylvania license plate you were probably in the Pittsburg or Philadelphia area. Plus, some of the programs I found were from areas near Philadelphia."

"I was a sommelier."

"A soma what?"

His expression and his thick accent made the corner of her mouth kick up and she was happy for the change of subject. "A sommelier. A wine expert."

"Interesting. Didn't know there was such a thing." He paused. "So, you are here—"

"Um, I will be working at Lake Village restaurant. I believe it opened not too long ago."

"Yeah, I'm familiar. Went to a wedding there a few

weeks ago."

"I was hired as their sommelier. I will also be working at the Purple Skies Winery."

He was quiet for a moment. "You're running." Another statement. His voice and demeanor changed. Strictly business. And she had to admit he had a pretty good angry cop expression. There was something in his eyes though that held concern.

"Yes," she said, drawing out the whispered word.

He took out a yellow legal pad and started writing. "Do you think you still might be in danger?"

She took a deep breath, let it out with a hiss, and stood. *Was she? Would Dante come after her? Or his family? They are probably pretty pissed that she alerted the cops to them.* "I don't know," she responded, still whispering.

"You said your ex-boyfriend came from an influential family. What did you mean by that?"

She turned away from Mitch and wrapped her arms around her waist. "The Angenellis. Ring a bell?"

"Angenelli?"

Her eyes met his. "Giovani Angenelli? As in the Philadelphia Mafia?"

Mitch's jaw pulsed. "And you decided to date this guy, why?"

She rolled her eyes at him. "Well, I didn't know he was part of the mob when I met him. I mean, honestly, I didn't know much about it. I thought it was something of the past, so when he gave me his name it didn't mean anything."

"Oh, they're still around," Mitch confirmed.

"When we started dating, someone at work mentioned that his family was part of the Italian mafia. I thought they were joking because when I met him, Dante said he worked as a supervisor at Delcox manufacturing. We had been dating for quite a while before I got up the nerve to ask him if he was part of a Mafia family. He said only by blood, then admitted his uncle was in the business. He said he wanted nothing to do with it. Dante has a brother that I don't think is involved either. He didn't live in Philadelphia, and I think Dante said he worked at a power plant. As far as his parents, he didn't talk much about them because they had died in a car accident several years before." She paced the floor and rubbed her hands together trying to keep from shaking.

The Philadelphia police had already taken her statement, and she wondered if rehashing everything was necessary. However, if they did try to track her down, she figured it wouldn't hurt for Mitch to at least have an idea of what had happened. "That was before he got laid off though. And after months of failed attempts to find a job, his uncle offered to help him out."

"I'm sure he did." His voice was loaded with sarcasm, and she bobbed her head in agreement.

"At first he acted like he didn't want anything to do with him. Then a few days later I found out he took the offer. I have no idea what he's doing. Whatever it is, it's not good. The few times I was actually around his uncle and his associates, there was no doubt in my mind he was up to no good."

"That's how they reel them in. Act like they are helping them out and then slowly bury them deeper and deeper." His attention went back to his pad where he scrawled something else down and continued to pepper her with questions. "How many people know where you are?" His question sent a shiver through her.

"My family and a couple of close family friends who helped me move." She paused. "Oh, and my mom's friend. Her sister owns the winery."

"Does he know where your parents live?"

"Yes. He has been to my dad and mom's place. They were taking an extended trip with their RV as soon as they got back home though, so they're on the road."

"How long will they be gone?"

"A month."

"Any sisters or brothers?"

"Two sisters. They both live out of state. He's never met them."

"Does he know the friends that helped you?"

"No. They work for my parents on their farm."

"Do any of your other friends know?"

"No. I told some that we were having trouble but never said anything about leaving and then when I actually left, it was very sudden."

"Does he know any of them?"

"He's met some of them, but I don't think he even knows their last names."

"And you haven't tried to contact any of your friends since?"

"No."

"You don't have any joint bank accounts or anything with him?"

"No. We kept our finances separate."

"And your phone?"

"I shut it off and got a new one."

"How about the people you worked for or the new people you will be working for?"

"I told my boss at the restaurant I had to resign immediately due to personal reasons but nothing else.

The couple at the winery know. The owners at Lake Village don't. I don't think. I will have to tell them though, because I want to use an alias. That way it will be harder for Dante to find me if he starts searching."

"What is your alias?"

"My name is Jessica Michelle, so I will go by Michelle Delano, which is my mom's maiden name."

"Okay. Where are you living?"

"Why?"

"I am going to set up a patrol in the area."

"Officer Gallagher—"

"It's Sergeant."

Rolling her eyes, she blurted, "Whatever. You don't have to do that."

"It's no trouble. And please, I'd rather you call me Mitch." Dropping his pen, he stood and walked around his desk. "Give me a minute."

She followed him up the hall to a room at the end. A smile broke across his face when he saw his son and daughter playing checkers.

Brandon lifted his head. "Hey, Dad. Are we going to leave soon? I'm getting hungry."

"Me too," Georgia pitched in. Mitch slid his phone out and clicked the button. Jessi glanced at the screen. Five thirty.

"You wanna get a burger with us?" Mitch asked catching Jessi off guard. *Is everyone this open and friendly in this town?*

She stared at him. Just like that he was back to being Dad. "Oh no. I need to get back to the house. I still have a bunch of unpacking."

"Do you need help? We can get the burgers and meet you over there."

She really needed the help. Her body ached and she had no idea how long it would take for the bruises to heal. On the other hand, she didn't want to be around anyone, even the handsome sergeant. "No that's okay. I'm still trying to figure out where everything goes and I'm sure you need to get home."

"Suit yourself. The offer stands. We can eat burgers at your place just as well as ours."

"Thanks. I think it would be better if I did it myself though." He tipped his head and stared at her long enough for her to suddenly feel exposed and her whole body to heated. Tearing her eyes away from his, she turned to go back up the hallway and heard him behind her tell the kids they would be leaving in five minutes. She walked into his office and retrieved the remainder of the photos from his desk tossing them into the box, then piled the other two smaller boxes on top. Wrapping her arms around the busted box, she tried to lift it and winced. Immediately grabbing her side, she let out a pained groan. From behind her, she heard his voice.

"Are you crazy? You're in no shape to be moving those. They're heavy. And I still need to tape the box up before the whole thing falls completely apart and spills everything in the floor." Glancing over her shoulder, she caught him leaning against the doorframe, then he took a step toward her. "Why don't I put them in my car, go get some burgers and drop everything off?" She gazed at him from the corner of her eye trying desperately to stay strong. "I promise I will only drop the stuff off."

Suddenly, she felt completely helpless. Flashes of the attack stole her thoughts. Her nose burned and tears fill her eyes once more. All she could do was turn away and nod. She was mortified that she couldn't hold it together in front of him and didn't know what she would do when and if he tried to comfort her. Except he didn't. He gave her space. It was like he knew. She could see him stealing glances as she tried to compose herself. Concern laced his features, but he kept his distance and went about stabilizing the box with some packing tape.

Once he solidified the busted edges of the box, he stacked the smaller ones on top, then picked them up, moved past her into the hallway, and out a side door. She followed him and watched as he placed everything in the trunk of the Camaro, then turned back to her. "Where would you like these delivered?" His voice was light, which helped her regain her composure.

She tried to recall the address without checking her phone. Unfortunately, her brain still wasn't fully functioning yet. Reaching in her back pocket, she dug out her phone. "Um, I know it's on Spruce." Her fingers tapped on her screen.

"You aren't at Dale Adkins' place, are you?"

Her eyes caught his. "Yeah. The cottage."

He nodded and said, "I know where it is," then stepped in the doorway where she stood. He wasn't much taller than her and as he passed by his body brushed against hers causing her skin to sting where he touched. His eyes lingered briefly making her wonder if he felt it too, then he continued up the hallway. "What kind of burger do you like?" he asked not looking back at her as he walked into his office and rounded his desk. Then his eyes met hers.

"Cheeseburger with everything."

"French fries or onion rings?"

Her mouth watered with the decision. "I haven't had onion rings in forever."

"Oh, you won't be sorry. Their breading is the best."

"Yeah, I think the last time I had onion rings…geez, I can't even remember."

"What do you want to drink?"

"Diet root beer?"

Mitch's brow raised. "Diet? Seriously? You want to ruin the whole meal for a few measly calories?"

His comment had a smile returning to her lips. "Okay. Okay. Root beer."

"That's better." His mouth twitched then lifted into a half smile. He dropped the pen on the pad he was writing on and stood from his chair. "Give me about thirty minutes and I'll swing by. He stepped around her and walked down the hallway to the breakroom. "All right troops. Circle up. We're heading out."

"Daddy," Georgia whined. "Brandon is cheating."

"Am not. You just don't ever remember you can jump backward when you are kinged."

"Come on." He motioned with his hand. "You guys are both getting grouchy. Let's go get something to eat." Both kids slid their chairs out and joined their dad and Jessi as they headed for the heavy metal door. Mitch keyed in the code and the door buzzed. He held it open until everyone was through then pushed open the glass door. "Tell Miss Maddox bye."

Jessi rolled her eyes. "Please. It's Jessi." Georgia wrapped her arms around Jessi's waist. She smiled and rubbed the strawberry blond curls that filled Georgia's head.

"I'll see you in a little bit."

Georgia smiled. "Are we coming to your house?"

Jessi nodded. Georgia clapped her hands.

Mitch broke in. "Just to drop off her stuff. We aren't

staying." Georgia's face fell.

"Let me get everything put away and I promise we will have a playdate. Okay?"

Georgia stared up at her and the smile reappeared.

Mitch shook his head. Jessi glanced up at him and noticed he was staring at her again. "She has manipulation down to a science," he said with a smile.

Her mouth lifted into a half smile. "That she does. She definitely knows how to work the system, and unfortunately, I think I've already been sucked in."

Georgia eyes volleyed back and forth between Mitch and Jessi. "I know you are talking about me."

Mitch crossed his arms and gazed at Georgia who gave him a toothless grin. "And what are we saying."

She shrugged. "That I have a system."

"And what does that mean?"

She shrugged again. Jessi gave Mitch the side eye and smirked.

He shook his head. "I know, I know. You don't have to tell me." She stepped through the door. "See you in a little bit." Nodding her head, she chirped the fob on her car.

Chapter Four

Mitch pushed the doorbell and stood back from the large box on the ground in front of him. Behind him was Brandon carrying the two other boxes and Georgia carrying the white sack of food. He heard movement behind the door and then the click of the handle. His heart skipped, and he let out an audible breath. *What the hell is wrong with me?*

Since his divorce, he had, for the most part, steered clear of the opposite sex. He could count on one hand the number of times he'd been alone with a woman and none of them had made him as nervous as he was right now. And he wasn't even alone.

His line of work was not conducive for lasting relationships as proven by the failed marriage he already had racked up. To his credit, he and his ex were still friends, which was better than most could say. She was a good person and deserved the best in life. It just wasn't with him.

Miss Maddox seemed like a nice person. Nice and his chosen career didn't mesh. *Why am I even thinking about this?* We are simply dropping off her stuff. Making her feel welcome. What she had gone through was horrible and he wanted to make sure she was safe. That was all.

Jessi opened the door with a crooked grin that made her eyes dance, and Mitch wasn't sure he was going to be able to move. His body stiffened as his eyes took in her form. All her form. She still had her long brown hair fixed in a high ponytail except now it spilled over her shoulders making it appear more like a mane. Tendrils of loose hair played against her bruised cheeks that were washed clean. A body hugging, hot pink, scooped neck T-shirt that said "may contain wine" in glittery light pink letters left nothing to the imagination and sat just above a pair of checkered flannel pajama bottoms that rested on her hips leaving a sliver of her toned stomach showing. Mitch suddenly felt like the nice cool evening had increased in temperature about twenty degrees. He only hoped she didn't notice his inability to speak or shift his attention from her. *Sticking around is not an option.*

"Hey." She motioned for them to come in and Mitch picked up the box, twitching his head to his kids to follow him inside. "I hope you don't mind me changing into my comfy clothes." She chuckled. "I figured if I was going to have to tackle this mess, I might as well be comfortable doing it." Mitch forced himself to avert his eyes to keep his body from spontaneously combusting. The place looked similar to when Dale's granddaughter, Bekah Ellington, lived there, aside from the piles of boxes and packing paper strewn across the floor. It had only been a few weeks since he had to drag her ex out of the house when he broke in and threatened her with a butcher knife. Now she was married to his friend Brant, and Mitch couldn't be happier.

"Where would you like this?" he asked, still cautiously holding the flimsy box in his hands.

Jessi's mouth made an O, but no sound came out and just the sight had Mitch sucking in a deep breath trying to calm nerves. *"Is this woman clueless to how sexy she is?* Her eyes darted around, then landed back on Mitch. *Don't make me go into your bedroom. Please for the love of God.* "Would you mind carrying it to my bedroom?" Mitch closed his eyes but gave her an affirming nod and trudged up the hallway. By the sheer weight of the container, not to mention it's instability, regardless of if she was hurt or not, he knew she wouldn't have been able to carry it anywhere. He was surprised it had fallen from the truck.

"Let Brandon know where you want those other two boxes." He hollered over his shoulder.

"What's in them?" Jessi called back to him.

"I didn't look." He raised his voice hoping she could hear him from her room although she didn't respond. Finding a place in corner that, surprisingly, had no other boxes, he set the box down and strolled back up the hallway. When he returned to the living room, Georgia was sitting at the dining room table taking a bite of Jessi's burger. "Georgia what are you—"

Jessi shot him a glare. "She was hungry."

What was he going to do with his youngest? She had ways of pushing every one of his buttons and Miss Maddox wasn't helping by giving into her every whim. "That's your burger, Miss Maddox."

"For the last time, it's Jessi. Unless you want me calling you Sergeant Gallagher. And don't worry about it. I'll eat hers." She glanced at Georgia and smiled. "She's not getting my onion rings though."

Mitch shook his head, wondering if Georgia was manipulating the situation just to hang out longer, and let out a loud sigh. "So, is it okay if we stay for dinner since my daughter evidently invited herself?"

"Nah, you boys go on your way. Us girls are going

to hang out."

His head jerked to her. Was she serious? He wasn't sure since her expression gave nothing away.

Like she knew exactly what he was thinking, she said, "I'm kidding," then snickered. "That is unless you need to get home. I mean, I kind of assumed there was no Mrs. Gallagher since—"

"They got divorced. Mom got remarried and moved to Poling with our new stepdad, Ron." Georgia said with a mouth full of burger, not making eye contact with anyone. Mitch's head fell back, and he stared up at the ceiling feeling the hairs on the back of his neck stand. He rubbed the prickly spot and wondered if his face was going to actually catch fire. *This child is going to be the death of me.*

"It's Poland," Brandon called from the living room.

Mitch shot him a glare and noticed he was still standing in the middle of the living room holding the boxes.

He slowly moved his gaze back to Jessi. "Where did you say you wanted the boxes?" Mitch asked, thankful for the chance to change the subject.

"What was in them?"

"I didn't look. I only searched the busted box and only to try to find out who it belonged to," he said feeling guilty for prying into her life.

Her eyes darted around the room again. "Just put them down where you are standing," she said to Brandon.

"I'll go get the other bag." Letting out a defeated sigh, he stepped over a pile of packing paper and headed to the door. "You can have my burger. It's basically the same as yours anyway without pickles."

"You don't like pickles?" She teased.

"Not on my burgers." Yanking the door open, he wandered to the car to retrieve the second bag of food and drinks and realized he still had her root beer. With his hands full, he leaned up against the door to shut it and strolled back into the house doing the same with the front door. "I forgot to give you your root beer."

Setting everything on the table, he opened the bag and fished out three other burgers, two fries, and some onion rings, handing one burger to Brandon, who was sitting at the bar, along with a pack of fries, then pushing the second burger to Jessi. Grabbing the rest, he set a bag of fries in front of Georgia then sat down at the bar and peeled open the paper of the plain hamburger with only pickles, dumping the onion rings onto the paper. Picking the pickles off the bun of the sparse meal, he happily remembered he had gotten some salami at the store and figured he could make himself a sandwich when he got home.

"I've got some lettuce, a tomato, and some cheese in the fridge. Why don't you let me take that one?" Mitch didn't move other than lifting his gaze. Jessi's eyes leveled at him and had a warmth that did a number on his psyche. The light above the table reflected in them giving their hazel color a golden cast. She had a beauty about her even with her injuries that made him lose his train of thought completely. "Mitch?"

"I'm sorry. What?" he said trying to refocus. *What the hell did she say? Shit, I can't be doing this. I'm just here to drop her stuff off.*

Her eyes narrowed giving him a somewhat bewildered expression, then she smiled. "I said I have some lettuce, a tomato, and some cheese in the fridge. I can grab it, and eat Georgia's burger."

"Nah, go ahead and eat that one. I'm good." He took a bite of the dry buns and meat and slowly chewed. When he glanced up again, she was still staring at him while he tried to swallow the gummy paste in his mouth.

"It's no trouble. I'll get the stuff from the fridge if you want to add it to the burger?" Her eyes pleaded.

"I'm good. Thanks."

She chuckled, got up, and went to the fridge. Setting lettuce, a sliced tomato, cheese, and some mustard in front of him, she said, "Don't be stubborn." Then, retrieving the ketchup, she plucked the pickles from the white paper that he had removed from the burger, gave him a wink, and walked back into the dining room. "Who wants some ketchup?" Mitch watched as she squirted some on her paper for her onion rings, then on Georgia's fries before placing the container between Mitch and Brandon.

He shook his head, questioning if he'd imagined what had just happened, and wondering if his body was ever going to cool down between his daughter's constant over sharing and Miss Maddox's…everything. *What did I do to deserve this torture?* He picked up the mustard and spread some on his burger then tore some lettuce and added some tomato and cheese to the bun. It definitely made the burger much more palatable. *How can Georgia like the taste of a burger with nothing on it? It's so…bland.* Staring at his daughter, he suddenly realized she was nearly finished with her burger, and she had eaten it with everything on it. Did she not realize what was on it? She didn't tear it apart saying she didn't like tomatoes or lettuce or pickles. She ate it all. "Georgia. Is that a good burger?" he asked. She looked like a chipmunk with her cheeks loaded full as she nodded. Mitch's eyes moved to Jessi. "You have the magic touch." Jessi stared at him in confusion. He put his hand up to his mouth to block Georgia from seeing him speak. "She doesn't do veggies," he said barely above a whisper.

Georgia glared at him. "You don't have to whisper, Daddy. Everyone knows I hate vegibles."

Jessi pinched her lips together, raised her brows and shrugged.

"So, since we are here, do you have anything that you would like us to help with?"

She quirked her mouth. "Well…" Her head volleyed back and forth scanning the room.

"Lay it on me."

"I have this rug." She pointed to a long rolled up rug lying on the floor behind her. "I want to put it under the sectional." She paused for a moment. "Oh, and they put my desk in my bedroom, and I need it out here somewhere." She scanned the area. "I thought about under these windows over here," she said gesturing to a set of windows just past the dining table. "But please, don't feel like you have to. It will get done eventually."

Mitch flipped his hand at her, shoved the rest of his burger and onion rings into his mouth, and dusted his hands against each other. Glancing at Brandon, he twitched his head motioning him to help. Brandon dredged a fry and shoved it in his mouth then took a swig of his root beer before hopping off the barstool. Mitch picked up one end of the rug while Brandon got the other. They carried it around the edge of the sectional and laid it down. He moved several boxes along with empty packing paper then unrolled the rug. "Do you want it running this direction?" He stood off to the side.

Jessi peered over the back of the sectional. "Yes. That's perfect."

Mitch tucked the rug under the end piece then moved to the next until the rug was secure. He stood and brought his hands to his hips. "The desk is in the bedroom?" Jessi nodded and Mitch gestured to Brandon to follow him.

After positioning the desk under the windows, Jessi had him rearranging several other pieces of furniture along with unpacking several boxes. By the time Mitch noticed the time it was ten. He had to admit, as he scanned the room, the place seemed much more livable. Brandon broke down several boxes while Georgia helped pick up and fill an entire garbage bag full of packing paper, then they carried them out to the outside trash. Once everything was cleaned up, Mitch helped Jessi hang a few things on the wall. His finger tapped at the corner of the shadow box of her dog Layla he had just hung, waiting for Jessi to let him know if it was straight.

She stood back with her arms crossed below her chest. "Perfect." He glanced at her, then quickly diverted his eyes back to the shadow box when he realized that the placement of her arms accentuated her full breasts. Backing away, he spied something shiny on the floor and picked it up.

"Did you lose a key?" He lifted it up and showed her. She took it from him and examined it.

"Not that I know of. It may be the previous tenants." She flipped it over checking it carefully. "I'll put it in my junk drawer in case they come after it." She walked into the kitchen and dropped it in a drawer, and Mitch suddenly realized his kids had gotten quiet. Georgia had gotten comfortable on the sectional and fallen asleep. Jessi followed his gaze and whispered, "Aw."

"I think that's all we can do for this evening," he quietly said handing her the tiny hammer she had given him to use.

"I don't know how to thank you." He quietly stepped up to the sectional and stared down at his sleeping daughter. Jessi stood next to him. "I feel really bad now for barking at you in the parking lot and threatening to run over your cart."

"Oh, I forgot about that," he said, amusement lacing his words. "You know I could press charges against you for threatening a police officer."

"Well, in my defense, you weren't in uniform, and you hadn't told me you were a cop yet."

"True." He tilted his head back and forth. "I guess I could let it slide."

Mitch slid his hands under the limp little girl and propped her up on his shoulder. He glanced over at Brandon who was playing a game on his phone and let out a "pssst." Brandon's head popped up and Mitch ushered him to the door with a flip of his hand then pointed his eyes at Jessi. "Where's your phone?" Mitch questioned in a hushed voice.

She picked it up off the end table and showed it to him.

"Program my number in it." Her brows lowered and Mitch continued, "In case something or someone bothers you."

"Can't I call the police?"

He smiled and shook his head. This woman was confusing the hell out of him. Flirting one minute and pushing him away the next. He needed to stay away though. "Yes. Yes, you can." He turned toward the door to leave.

"I think I would feel safer if I had your number though." He heard her say over his shoulder.

His fingers rubbed the ridge in his forehead. "It's six-nine-seven-four-eight-six-twenty-twenty," he called back, turning slowly to face her.

"Six-nine-seven-four-eight-six-twenty-twenty?" she repeated back as she typed it in.

"Yes. And I'm serious. If something seems suspicious, don't wait. Call me. If I can't help, I'll send someone who can."

Her voice softened. "Okay."

"I mean it. Especially if something raises a red flag."

"Got it."

He pulled open the door and walked out. She stood in the doorway with her arms hugging her waist. He could feel her eyes on him as he buckled Georgia in her seat then slid beneath the wheel. As he backed down the driveway, he lifted his fingers when he saw her wave. Easing out onto the street, his chest tightened working through everything that happened during the day. He hadn't had that much fun in a long time. Even though she had put him to work, he enjoyed it. His phone buzzed. Reaching into his back pocket, he slipped it out and set it in the cup holder. Slowing to a stop at the stop sign, he clicked the button. It was an unknown number.

—Thank you for helping me tonight. I feel like this place is home now, and it's all because of you and your amazing kids. I don't know how to repay you, but I thought maybe if you wouldn't mind, I would love to treat you to dinner sometime—

Mitch smiled. *What? Is she trying to kill me texting me while I'm driving?* He drove through the downtown area. Most of the shops had closed for the evening. He liked driving through the old part of town. Taking in the historical buildings somehow gave him comfort. Eased his mind. He was excited that he had the chance to raise his kids in the community that he loved and enjoyed protecting.

Protecting it brought his mind back to Jessi. Did she need protecting? Was she in danger? He didn't want to take any chances since her ex was connected to the Mafia. It wouldn't take much to ensure she was safe. The question was, would he be? Thinking about their evening together, he knew she was definitely not safe for him. Being around her did something to him. It had been a long time since a woman distracted him like she did. In fact, he couldn't remember any woman since his wife that had thrown him that far off kilter. He needed to keep his distance and not get tangled up with her. Not when he just got full custody of the kids.

Moving to Poland was the hardest decision his ex-wife probably had to make, and he had no idea what being a full-time dad would be like. The last thing he wanted to do was screw it up. He needed to figure out how to keep Jessi safe while staying far, far away from her.

He tapped a button on his rearview mirror as he pulled into the driveway and the garage opened.

Mitch grabbed a beer and sat on his sofa after tucking the kids in bed. He propped his socked feet up on the coffee table, crossed his ankles and stared into the empty fireplace. The house was quiet. His eyes tracked up the stairwell to where the kids slept. They were home for good. No shuttling them back and forth. No making arrangements for the holidays. They were there for the foreseeable future. He was happy. Wasn't he? Sitting in the now quiet house, the truth was, he wasn't. He was happy they were there, but it had become painfully evident after the impromptu dinner date, just how lonely he'd been.

His ex-wife's marriage had hit him harder than he expected. Mitch had to come to grips with the fact that he wouldn't get to see her much now. Most of the time when he'd get the kids for the weekend, she'd stay in town, and they'd do lunch. That wouldn't be happening anymore.

She had found someone new who made her happy. He wanted that for her, but them moving halfway across the world was going to be harder to get used to.

When she and her now husband decided to marry, she told Mitch she planned the wedding in Georgia so her dad could walk her down the aisle again. Years of cancer and treatment had taken a toll on him. Mitch knew it would be awkward for him to be there, so he was glad she was getting married so far away. He didn't think he could take seeing her marry another man.

Looking around, he could still feel her there. Though the photos of them as a family had disappeared long ago, she still lingered in the walls and rafters. So many memories were made. The house was an older craftsman. They had bought it together. The minute he saw it he knew he wanted it. He was like that. There were certain things that he knew from the first minute he laid eyes on them, he wanted them. The same thing happened with the Camaro. The same thing happened with Lorrie. It was like they were already his. It was just unfortunate he wasn't hers.

Lifting the bottle to his lips, he took a drink as the memories came flooding back like an old eight-millimeter movie.

The minute Lorrie Williams walked into his junior world history class Mitch knew he was toast. Her strawberry blonde hair was cut in a way that brushed her face and accentuated her dimples. She slid into the seat next to him and gave him a shy smile. He figured he had no chance with her since she was the prettiest girl he had ever seen, and he had nothing really to offer. He was an average Joe with dark wavy hair that was going gray at a rapid rate.

Weeks passed. And from the few times he'd gotten up the nerve to speak to her, he found out her family had moved from Georgia when her dad was hired to head a large commercial construction project. The project was estimated to take about a year. The move was temporary. *She* was temporary.

Signs went up for the homecoming dance and he desperately wanted to ask her to go with him. After a terrible baseball practice that made him wonder why he ever wanted to play, he noticed her sitting by herself on the rickety wooden bleachers by the dugout. Something was wrong. She was crying. He took a deep breath and hopped up on the bottom bleacher. When he tried to take the next ones a few at a time, he tripped, and faceplanted against a plank of wood. Slowly raising his head, he noticed her mouth gaped open then it quickly became a smile and she let out a soft laugh. Well, that's one way to change her mood. Wasn't his choice. It was kind of painful. However, if it took her mind off whatever had upset her, he would take it as a win. Carefully climbing up the rest of the bleachers, he sat down beside her.

She said she was having trouble in some of her classes, and she was worried her parents were going to make her quit the volleyball team. School came easy to him, so he offered to help her. Once she had agreed, he thought he might as well ask the big question. To his surprise, she said yes right away and told him she had hoped he would ask her. That's where it all started. And it seemed nothing could separate them. Not when her dad's job ended. And not when he was later diagnosed with cancer. Every trial they faced, they came out on the other side, together. Until they didn't. Until the day she told him his job was too much. The job he had dreamed about since he was six. The job he had worked so hard for, waited so long for. The job she asked him to choose between. It or her.

How had he screwed everything up so badly? A small part of him had always thought they would work things out, but not anymore. She was gone, and it was his fault because he chose his job over her.

He loved his job. It gave him a rush when he was able to help someone. But he knew it had taken away what truly made him happy, coming home to his wife and kids. He made a shitty choice that would forever change his life.

Work demanded he stay focused, so he didn't have time to think of much else during his shift. When he wasn't working though, he was lonely, and no amount of working out at the gym or hanging out with his buddies changed that fact. His guard was always up.

Another swallow from his beer, and he thought about how his life was about to change and his mind flipped to Jessi. The surprised expression on her face when Georgia hugged her, and the way she wrapped her in her arms and defended her. And that mouth. God help him, he wanted to plant a kiss on those luscious cherry-tinged lips just once to see if she tasted like sweet cherries like he imagined. He shook his head hard. *Not happening. I have kids to take care of. I don't have time for a woman in my life. Hell, I don't know anything about her.* Staring at her message again, he responded.

—*No need for repayment. Just happy we could help*—

Chapter Five

Jessi stared at her reflection in the mirror. It had been two weeks since she packed her things and headed south. Two weeks since Dante had shown her he wasn't the man she thought he was, and two weeks of recovering from what he did to her. The swelling was gone and there were only a few areas that were still discolored, although they were easily hidden with makeup if needed. The emotional scars were healing too. It helped that everyone she'd met had been extremely nice, especially one sergeant and his two sweet kids. There was something about him that she couldn't shake. She knew she should be heartbroken and scared from the way her relationship ended, and she was. But there was something about the town and Mitch that lit a candle in her pitch-black soul and wouldn't let her spiral into the pits of hell.

She rubbed her finger under her lip to fix her gloss then straightened her earring. In a form fitting, cream-colored, long sleeved, wrap dress, she thought she looked presentable to meet her new bosses. She had called the restaurant and winery to set up appointments with each to meet and discuss her positions before she was scheduled to start the following week. Tapping the screen on her phone to check the time once more, she spritzed a light mist of perfume then hurried out of the bathroom. Just enough time to make a quick stop before meeting *the* Anson Carothers at the restaurant. She'd Googled him after the owners had said she would be meeting with him. He was a highly acclaimed chef that had worked in a fairly well-known restaurant in Las Vegas. It made her wonder why he left to work in Dalton.

She grabbed the foil-wrapped tray off the counter, then her purse off the small table next to the door and headed to her car. A smile crossed her face. She peeked in the rearview mirror and fluffed her hair. Mitch had nixed her idea for dinner which disappointed her. She wasn't, however, going to let his good deed go unnoticed. It meant a lot to her for him to help her get her place in order and even more to have her stuff back. She had to find a way to repay him, and the best way she knew, was to feed him. Brownies, specifically. With powdered sugar like her grandma made. The smell currently wafting through the car made her wish she had eaten something more than a salad for lunch. Her pulse increased a beat as she drove up to the front of the station. She picked up the plate and stepped out of the car. The wind caught her hair and blew pieces across her face as she opened the door to the station. Leaning her head, she combed the wayward hair with her fingers and pushed it over her ear trying to put it back in place. An older lady with wire rimmed glasses greeted her at the front window.

"May I help you?" the lady said through an intercom.

Jessi leaned in "Is Sergeant Gallagher in?"

The woman's face brightened with a kind smile. "Is he expecting you?"

Jessi wrinkled her nose. She had no idea what his schedule was, so she was taking a chance on him being at work. "No." The woman held up a finger for her to wait, then disappeared. Jessi heard a loud buzz of the door next to her and the lady appeared.

"Come on back." As Jessi stepped into the dimly lit hallway, she could hear Mitch's voice. Drawing closer to his office, she heard a second male voice.

"…and Poppi said some bags of feed have come up missing too in the past few weeks."

"And you haven't noticed anything odd on your property?"

"No. Nothing that I can think of."

"You don't think he's lost count of how many he used, or got shorted on the ones he bought?"

"Anything is possible, I guess. I'm telling you Mitch, something strange is going on though. I've been helping him for quite a while with those horses. The guy is as sharp as a tack. I can't put my finger on it, but something's not right."

"I will make sure there is a patrol car in the area. Just keep me posted on anything else that comes up missing or any other odd activity. Let me know if you see any strange vehicles around the area."

"He'll be with you in a minute. You're welcome to have a seat." Jessi heard the woman's muted voice behind her, and she quickly spun around.

"Thank you."

The woman nodded and disappeared through another door. Jessi glanced at the plastic chair against the wall outside Mitch's office, then her focus shifted when she heard the scrape of the chair against the tile floor and caught sight of him. Dressed in his blue uniform, Jessi couldn't take her eyes off him. And by the expression on his face, she thought she might have scored in the outfit department herself.

A playful grin spread across his face lighting up his eyes. "What are you doing here?" God, his southern accent sent steam directly into her bloodstream, flooding her with so much heat she nearly began fanning herself. She wanted to listen to him all day long. He glanced back at the scruffy cowboy with him, and the friendly expression he had, vanished. He had business to tend to.

"Ben. This is a friend of mine, Jes—"

"Michelle," she quickly corrected and held her hand out, "Michelle Delano."

"Ben Corbett." He took her hand and gave her a head nod then returned his attention to Mitch.

"I'll keep an eye on Poppi's place," Mitch assured. "Thanks for coming by and letting me know." With another nod of his head to Jessi, Ben donned a black cowboy hat and disappeared up the hall, and Mitch's attention returned to her. All of her. The way his eyes raked over her body singed her skin. She had just gotten her temperature under control when the heat returned, filling her cheeks so fast she wondered if she spiked a fever. Her stomach fluttered and she sucked in a deep breath. *What exactly am I here for again?*

"What did you do?" The amusement in Mitch's voice managed to drag her out of her fog but only heightened the fluttery butterflies in her stomach.

"I-I know you said you didn't need any repayment, but I really do appreciate what you and your kids did for me, making my place more livable and returning my stuff. I couldn't let your good deeds go unnoticed." She held out the plate and gave him a cheesy smile.

Mitch huffed, feigning irritation, but she could see the twinkle in his eye as he hesitantly took the plate.

"You really didn't have to…" his eyes widened as his words evaporated and he sniffed. "Is that chocolate?" The corner of his mouth slowly lifted into a crooked smile. His fingers pinched the corner of the foil, and he raised the wrapping enough to see what was under it. "Brownies?" Jessi dug her teeth into her bottom lip. "Who told you that was my one true weakness?"

She chuckled. "Isn't it everybody's?" He leaned into the door and rolled his arm signaling for her to follow him. She stepped through the doorway into to his office and he followed behind her, walking around his desk and setting the brownies down before taking a seat.

"Wow! Thank you." He peeled the wrapper back, slid a powdered square from the pile, and quickly popped it into his mouth. Then his eyes slowly closed, and he let out a low moan that instantaneously sent goosebumps all over her body. "Oh my gosh. These are amazing. Seriously, brownies are my favorite. I am going to have to take these to the break room or I will sit here and eat the entire plate before I leave. No joke."

"Yay! I'm so glad. I am just grateful that you found my stuff and helped me out. The place would probably still have boxes piled up and paper on the floor if you hadn't."

Mitch swallowed hard and wiped his mouth with his fingers. "Speaking of stuff, I found a couple of pictures under some papers that didn't make it back into the box. Turning in his seat, he reached over to grab the photos. They were photos showing some of her injuries. He glanced at them then back at her as he scooted them across the desk. She picked them up trying desperately to keep the photos out of her line of sight and dropped them in her purse. "You look great by the way."

"Yeah? The bruises are almost gone," she said brushing her cheek with her fingers.

"I can see that, although I meant…"

"Oh," she said almost in a whisper suddenly feeling flustered. "I've got appointments to talk to my bosses about the jobs today. Getting my schedules and figure out what I'll be doing." Spying the time on Mitch's computer screen, she added, "In fact, I probably should be going. I didn't want to bother you, just drop off the brownies and tell you thank you."

"Well, I appreciate it." He paused. "Did you get all settled in?"

"Yes, thanks to you guys. I really like it. It's very warm and comfortable."

"I have a patrol set up to keep an eye on the place. You can't see the cottage from the street, which is good. I still feel better though having someone keep an eye on the area. At least for a while." Mitch stood and snuck a second brownie before walking around his desk.

"Thank you. So far, I haven't heard anything from him and neither have my parents. So, that's good."

They walked out of his office and up the hallway. "Well, let me know if you need anything." He tapped in a code and the door buzzed.

"I will."

"Thanks again for the brownies. I promise I will take *a few* to Georgia and Brandon." He gave her a sly smile.

She returned it saying, "you better," before pushing open the door.

The sun shone bright in the cloudless sky, but she knew that wasn't why her skin felt hot. Jessi opened the door to her car and climbed in. A grin slowly spread across her face. Leaning her head against her steering wheel, she wondered what to think of her law enforcement friend. She was crushing a little bit on him. Unsure of what his reaction would be today since he declined her dinner offer, she was very excited that he seemed happy to see her. And there was no mistaking, from the way he examined her, that he liked her outfit. The butterflies returned again just thinking about it.

She inhaled deeply to still her heart that was beating a mile a minute. When she finally raised her head, she glanced at the glass door in time to see him walk away. *He probably thinks I'm crazy. Hell. I am crazy. What the hell am I doing? I shouldn't be teasing him with brownies. I should be running in the opposite direction. The last thing I need is a man in my life right now. I just got rid of one.*

Pulling away from the station, she shook her head trying to clear her thoughts of him. However, nothing could take away the vision of him and the childlike expression on his face when he saw the brownies. He was adorable for having kind of a gruff demeanor. Kind of like his son's when he gave him money and told him to get a root beer. Wide eyes. Gaped open mouth. The whole bit. Her heart tumbled. The buzz of her phone had her blinking back to reality. Nothing could keep the smile from forming on her lips when she saw who it was. *Speak of the devil.*

—I'm making myself sick—

Jessi chuckled. There was another buzz. A photo popped up of the plate she had given him heaping full of brownies minutes before, that now was half empty.

—Dear Lord. I hope some of those were eaten by others at the station—

— Some. Not many. I won't need to eat dinner

tonight. I hope you aren't texting and driving—

—Leave some for your kiddos—

—One each—

—Give them at least three each—

—One—

—Aw. You're mean. They helped me get settled in too—

—Have you been around kids who are full of brownies? Just be glad I'm giving them some. You didn't answer me. Are you texting and driving? —

— Well, if you are worried, why are you texting me? And no. Stopped at a stop sign. I'm getting honked at. Gotta go—

—Good luck at your meetings—

She smirked and shook her head. *God, I need to stay away from him and he's making it so hard.*

A few miles up the highway a sign appeared for Lake Village Restaurant, and she turned down a winding road flanked with pine trees. At the opening stood a Spanish villa that looked like it was picked up from the Mexican Riviera and dropped in Arkansas. The winding driveway guided her to a large parking lot with a handful of cars. She parked and walked up to two large wrought iron gates that opened into a courtyard with a huge fountain and gardens filled with multicolored rose bushes. Benches and bistro tables with chairs were placed around the flower beds for guests waiting to be seated inside the restaurant.

She pushed open a heavy wooden door and was immediately greeted by an older Hispanic lady wearing black pants and a white button-down shirt.

"I'm sorry, we aren't open."

"Oh, I have an appointment to see Anson

Carothers."

The woman gave her a shy nod. "Wait here, please."

A man in a double-breasted white chef's coat appeared around the corner several minutes later. A black apron was cinched around his waist, and he was drying his hands on a towel he had slung over his shoulder. His thick dark hair was closely cropped, and he had just a hint of five-o-clock shadow.

His brows were drawn together. "Can I help you?" The sound of his voice let her know she was interrupting his day.

"Yes. I spoke to Peggy on the phone last week about coming out to tour the restaurant. She said I needed to speak to you."

"She did, did she? And why exactly do you need a tour? Are you with a magazine?"

"Oh, no. The owners hire—"

"You seem familiar." Anson crossed his arms over his chest and cocked his head.

"I do?"

"I'm sorry. Continue. I just feel like I've seen you some place before."

"Oh." Heat rushed up her neck. She had won many awards and had become fairly well known in her field. However, she doubted that was the reason he thought she looked familiar. "I was going to say, the Valentis hired me to be the restaurant's sommelier. I'm Jessica Maddox."

As she said her name Anson joined in. His eyes rounded in surprise and his hard, no-nonsense expression faded. He clapped his hands together once and smiled. You worked at Austere Nouveau."

"Yes."

"I read the article in Flawless Palate magazine about you. You have won awards all over the world."

"Well, I wouldn't say—"

"What in the hell are you doing here?"

Her body stiffened. She had no clue what had been shared with the Valentis as to why she needed to get away, and as of yet, she hadn't had to come up with a good story. What could she say on the fly?

"Things were getting a little too much for me in the big city, so I decided to get some fresh air. The Detwilers hired me at their vineyard, and I guess they know the owners of this place because they got to talking and, well, here I am."

"Yes. The Detwilers and the Valentis are good friends. We have several of their wines in our cellar." He paused not releasing her from his gaze. "I must say, I am honored to have you on board. When do you start?"

"I was told next week, although I guess it's up to you."

"Then, by all means, let me show you around." He headed back the way he came, and Jessi followed. The state-of-the-art kitchen, filled with stainless steel tables and workspaces, had an aroma that could only be described as mouthwatering. She prayed her stomach would not make itself known as Anson spoke about his staff. Several people in black chef's coats were scurrying around chopping and stirring. Anson stopped talking to watch his crew at work. His eyes narrowed and head moved as he studied the room.

"We started out with me and three others when the place opened a few months ago. Now we are up to sixteen, working different shifts."

"Wow. That's incredible. What brought you here?"

"The same thing as you. I was working in Vegas at Private Reserve, and it was killing me and taking a huge toll on my marriage. I noticed an ad in one of the food magazines about this restaurant needing a chef. My wife is from this area so I thought it might be a good change. It was the best thing I've ever done. I love it here." He motioned for her to follow him out a door and down a few steps. "This place was built by Paul Morrison back in early eighties. He was a big oil tycoon. When the oil bust hit, he took a hit and wound up walking away from the place. It sat for years. Someone bought it and tried to fix it up but ran out of money, so it sat a little longer. Then the Valentis bought it at a bank auction with the idea of making it a nice restaurant and event venue. We've already had a couple of weddings."

They entered the wine cellar filled with dark-stained wooden shelves containing bottles of wine. Jessi's eyes wandered to all the shelves. "Now this is my happy place."

"It's not quite fully stocked yet. We have a good selection though."

She stepped away from Anson and wrapped her arms around her waist feeling the coolness in the room. "You really do." Jessi's fingers ran along the edge of the shelves reading the labels. The few she didn't recognize she would need to become familiar with. Dragging her phone from her pocket, she snapped photos of the bottles to refer to later. As she continued examining the shelves, she stopped and gasped in surprise as a grin filled her face. "You have Salishan?"

"Are you familiar with the Salishan Cellars Winery?"

"Yes. I actually got to tour it a couple of years ago."

"How did you manage that?"

"I was invited to speak about wine pairing at a small university in Washington and I found out the winery wasn't too far away. Several of their reds and blends had become some of my favorites, so I took a chance and gave them a call to see if they would give me a tour. I didn't realize it was a family business, and they were some of the nicest people I've ever met. Cooper Miles, the Head Grower for their operation, showed me around the vineyard and talked about all the different varieties of the grapes, and the process they use. He was hilarious. Said, 'the key to great wine is to talk to the plants.' When we went into the wine tasting room, I got to meet a few of the other family members, and they let me taste some of their new blends. They have a two-thousand fourteen cab that is amazing. If you can get your hands—"

"Has flavors of caramel and pepper—"

"That's it!" Her hand flew to her chest. "I absolutely love it."

"The perfect blend."

"That's what made me want to tour the winery." As she finished perusing the wines Anson joined her.

"Let me take you up to the dining area." She followed him up the stairs to a bright and airy dining hall with windows spanning floor to ceiling along two sides. Tables covered in white tablecloths and purple fabric chairs were set strategically throughout the area. Purple, gold, blue, and red light fixtures that resembled a field of pansies hung from the ceiling.

"Wow! This place is beautiful." Her eyes were drawn to the veranda that overlooked the lake. Fiberglass tables in the same hues as the light fixtures filled the area with coordinating chairs. "Oh my gosh, the view."

Anson opened the doors to the outside overlooking a large lake. "Pretty spectacular."

"No kidding. I definitely didn't get a view like this at the last place I worked."

"I have to say, I'm much happier working here. The pressure is gone, the view is amazing, and I still have the ability to create." He strolled back inside. "Through here we have our party room or event venue." The room was wrapped with windows that took advantage of the lake view and also had a private patio.

Turning his attention to what he required of her, he walked her through the rest of the restaurant to the office where they sat down so she could fill out the paperwork. She took the opportunity to elaborate on her move to Arkansas and the reason she would be using an alias. He didn't bat an eye.

With a schedule in hand, and several bottles of wine to sample, she said her goodbyes and drove away, never meeting the couple that hired her sight unseen. Her next stop was Purple Skies Vineyard which was a few miles away.

The winding road brought a beautiful two-story Victorian house surrounded by acres and acres of grapevines and lavender into view. The front of the house had a long walkway with lavender and wildflowers lining the path up to a set of stairs and a wooden porch with several white rocking chairs. Her hand brushed against the bushes eliciting an intoxicating smell.

Pushing the door open, she scanned the gift shop area filled with wine glasses, mugs, T-shirts, stained glass, and other items. At the back of the store was a woman, with short brown hair and dark red glasses, standing behind a counter. The woman peeked up and smiled as Jessi approached.

"Hi. I'm here to see Vicki or Burt Detwiler?"

The woman held her hand out. "You must be Jessi. I'm Vicki. It is so good to finally meet you." Jessi took her hand. "Let me go get Burt, he will take you on a tour." Vicki disappeared through a door and moments later she returned, followed by a giant of a man with thick auburn hair and a bushy beard. Dressed in a red checked flannel shirt with the sleeves rolled halfway up his arm, he resembled a lumberjack. A large tattoo peeked out from under his right sleeve, as he reached out his hand to shake hers, and made her curious as to what it was. His hand dwarfed hers, and he could probably crush it with one squeeze, although with the smirk he was wearing and the twinkle in his eye, she figured he was a big Teddy bear.

"Nice to meet you, Jackie," he said gently shaking her hand.

Vicki backhanded him and let out a playful sigh. "He's messing with you. He knows your name." The low rumble of his chuckle made her realize Vicki was right.

"Let me take you out back to the vineyard." He motioned for her to follow him through the door. "The first thing you need to know is, although you look very pretty and professional today, you will get dirty. I suggest jeans and a T-shirt, maybe with a light cotton long sleeved shirt to block the sun, and sneakers. We do have some shirts with our logo on them that we can provide."

"Okay." She could do jeans and sneakers. Beats wearing heels for hours any day. *This whole moving across country thing might be a lot better than I expected.*

They hopped in a utility vehicle and sped off up through the vineyard. "We've had this place for ten years," he stated. "A little over eighty acres total. We started out growing an assortment of crops. The last seven years we have been primarily growing grapes and lavender. They both do well in this climate and soil. Some of our grapes came from a crop that survived a massive fire out in California. I've been pretty picky with what I've planted. After three growing seasons we started producing, and the wine sold so well at the herb festivals and farmers markets that we decided to turn the first floor of the house into the storefront. We've been open for about two years now."

"What exactly will my job entail?"

"Basically, you will have your hands in every area. Buying the best plants, harvesting, processing, tasting the wines to make sure the blend is correct, and, of course, marketing." He pointed. "This is my favorite area. These grapes are perfect globes and have such a robust flavor. They are almost spicy." He hopped out, so she did the same. Lifting some clusters of deep red grapes, the size of large gumballs, he motioned. "There are about six acres of these. We started out with around ten plants to begin with. I found them not too far from here over in Missouri. The heirloom vine came from Germany." He walked along row after row lifting different clusters. Although she had toured several vineyards, she really hadn't gotten that up close and personal in any vineyard other than Salishan. "The position you would fill isn't a full-time job. Certain times of the year, your hours would be cut back considerably. That's why Vicki thought to call Peggy Valenti. They're great people and we can work with them on your schedule, so you aren't run too ragged." He walked back to the utility vehicle. "So, you think you would be okay with this end of the wine business?"

"Absolutely. I'm actually very excited to get started," she said without hesitation.

"It won't pay near what you were getting in Philadelphia."

"That's not a problem. The cost of living is much cheaper, I've noticed, than Philadelphia. So, I think I will be fine."

"Next weekend is the herb festival downtown. We will be presenting several of our wines. We would like you to represent us. I think with your expertise, you would be able to put the best face on our wines."

"I would love to."

"We will work out the details and get you up to speed with the wines we would like to market at the festival."

They arrived at another building across from the house, and he took her on a tour of the processing room then the bottling area and finally the tasting room. He retrieved several bottles from the shelves and put them in a box and said, "I want you to give your critique of these," then set the box on a table. "I've selected a variety of reds and whites. Some, we plan to have at the festival. I'm not going to tell you which ones because I don't want to influence your critique." *I think I'm going to have a very interesting weekend.* "Let's go back to the house and I'll get you a few shirts. We open at ten on weekdays, nine on weekends. What is your schedule for the restaurant?" She pulled a paper from her purse and handed it to him. "I'll have you come in at nine Monday and we will get you set up and have you fill out your paperwork then."

He pushed open the door and they returned to the gift shop. "Vicki, she needs some shirts."

"What's your size?" Vicki asked as she shoved a stack of sacks under the counter.

"Medium?" Vicki moved past Burt and went through the door.

"I'll take the box out to your car."

"That would be great." She opened her purse and fished her key fob out and hit the button. "It's the blue Jag."

"A Jaguar? You really were paid well up there." He turned and headed to the front door.

Vicki returned with a bag and passed it to Jessi. "I got you both short sleeve and long sleeve in the Ts and also some of the cotton button ups in a few colors."

Jessi took the bag. "Thank you." She watched Burt through the windows as he placed the box into her car. Vicki leaned on the counter and did the same.

"Is there anything else I need to know?"

Vicki laughed. "It looks like he's given you plenty to work on. Don't worry if you don't get through all of them. You have plenty of time."

Jessi smiled. "Do you have a favorite?"

"Oh. I don't know. They are kind of like kids. You put the work into them and when they turn out good, it gives you a sense of pride." She chuckled. "Don't be afraid to really let us know what you think though. We want to have a quality product. We know there are things we can improve on."

"Okay. I will do my best."

Burt returned through the door. "You are all set."

"Okay. I guess I will see you Monday then." She shook Vicki's hand then Burt's.

"See you Monday, Joanie." Jessi giggled as she opened the door.

Chapter Six

Mitch stared at his computer screen, scrolling through social media apps, searching for any signs Jessi's ex was trying to find her. He had put a call into the cyber unit in Little Rock to keep an eye out. So far, they hadn't responded so he decided to conduct a search on his own for any evidence Dante Angenelli was searching for Jessi. As of yet, he'd found nothing. In fact, he'd found hardly anything on Dante at all. He'd scanned page after page and come up empty. Still, something didn't sit right. He wasn't convinced she was completely safe.

The chime of his phone caused him to jump. It was Kathy, his kids' babysitter. His gut plummeted thinking something was wrong. It happened every time she called. He figured every parent went through the same thing. It's every parent's worst nightmare to get a call with bad news about their kid. He took a deep breath to calm his voice. "This is Mitch."

"Hey. It's Kathy. Would it be okay with you if Georgia and Brandon spent the night? Michael and Ashley have been begging me for over an hour."

He let out the breath he was holding. "Are you sure? You have a house full as it is."

"Two more won't make a bit of difference. I cook for an army anyway. And to be honest, it at least keeps those two of mine occupied, so I only have to deal with the other three."

"If you are sure. I'm good with it. I'll swing by around ten tomorrow, if that's okay?"

"That sounds great."

Disconnecting the call, he sat back in his chair and rubbed his eyes. He loved his kids, but they were a bundle of energy, and after a couple of weeks with them, he was mentally and physically exhausted. Refreshing his screen, he checked the time. Thirty minutes until quitting time. He had been on the evening shift for over three years but when he found out he would be getting the kids permanently, he put in for a transfer to day shift so he could be home when they got out of school, and it was accepted. He liked it much better and looked forward to the possibility of a social life. His phone buzzed. Jessi.

— So how many are left? —

He snickered at her comment and stepped away from his desk to walk to the breakroom. Truth be told there were several who had partaken of Jessi's delicious brownies, although he didn't have to tell her that. He took a photo of the plate with only four brownies left, then hit send. Within seconds the little dots moved along the bottom of his text screen below the photo.

— Oh my gosh. That was a double batch. How many of those did you eat? Did you save any for Brandon and Georgia? —

Mitch's fingers hovered over the screen trying to come up with something clever to say.

— Let's just say I probably won't be sleeping any tonight. Brandon and Georgia are spending the night with some friends so too bad so sad. More for me—

—Save the rest for them. You don't need any more—

He smirked and thought about what to say. The bubbles popped up again.

—So, Mitch, if you are going to be all by yourself this evening, would you be interested in joining me in taste testing some wine? —

His stomach tightened. He spent the last two weeks giving himself reasons why Miss Jessi Maddox was not a good idea. Which meant he spent the last two weeks continually thinking about her. The idea that she could be in danger had him obsessed with making sure she was safe. He had officers, including himself, patrolling her neighborhood four times a day. And countless hours were spent searching the Internet for anyone searching for her and researching the Angenelli family. The more he delved into their history the more he wanted to ramp up her protection.

Maybe it would help if he got more information from her. If he did accept her offer, he might be able to find out more about her and the Angenelli family and maybe, just maybe, find out how to guarantee her protection.

— You cooking? If you can cook like you can bake, I might be persuaded—

He watched the dots dance again on his screen and failed miserably at trying to keep the smile from spreading across his face.

—I'm not too shabby. What do you like? —

—Brownies—

—I think you've had enough, don't you? —

—Never—

—I think I may have created a monster—

— What exactly did you put in them? I am feeling kind of strange—

—Trust me. It's my grandma's recipe. Everything is legal and organic. It's the sheer volume of chocolate you have ingested, I'm sure. You are on a caffeine high. No more for you sir—

—Forever? —

—Are you coming by, or not? —

—I guess so—

—Six thirty then? —

—Fine—

****

It was the perfect day. No clouds in the sky except a few jet streams. The winds were calm, and the temperature made you want to be outside. Mitch drove through town with his sunroof open, and windows down, and noticed several people, sitting outside some of the local businesses, visiting. He thought about stopping to find something he could bring as a gift for Jessie. What though? She obviously already had wine, and flowers seemed inappropriate. Chocolate? Well, if he was being honest, he'd had enough to last him a lifetime. There was no explanation of what had come over him when he was texting her earlier. He wasn't lying when he said he felt strange. Almost like he was drunk.

When he had come to his senses after he got home, he thought about calling her and cancelling. He didn't though. He didn't want to sit at home alone again. And the more he thought about it, the more he liked the idea of spending some time with her even if it was to get more information that might help keep her safe. He pulled up in the driveway and stepped out of the car. The front door opened before he even had time to shut his car door. Jessi stood in the doorway in a navy tank top and a long, flowy, blue and white skirt. Her hair was half up with loose pieces that framed her face. She was gorgeous. Mitch's heart stuttered so violently he had to suck in a deep breath.

"I heard you pull up," she said casually leaning against the door frame. "I love cars that growl."

Mitch smirked and walked up the driveway. "One of the reasons I bought it."

Jessi moved out of the doorway as he approached. "Come in. Dinner isn't quite ready. I'm waiting on the scalloped potatoes and bread to get done."

The smell of the food hit Mitch's nose when he entered the living room and his stomach growled. "Whatever it is you're cooking smells delicious."

"Just something one of the chefs taught me." She walked back into the kitchen. "Make yourself at home." She called over her shoulder. "Do you like seafood?"

He found a spot on the sectional and sat down. "Love it."

"Good. Since I didn't know, I have a little surf and turf planned." Mitch peered back at her. "I couldn't decide if I wanted to start off with red or white wine first because we could go either way." She walked around the bar with two glasses of red wine. "I decided we would start with a cabernet from the Lodi wine region of California, then maybe move on to a Sonoma white, although I have some others we might try."

He gave her a sidelong glance when she handed him his. "Exactly how many bottles of wine are we sampling?"

"I have fifteen."

Mitch's whole body jerked. "Fifteen? You don't plan—"

"No silly," she snickered. Her nose wrinkled with

her comment and Mitch lost all ability to think for a second. "We aren't going to drink all fifteen. We'll drink some and maybe taste some. And yes, there is a difference." Jessi walked back into the kitchen and Mitch heard her banging around, so he stood and strolled toward the noise.

"Can I help with anything?"

She set two place settings on the bar and responded, "no," then scanned the food on the counter. "Well, yes. You can help yourself to some food. We have steak, scallops, roasted Brussel sprouts, and scalloped potatoes." She studied all the dishes on the counter. "Oh, and garlic bread." Pulling it from the oven, she set it on the counter and began slicing it.

"It all smells delicious." He picked up his plate and moved around the bar to get to the food. Grabbing a spoon, he ladled some Brussel sprouts onto his plate then reached for the steak bumping into Jessi who was doing the same. "Sorry." He spun around to get some potatoes instead and bumped into her again. "Okay. I'll wait until you get yours."

"No, you are the guest. You get yours first."

"Ladies first." Jessi rolled her eyes and let out a huff. Mitch stood his ground. "Hey. I had a southern momma who taught me to be a gentleman. Now shut up and get your food." Jessi smirked and shook her head, then filled her plate. She waited for him to fill his before they sat down at the table.

"So, tell me, what is this simil, somel—" he cut into his steak and took a bite "—oh my gosh this is delicious."

"Sommelier," she filled in. "And thank you. I kind of dated the chef at one of the restaurants I worked at, so I got to learn a few tricks of the trade."

"Yeah, you did," he said after biting into half a scallop.

"A sommelier is a wine expert. You've probably had one, at some time, come to your table when you've been out to eat." She shoved a bite of potatoes in her mouth.

"Honestly? I don't know that I have. There aren't many high-end restaurants around here. We didn't have the money to go to those restaurants anyway when we didn't have kids, and when we did, we wound up being a fast food family."

"Do you know how to tell if the wine is high in alcohol?"

"Maybe. Does it have to do with, how the residual drips down the glass when you tip it?"

"Ding. Ding. Ding. Good job. The more legs, the higher the alcohol content. Also, the slower it moves down the glass the sweeter the wine."

"Seriously? That's interesting. I didn't know that."

"Basically, I learn everything about the wines. Their fragrances. What flavors they convey. How sweet or dry they are. How they feel on the palate. How they finish. And what foods they go with. That way, when a customer is needing a wine to go with their meal, I can help them find the perfect one."

Her hand caressed the glass as she described each element, and her voice took on a rich sultry tone that showed how much passion she held for her trade. Mitch was mesmerized.

"Wow. So where did you learn to do that?"

"I got interested when I started working as a server at a small restaurant in Wicker Park just outside of Philadelphia. Then I moved to another restaurant closer to the city that was a little more upscale, and apprenticed with the sommelier there. He told me about a school in California that was one of the premier schools in the world. I was certified as a sommelier there, then had the opportunity to train in France and Italy."

"That's impressive. And you get to drink wine."

"In the grand scheme of things, not so much. I taste wine. Again, there is a difference." She cut a piece of ribeye. "So, what made you want to get into law enforcement?"

"Honestly? I have wanted to be a police officer since I was little. I just always knew."

"Do you like the work?"

Her question should have put him on edge. He was expecting the accusatory tone that Lorrie's voice always held when his job was discussed. He remembered countless arguments about his long hours, and the dangers of the job. But Jessi's tone held no edge. She sounded genuinely curious. "Yeah, I really do. I mean it can get boring sometimes like when you have to pick up stuff out of the road." He sucked in his cheek, trying not to smile, and glanced off knowing Jessi was throwing darts at him with her eyes. "But for the most part it is extremely rewarding."

"Have you ever had to shoot anyone?" His thoughts went back to his buddy Cody and the night he took the life of his dad. The thought put an ache in his chest. Although, if he had to do it over, he wouldn't have changed anything. It saved Cody's life. Still, it didn't keep him from feeling a tinge of guilt.

"Yeah." He could see the sadness take over her expression.

"I'm sorry. I didn't mean to—"

"It's part of the job. I knew going into this field that

it was dangerous, and I might be called on to make tough decisions. It's what we train for." He took a bite of his garlic bread and decided the mood had gotten too serious. "Do you like what you do?"

The twinkle in her eyes immediately returned. "I do. I didn't exactly choose it. It kind of chose me. I like that it doesn't conform to the norm. It fits me." He was inclined to agree. Something about her didn't conform to the norm. She had an edge, and a strange mix of gentleness and confidence that he was finding harder and harder to resist. He lifted his glass and took a sip. "What do you think of this wine?"

"It's good." He swirled the liquid around the glass and then set it down. "Very smooth." Sitting back in his chair, he crossed his ankle over his knee and tipped the glass, studying the residuals coating the sides. His eyes lifted to Jessi's and met her amused gaze.

"Tip the opening to your nose and tell me what you smell."

He breathed in deep. "It smells sweet…and maybe a little smoky?"

"Good. Now take a drink and hold it in your mouth for a bit before you swallow."

He watched and followed as she took a drink then paused before she swallowed. "It has a spiciness to it, like a black pepper taste."

"Yes." Her face lit up with excitement. "Okay. What do you get as the aftertaste?"

He smacked his lips together and gazed up to the ceiling. "It almost has a—" he rubbed his fingers together like he was trying to come up with the right term, "—grapey flavor."

Jessi picked her napkin up and threw it at him.

"What is with you today. First you eat the plate full of brownies and now—"

He held his hands up. "I'm sorry. I think it's the lack of sleep. I'm still getting used to having the kids full time and it has taken its toll."

Jessi's brows furrowed. "You don't have them all the time?"

"No. I actually just got full custody a couple of weeks ago."

"Oh. What happened?"

Mitch sat back in his chair.

"You don't have to tell me. I don't mean to pry," Jessi added quickly.

"No, it's fine. Their mom and I have been divorced for a little over four years. It was an amicable split. We are still friends, and shared custody until she got married recently and she and her new husband moved to Poland."

"Ah yes. Georgia mentioned that."

Mitch nodded remembering his little girl's announcement. "We got married young and me being on the police force was hard on her. It can be intense sometimes and once the kids were born it was too much for her. We went to counseling. She said she couldn't handle the stresses of the job and gave me an ultimatum. The job or her."

Jessi gasped. "You're kidding me."

Mitch shook his head. "She told me to quit the force. I balked because I really do love my job, and she took that as my answer. That was the beginning of the end. She agreed to continue with the counseling. I thought maybe we would make it through the storm. Then she met someone while she was volunteering at Brandon's school, and I came home early one day to find her and her *friend.*

"Oh my gosh, Mitch. I'm so sorry."

"They weren't actually going at it, but their relationship was far from innocent and things kind of disintegrated from there. She finally filed for divorce."

"How old were the kids?"

"Georgia was two and Brandon was six." His thoughts zeroed in on the day they sat Brandon down and told him, and the usual ache filled his chest. "Anyway, she found someone that makes her happy and they got married two weeks ago and his job is taking him to Poland. She thought it would be best for the kids to stay in the U.S."

Jessi sat for a moment. "Wait. So, did you get the kids the day we met?"

"Yeah. I stopped at the station to get the box of photos after I picked them up at the airport. I was going to take it home to see if I could find any more clues to the owner."

Her mouth dropped open, and her face filled with shock. "Oh my God. I feel horrible. I can't believe I did that to you."

"Did what? We had a great time. Georgia loves you. She wants you to come over to play sometime."

She tilted her head. "Aw, really? I love her too. But seriously. I'm so sorry."

"No need to apologize. Again, we had a great time."

"Did you really? I mean, I did. You guys made unpacking so much better."

"The place looks great by the way."

Her eyes darted around. "Thanks. It's really starting to feel like home."

"I have to ask something though." Her brow tipped

up. "What's the story of the dog?"

"Layla?" She glanced at the photo on the wall. Mitch nodded. "She was my best friend. I got her when she was a puppy. She was my constant companion. We went through so much together. She met all my boyfriends. Liked some, didn't most. She knew before I did if they were good guys or not." Jessi let out a scoff and shook her head. "She wasn't very fond of Dante. Go figure. I should have known. I had her for thirteen years. She passed away from cancer two years ago. I was devastated."

"I'm sorry. I know how you feel. I had a German Shepherd growing up named Frosty." His mind flashed on the furry companion he had for so many years. "She wasn't the standard shepherd colors. She looked like she had a dusting of snow on her. Great dog. I never went anywhere without her. When she died, it nearly killed me." He shook his head. "I wanted to get a dog for the kids but by the time they were big enough my marriage was struggling."

She gazed back at the shadow box for a long minute then slowly brought her focus back to Mitch. "Are you ready for round two?"

He knew the subject had gone as far as she was comfortable, so he left it alone. Gazing at her from below his brow, he asked, "Of?"

"Wine tasting." She stood and held her hand out to gather his plate. Instead, he stood and picked his and hers up and walked to the kitchen with her following him. "Actually, what we are doing is drinking not tasting." While he placed the plates in the sink, she opened the refrigerator, stood for a moment, then took out two bottles. "I have a Rose` from Purple Skies, or a Zin from

92

the Sonoma Valley. Take your pick."

"What's the difference?"

"You aren't much of a wine drinker, are you?"

"I don't mind it. I just don't have the occasion to drink it much. It's more of an intimate setting drink. A nice dinner drink. I'm usually eating fast food or store-bought pizza, so my go to drink is beer."

"Gotcha. This Zinfandel is a blend, meaning it is a mix of white and red wines. It's a fruitier wine. Tends to be a little sweeter. Whereas the rose` is a white wine that has been exposed to the grape skins for a short period of time. That's where its light pink color comes from. The flavor is still light although more complex on the palate."

"Let's go with the rose`."

"Good choice." He playfully swiped the bottle when she picked up the wine opener. Her mouth curled up in one corner as she studied him, then handed over the opener. He uncorked the wine while she washed the glasses before he poured some in each. His eyes locked on hers as she smelled the wine. "What do you smell?"

Slowly tipping the glass, he breathed deep. "It kind of smells like pineapples."

A smile filled her face. "That's what I got too." She tipped the glass to her lips, and he did the same.

"It's really smooth. I definitely taste vanilla."

She nodded her head then tipped it just enough to clink his, then walked around the bar to the living room. Folding her legs under her, she sat back on the sectional. Mitch sat down and crossed his ankle over his knee.

"You have me curious. You said there is a difference between drinking and tasting."

"Tasting is just that. You don't drink the wine; you swish it in your mouth then spit it out."

"Seriously?"

"Yes. Are you kidding me? I can't drink all that wine in there."

"Why do you have so many bottles?"

"I was not familiar with some that the restaurant had, so I needed to get familiar with them. Burt from Purple Skies wanted me to critique some of their wines in case they needed to tweak them a little. Also, they are going to be at the herb festival next weekend, and I need to get familiar with the wines before I represent them. She ran her fingers through her hair. "I picked out a couple I liked that I thought maybe you would like to try this evening. The rest I will be tasting not drinking. Unless of course I really like it then I will cork it and save it for later."

"What was the red wine we had?"

"It was a California cabernet. It's usually a safe wine. Not too dry or sweet."

"I liked it." He stared at his glass. "I like this too. It's sweeter though."

"We could have gone either way. Usually, red wines pair better with red meat. They have a bolder richer flavor that brings out the flavor of the beef. On the other hand, white wines, along with blush or rose`, have a lighter flavor and mouth feel, and pairs better with fish and seafood. Since we had both beef and seafood, I thought I would bring out both."

"So, tell me, did you grow up in Philadelphia? I kind of got the idea you grew up maybe in a suburb or a smaller town."

"I actually grew up in a small town in Delaware named Carlin." She moved the pillow behind her to her lap. "Made this place seem like a metropolis. There was nothing there. That's why I decided to move to Philadelphia."

"And that's where you met Dante?"

"Yeah, when I was working at Austere Nouveau. He came in with his brother one night."

"And his family—"

"I think they all live in and around Philadelphia and were from the area. I'm not sure where his brother lives. It's outside of Philly."

"Does your family still live in Delaware?"

"Yes. My mom and dad bought some land and have a small farm with a pond."

"The farm sounds fantastic. I'd love to be able to go out and do some fishing in my own back yard."

"It is. Mom has a big garden and some animals. I caught a pretty good size bass at the pond the last time I visited."

"You did not."

"Why do you say that? You think I can't fish?"

"You don't strike me as a girl who would like the art of fishing."

"Well then you would be wrong. I fish."

"Well, I am—"

"And I will let you in on a secret."

He sat back and propped his leg up. "What's that?"

"I hunt."

"Seriously? What's the largest thing you've shot?" She stood and walked into the kitchen. Returning with the bottle of wine, she refilled Mitch's empty glass then added more to hers.

Settling back on the sofa, she said with a smirk, "I got an eight point buck a few years back." Mitch's brows rose and he held up his glass in congratulations, for her to clink it, And she did. "My dad was so proud. I haven't been hunting in several years though." She propped her elbow on the arm of the sectional and leaned her cheek against her fist.

Mitch gazed at her. She was so effortless with her beauty. He shook his head trying to dispel the fantasies that were playing out and focus to the conversation. "The last time I went hunting I thought I got shot in the butt."

Jessi's eyes widened. "No. Really? What happened?"

Mitch took a drink of his wine and chuckled. "The key phrase is 'I *thought* I got shot.' Four of us went out early one morning. It was about three years ago, I guess. We were heading to two blinds on this property outside of town, in a heavily wooded area, and it was barely breaking daylight. I spotted a huge buck not probably a hundred yards away. He had to have had twenty points. I kid you not. It was the biggest buck I had ever seen. We all stopped, and I lifted my gun. The deer started walking off slowly, so I took a few steps forward and followed trying to get my shot. Suddenly something popped me in the butt, and I yelped. My gun went off and the deer disappeared. I thought one of the guys lost sight of me, and thought I was the deer. Turns out I stepped on a large stick just right and it flipped up and swatted me in the butt."

Jessi started giggling. "I can see it." Mitch watched as her giggles transformed into a full out cackle which caused him to burst into laughter. Their laughter fed off each other to the point they were both gasping for air. Jessi wiped the tears from her eyes, still trying to catch her breath. "I really like this wine," she snorted.

Mitch had his hand on his chest trying to catch his

breath but with her comment another fit of laughter hit him. It all came to a screeching halt though when a loud thump came from her bedroom. Mitch jumped up, trying to clear the tipsy fog from his head, and listened for more sounds. His heart raced with the thoughts flying through his head.

"I left the window cracked, so something probably blew over."

"Stay here," he quietly growled and headed for the hallway. "Do you have a gun?"

"Yes, in the bedroom." Mitch let out a huff of frustration and flattened himself against the wall. The bedroom door was slightly ajar, so he slowly pushed it open and noticed the window was halfway up. White muslin curtains bellowed in the breeze. A box was flipped over on the floor and note pads and pens had spilled out. Mitch cautiously stepped through the doorway and scanned the room. He pushed open the bathroom door partially and did a cursory scan then went to the closet. Finding nothing, he breathed deep and turned to head up the hall, then stopped short seeing Jessi standing in the doorway. "I told you to stay there."

"I did…for a minute."

"What if someone had broken in? What would you have done? You could have been hurt." He walked over to the window and noticed the screen was loose. Making a mental note to fix it later, he closed the window and locked it.

"Aw. You're trying to protect me."

"Um, that's kind of my job. You know, 'to serve and protect'?"

"I could ask you the same thing. You don't have your gun."

"I've been trained in this situation. You haven't." Another noise sounded from the bathroom. Mitch pushed Jessi behind him and as both peeked in, a squirrel bounded straight for Mitch. Jessi screamed. Mitch jumped back, lost his balance, and landed on his butt on the floor. The squirrel bounced across the dresser onto the bed and out the doorway.

Mitch scrambled to his feet and ran up the hallway with Jessi close behind. "Do you have anything I can use to trap him?" His head darted back and forth searching for the frisky rodent.

"I can't think of anything." Jessi stayed close behind Mitch. The squirrel ran directly at them, and Jessi latched onto Mitch's shirt, dragging him in close, using him as a shield until it bounded across the living room.

"Do you have like a laundry basket?" She nodded and took off up the hall. When she returned, she had a small blue basket that she handed to him. Mitch carefully walked into the living room scanning the area. He finally spied a fluffy tail behind a teal curtain and slowly moved closer, reaching the basket out. As he lunged to drop it, the squirrel leaped from behind the curtain and scurried across the wooden floor right toward Jessi. She let out a high shrilled scream and jumped onto one of the dining room chairs. The squirrel immediately dodged past the table then leaped up on her desk. "Shoo him away. It will be easier to catch him on the floor."

"Are you kidding me?" She tentatively stepped off the chair and moved her hand slightly, trying to keep the animal from jumping at her. It made eye contact with her and crouched down. She moved her hand shooing it toward Mitch and the squirrel hurled himself right at his face. He yelped and threw the basket. Jessi snickered.

"Not funny." Reaching down and grabbing up the basket, he caught sight of Jessi doubled over in fits of laughter. His head swiveled trying to spot the squirrel and jerked when he heard a crashing noise and watched the squirrel as it perched on a small table. "You want to come help, or are you too busy laughing at me?"

She tried to speak but nothing came out except a snort. Mitch shook his head and returned his focus to the squirrel who had hopped from the table to the floor. He flung the basket at the furry creature, and it hit its mark, trapping the squirrel. Mitch jerked his head, surprised at the capture, and Jessi clapped her hands together.

"Yay! You got him."

"Yeah. No thanks to you." Mitch watched as Jessi tried to stifle a smile then busted out laughing again.

"I'm sorry. The expression on your face—"

His hands landed on his hips, and he stared at her. Shaking his head, he pretended to be mad, but her laughter had sent a torrent of heat through him. Turning away, he tried to quell the urge to drag her into him and teach her a lesson about what happens when someone laughs at him. "Do you have any of your boxes left that I can break down?"

Wiping the tears from her eyes, she took a shaky breath. "Yes." Trotting up the hall, she quickly returned with the box. "Do you want me to break it down?"

The squirrel pushed the basket and Mitch held it down to make sure he didn't get out. "If you would, then I can keep my hand on the basket." She took out a kitchen knife and ripped the tape to flatten the box. Handing it to Mitch, he slipped it under then flipped over the basket, and carried the squirrel out the door, setting it free. He glanced up to see Jessi standing in the doorway. "You might want to make sure the window is closed, or he will be back in your bedroom snuggling up to you tonight." Her eyes widened and she quickly disappeared. Mitch chuckled as he walked back into the living room with the basket.

When Jessi returned, he held out the basket and lifted his eyes to her. She busted out laughing again. Mitch put his hand on his hip. "What's so funny?"

She tried to stifle the laughter. "You." Her hand reached for the basket.

"I'd like to see your reaction having that flea-bitten rodent leaping at your face. Have you seen their claws?" He tried to give her his best angry face, but she snorted again which made him chuckle and shake his head again. He couldn't help smiling at her even though he knew she was laughing at his expense. She waved her hand in front of her face trying to calm down and suddenly the fire was back with a vengeance, and he had to fight like hell not to take her in his arms and kiss her.

Chapter Seven

Rejection was a real possibility when Jessi decided, last minute, to invite Mitch over. She knew it. He had every reason. She had a ton of baggage. Although, with the kids gone, what could it hurt? All he could do was say no. She was happily surprised when he didn't. That alone made her heart race. She knew exactly what she wanted to cook. It was one of her go to meals. There were a few that she had learned from working in a restaurant for so long. The meal wasn't the issue. She could nearly create it in her sleep. The outfit on the other hand, was. She changed three times trying to figure out what he might like. Why was she so nervous? What was it about him?

This man had taken over her thoughts, and she knew it was the last thing she needed. She knew she should avoid the opposite sex like the plague right now. She worried she was subconsciously trying to fill the void Dante left which was almost laughable because Mitch was nothing like Dante. In fact, he was nothing like any of the guys she'd dated. But damn, the more she was around Sergeant Mitch Gallagher, the more he dug his claws into her. And she liked it. The minute she saw him her entire body was engulfed with goosebumps. There was something about the way he moved. His walk. It was so confident, and it set her world on fire. And there was something else. Since the attack, everything set her on edge…except him. She should have been afraid. And yeah, he'd scared her when he walked up to her window at the grocery store. But when she met him face to face, her mind calmed. The fear was gone. Even when he peppered her with questions, she knew when he told her he would protect her, he would. She felt strangely safe.

And that laugh. I've never seen a guy break into uncontrolled laughter like that. It wasn't one of those obnoxious laughs either. It started with a raspy chuckle, and the longer it went on, the tears filled his eyes, and he couldn't catch his breath, and there was no way she could keep from joining in. He was so stiff when she met him; so reserved. Tonight though, he surprised her. Probably the wine, she guessed. He tried hard to put on the tough man persona, but deep down he was freaking adorable. She couldn't help laughing when the squirrel leaped at him. The expression on his face was priceless. Now though, the look was entirely different. Was he attracted to her? Or was she wishful thinking? The problem was, she wasn't thinking. She didn't need to be wishing for anything to happen. She couldn't stop it though. He made her feel pretty, the way he stared at her, and regardless of how he interrogated her to begin with, she enjoyed talking to him, and she didn't want this night to end.

Jessi sat back down on the end of the sectional. "So, since I have taught you a little bit about the art of wine tasting and we both have mastered the art of squirrel wrangling, what else can we tackle tonight?"

Mitch dug his phone out. "Eight twenty."

"It's still early."

"For you maybe, I'm still learning the art of being a single dad and it's kicking my ass."

"Well, you can't go home yet. You don't want to get pulled over for DUI."

He slid his teeth over his bottom lip. "That probably wouldn't look good on the department."

She scrunched her face. "Not so much." Silence fell between them as she thought about how much she enjoyed their dinner. Then it hit her, and she jumped out of her seat. "With all the squirrel wrangling I nearly forgot. I have dessert."

"Please tell me it's more brownies." His voice called out behind her.

She glanced at him over the bar. "No more brownies for you." Her eyes narrowed. "I can't believe you didn't save any for your kids."

"They didn't come home."

"Doesn't matter. You could have saved them for when they did."

"No. Don't you know the cardinal rule of brownies? They have to all be eaten in one day or it's bad luck."

"There is no such thing," she said skeptically. Retrieving the glass container she left to warm in the oven, she picked up a spatula and served up two squares of peach streusel then squirted whipped topping on both. Before she could look up, she felt his presence behind her.

"What is that? It smells delicious," he said, pointing at the dessert on the counter while picking up the container of whipped cream and spraying some in his mouth.

Jessi's mouth dropped open in disbelief, though she fought back a smile. "What are you doing? You contaminated my whipped cream."

His eyes locked on hers and widened at her scolding,

then the corner of his mouth slowly lifted in a mischievous smile. He swallowed and wiped his lips with his thumb. "Don't tell me you have never eaten a can of whipped cream before, because I won't believe it." Her eyes darted away. "Eh." He pointed the tip of the can at her. "I saw that."

"Okay maybe I've done it once...or twice. But it was mine." She shoved the desserts onto the bar. Mitch started to shake the can.

"I know what you need." He walked around the bar and stood in front of her. "Open your mouth." She shook her head and pinched her lips. "Open your mouth," he demanded, grinning as he pointed the can at her mouth. Her mouth opened slightly. "Wider," he encouraged, drawing out the word. Her teeth scraped her lip trying to decide whether to trust him, then her chin dropped more. He filled her mouth with the sweet substance to the point she had to back away. Whipped cream spilled out and she captured the excess with her fingers, then quickly, spread the sugary cream on Mitch as her cheeks expanded to accommodate the growing foam. He shook the can and took a step toward her holding his hand out trying to avoid another swipe with her sticky fingers. "Good isn't it." She nodded and moaned still trying to swallow all of it. Licking her lips to get all the excess that had escaped, she then wiped around them with her fingers. Grabbing her hand, he pulled it away from her face. Her eyes met his and with the tip of her chin, his lips were on hers. Softly at first. One sweet kiss and he backed away. She licked her bottom lip and her eyes slowly lifted to his. His thumb came up and rubbed the wetness, then his hand wrapped around her cheek and his mouth captured hers again. This time seeking more. Her lips parted and he swept in. The sweetness of the cream swirled as their tongues collided. He leaned against the bar, set the can down, and with his hand circling her waist, he dragged her to him. Every move he made felt effortless like a dance they had done thousands of times. His thumb caressed her cheek while his fingers massaged her neck. His touch was gentle, though it sent an electric current coursing through her that lit her up like a lightning storm. *Mercy, that mouth of his.*

Backing away, he placed several small pecks on her lips then leaned his forehead to hers and gazed down at her. She melted into the intensity of his gray eyes. His mouth twitched like he wanted to say something although nothing came out. He stood stock still, staring at her with an almost bashful expression on his face.

"You okay?"

"I-I haven't done that in a while."

"Well, you definitely haven't lost the skill," she blurted, still a bit stunned. The corner of his mouth curled up and he ran his fingers through his hair.

His brow slowly lifted, and he let out a hesitant chuckle. "You, you aren't so bad yourself." His eyes moved to her lips again and remained. Her breath caught thinking he would continue his assault on her mouth. Then, they moved back up to her gaze. "Maybe we should have some of this delicious dessert before I get myself in trouble."

She leaned into him and whispered in his ear. "I don't mind a little trouble."

He whispered back. "Don't tempt me." His hands rubbed her arms, and he brushed a kiss on her lips then moved around the bar and picked up his dessert. She rubbed her lips that were still tingling from the kiss.

Slowly, she stepped around the bar and picked up her dessert.

"So, what is this?" He questioned, obviously trying to break the tension.

"It's peach streusel. Normally the only sweetness in it is the peaches and a smidge of sugar. I like to add the whipped cream and if you pair it with your wine all the flavors and sweetness are enhanced."

He wandered over to the sectional and sat down in a relaxed position with one leg propped up. "I'm surprised our glasses are still upright. I figured the squirrel would have spilled them everywhere." She sat down against the opposite corner and propped both of her feet up. Mitch took a bite of the dessert and a sip of his wine. Jessi watched him, examining his facial expressions. He bobbed his head back and forth not saying a word.

"I'm not the best at making the crust."

"No, it's delicious and you are right. The wine really changes the flavors."

"Isn't that cool?" He suddenly quieted and tilted his head, studying her to the point she could feel the heat creeping up her neck.

"You are very interesting. You know that?" he finally said.

"I am? Seriously? You know people have called me all kinds of things. Unique. Odd. Quirky. Never once have I heard someone refer to me as interesting."

He shoved another forkful in his mouth. "You are. And I like that."

She wanted to believe him, although she never really thought of herself that way. They sat in silence for a long minute.

"I enjoyed tonight. Thanks for inviting me." His

words surprised her.

"Really?" He nodded and slowly licked his fork.

"Even with the squirrel wrangling."

A soft laugh erupted as his comment conjured up the whole escapade again. "I did too."

Picking up his glass, he took a sip. "I was thinking." His gaze remained on her as he set his plate on the table. Her eyes followed his movement until their eyes connected. "Maybe, if you are interested, we could do this again sometime." She could hear the hesitation in his voice, and she could barely contain her smile. He was nervous. "Preferably without the squirrel wrangling."

She pushed her foot out to where it was touching him. "I think I would like that."

"Good." Mitch brought his foot to the floor.

"You aren't leaving, are you?"

"I really need to. I am exhausted. I can call an uber and then get one of my buddies from the gym to drive me over tomorrow to get my car."

"Oh? What gym do you go to?"

"Do you like to go to the gym?"

"Are you kidding me? I hate going to the gym. Anyone who says they enjoy going to the gym is lying. Unfortunately, I have a terrible sweet tooth, if you haven't noticed. So, I have to do something, or I'd be the size of a house."

"I go to 24 to Life. It's not too far from here…well nothing is too far from here, but it's on this side of town."

"Do they have classes?"

"Yes. Anything you can think of. The girl, who lived here before, is teaching a yoga class, and I hear she's good. They also have cardio equipment and free weights."

"That sounds perfect. What time do you normally go?"

"It varies since the kids are out of school for the summer. Mostly, before I head into work."

"Maybe we can go together sometime."

"Sounds good. But hey, I'm going to need to go, otherwise I'm going to fall asleep right here. With the shift in my schedule and trying to keep up with the kids, and the wine, I'm fading fast."

She sat for a moment. "It would save you trouble and money if I let you sleep on the sectional."

"Jessi, I don't think—"

"Completely innocent. You sleep out here. I sleep in my room." She could see him studying her. Truth be told, she wasn't sure why she wanted him to stay so badly. She just really didn't want him to go.

"I appreciate it—"

"One other thing people say about me." She poked him again with her foot. "I'm kind of stubborn."

He reached down and rubbed her foot then tipped his eyes to her. "Are you sure?"

She chuckled. "Pretend you are protecting me from that crazy ass squirrel."

"I'm not so sure you shouldn't be protecting me."

Her brow inched up. "True. He seemed to have it out for you." Silence drifted between them, and she decided to use her last weapon in her arsenal. "I make a pretty mean omelet. Just sayin'."

He tipped his head and rubbed his hands down his cheeks. "Ahhh," he growled. "I may regret this." He let out a sigh and nodded. "Okay."

She clapped her hands together and put her feet on the floor. "Great. I'll get you some linens and a pillow."

With a wink, she hopped up and trekked up the hall. Pulling linens and a pillow from the closet, then a blanket from a chest at the end of her bed in her bedroom, she marched back into the living room with her arms full and made quick work of fixing the sheets to the cushions then added the blankets and the pillow. Her hand patted the blanket. "Now get comfortable and I will see you in the morning." She started to walk away but his fingers circled her wrist and he flipped her around.

Wrapping his arm slowly around her waist and nestling his other hand in her hair, he pressed his lips to hers in a hungry kiss. A wave of heat washed through her, and she leaned into him wrapping her arms around his neck, and digging her fingers into his hair. His kiss was needy; almost desperate, making his entire body tense, and with every movement she became putty in his hands. He backed away and she leaned her head on his shoulder trying to catch her breath and filling her nose with his scent. "I thought we agreed to keep this innocent."

"I needed to give you a good night kiss."

Lifting her head, her eyes widened with his comment. "You take kissing to a whole new level." His thumb wiped her lip, and she smoothed her hands down his shirt and patted his chest. "I'll see you in the morning." She stepped back and headed up the hall. When she got in the room, she peeked back around the door and watched as he pulled his shirt off revealing his toned chest. Her teeth grazed her lip wishing he had made more of a move on her. But she knew it would be a bad idea. Her body sure didn't though. That kiss was seared into her brain, and she craved his hands on her.

Changing into a soft pink camisole and loose gray

cotton shorts, she crawled in bed. The wind had picked up and she could hear the branches of the trees blowing against the window. The shadows they made from the streetlight outside were ominous and set her on edge, but the thought of Mitch sleeping not far from her made her feel safe and she quickly drifted off to sleep.

****

Her throat was on fire, and she could only manage short gasps. Each stair he dragged her down pounded against her already injured ribs and sent such a sharp stabbing pain through her she thought she was going to pass out. "Dante, stop." She cried, trying desperately to get free. "Please. Don't do this." Fury filled his eyes and he stayed silent. She could feel the vibration in his body as he growled. His hand wrapped around her wrist so tight it felt like it would break. She kicked at him with everything she had, but he only tightened his grip. Her strength was waning from the pain. How was she going to get away? Her vision blurred and the room began to spin. He picked up the gun at the bottom of the stairs. "No! Please, Dante, don't." She screamed.

"Jessi?" someone called out. But it wasn't Dante. It was strange; distant. She screamed. Hands latched onto her shoulders. She screamed again and jerked, trying to get away. A hand softly stroked her cheek. "Jessi." The voice was closer now. "Wake up." She moaned and sucked in a deep breath. Her eyes flew open. Cold sweat dotted her face. Her chest heaved trying to gain more air. *Where am I?* Trembling, she sat up and took in her surroundings. Tears filled her eyes and spilled down her cheeks. "It's okay. You had a bad dream." She heard the voice say. His arms swept around her, and she thought about fighting back, but somehow, sensing she was safe, she leaned in. Pressing her cheek against his soft warm skin, she let her emotions take over. His hand stroked her back, rubbing gently up and down. The heat of his breath caressed her cheek when he softly whispered, "You're safe, Jessi." He continued to rub circles gently up and down her back and little by little she relaxed. Finally clearing her head, she realized it was Mitch holding her, letting her cry on his shoulder, gently soothing her with his calming whispers.

She backed away and wiped her eyes. Mitch had switched the hall light on, and gazing at his face, he looked like an angel with the glow of the light behind him.

He slowly stood. "How about I get you some water?" Though she wanted desperately to say something, she was still too shaky, so she nodded slightly. "I'll be right back." His tone was reassuring. She was safe. Reaching over to her nightstand, she grabbed a tissue and blew her nose. *How embarrassing.* Although she'd had some nightmares since moving to Dalton, she didn't think about it when she invited Mitch to stay. Her mind had been preoccupied with other things.

Sitting up against her pillows she scooted her knees up, wrapped her arms around them and leaned her head down. Her body buzzed from the adrenaline racing through her veins. There was no way she was going to be able to sleep. The memories of that night were flipping like a slide show through her head now. Although the bruises had healed, the pain felt fresh. She dabbed her eyes as new tears wet her cheeks.

The floor creaked and Mitch stood in front of her. He'd brought her the glass of water. That's when she noticed he was in his boxer briefs. He handed her the water and slowly sat back down on the bed.

"Thank you," she said groggily and took a sip.

His hand squeezed her leg through the covers. "Are you okay?"

"Yeah. I'm fine. Just mortified." She let out a huff and set her glass on the nightstand. "I'm so sorry."

"Why are you sorry? You had a bad dream. It's not like you can control that."

"I know, but I invited you for a sleepover, not to take care of me."

"Don't worry about it." He patted her leg and stood. "Do you need anything else?" He stretched as he spoke.

She knew she shouldn't ask. She didn't want him to know how the nightmare affected her, but she didn't want to be left with her thoughts. "Don't go," she said under her breath.

"Excuse me?"

"I don't want you to go." Her throat thickened as tears threatened again. "Please."

Without a word he flipped off the light, moved to the other side of the bed, lifted the covers, and crawled in. She scooted back down, tucking her long hair over her shoulder. He dragged her to him wrapping his arm around hers. His lips gently kissed her shoulder and she snuggled into him. Her anxiety slowly dissolved, and her body relaxed. The feel of his body pressed up against her gave her the security she needed to drift off to sleep.

****

Thunder rumbled ushering in a summer storm. The windowpanes rattled with the low boom waking Jessi. Her hand moved brushing up against a warm hard surface. Slowly opening her eyes, she gazed at the silhouette of the man facing her. In the low light, she could make out his facial features and a little bit of his muscular arms she felt earlier wrapped around her body. She wanted to reach out and touch them again, but he was sleeping peacefully.

She propped herself up on her elbow and stared at him letting her eyes adjust. His hair was messy and the stubble on his face was darker. Gone were his steel gray eyes beneath the vail of thick dark lashes. Those lips that were so soft and sweet and had kissed her like there was no tomorrow, were parted slightly, and it took everything she had within in her not to lean down and taste them again.

The covers sat just below his chest revealing the etchings of his muscles and a slight dusting of pepper colored chest hair. She watched it rise and fall with each slow breath. He was so different and so handsome.

Her thoughts went back to the night before, wondering what he really thought of her. *Probably needy.* Nevertheless, he stayed. He didn't leave her. She'd developed a crush on him the first time she talked to him, then fell for him even harder last night when he was so gentle with her after she woke up disoriented and confused.

Slowly, she scooted into him, gently wrapped her arm around him, and breathed in his scent. He smelled like cedar and cinnamon. His arm, that lay between them, moved to her hip then slowly tugged her closer. Her cheek pressed against his chest, and she closed her eyes.

Chapter Eight

It was all too much. Mitch had not shared a bed with a woman since his wife left. Not even shared a kiss. He'd only been on a handful dates with women, and in the end, nothing came of any of them.

When he accepted Jessi's invitation, he had no idea what he was getting himself into. He knew he should have said no. There were so many reasons it was a bad idea, yet the way she effortlessly made him drop his guard and had him laughing made him rethink everything.

She had already become his obsession. From the first time he laid eyes on her photos, something about her haunted him. Meeting her face to face, he noticed a strength about her, even with everything she'd gone through. And when she finally broke, she suddenly became too much. Her laugh was too much. The mischievous twinkling of her hazel eyes was too much, and her smile, with those plump wine-colored lips, and the way she used that mouth, was way too much. The control, which he was barely hanging onto, was quickly being whittled away.

But who was he kidding? Watching her lick the whipped cream off her mouth last night snapped his last thread of self-control like a dry twig, and his mouth wound up on hers. He couldn't stop himself. He was barely able to pull himself away before he threw her on the table right there and lived out his dirtiest fantasies. Now, she was lying in his arms, molded to his body, fitting perfectly. Exactly like he knew she would. And oh, was he in trouble.

It tore him apart when his marriage ended knowing much of the reason had to do with his job. It wasn't the only reason. But he felt the primary blame landed on him. He unintentionally chose his job over his marriage.

Why did he love his job so much? It was unpredictable. It was dangerous. It was long hours that sometimes carried over to his homelife. All things his wife had thrown at him. All true. Still, he couldn't imagine doing anything else.

When his marriage ended, he decided he needed to avoid relationships if he wanted to continue working in law enforcement. He buried himself in his work and making sure his kids were taken care of, not leaving himself any time to date. On purpose.

It had been four years. Four years of telling himself he needed to stay focused. Four years of reminding himself that the job wasn't conducive to relationships. And if he were honest, it was four years of anger and loneliness. Four years of feeling empty. Four years, until last night.

He came extremely close to saying no to the invitation. But something inside him said enough. He loved his job and if truth be told, he was tired of apologizing for doing what he loved. He was tired of feeling guilty.

Maybe it had something to do with his ex-wife getting married. Maybe not. Whatever it was caused him to pull the trigger, and he was glad he did. He couldn't remember a time he laughed so hard or had so much fun even if it was chasing a rogue squirrel. It was like Jessi gave him permission to breathe again. Something about her made it easy for him to let go. He had been so closed up, had his walls so firmly in place, for so long, that he forgot how to enjoy life.

Her hand moved from his chest to the small of his back. The scent of her hair captured his nose as she snuggled into him. Vanilla. Without opening his eyes, he reached up, grasped her hip, and brought her closer. Her leg draped over his and his fingers fanned out, slowly moving up her bare leg, up over her soft shorts. Her head moved against him, and he felt her lips softly pressing against his chest causing him to shiver.

His eyes popped open. Daylight was taking over the darkness in the room. He could hear the patter of the rain against the windows. Jessi's hair was a mass of waves scattered everywhere. His fingers threaded through the silky brown strands, pushing the hair out of her face and he met her heavy-lidded eyes. "Don't start something unless you are ready for me to finish it," he whispered hoarsely. Her body rubbed against him as her lips met the hollow of his neck and her teeth scraped against his skin. He let out a strained warning growl. "Jessi?" She continued her assault until she made it to his lips.

"Please, Mitch," she whispered. Her fingers danced over his skin, and he squeezed her hips to his as he rolled her underneath him and deepened the kiss. Was he really going to do this? The hunger within him surged making him feel like his body had a mind of its own. He shifted his weight leaning into her. His hand roamed her body, brushing against the bare skin of her belly and slipping beneath her camisole. God she was so soft. His lips took what they wanted, moving quickly down her neck to her shoulder. He couldn't get enough. She tasted like a sweet peach and with each taste his hunger grew. Her whimpers and the way her fingers were kneading into his back only intensified his need. He lifted her top over her head and paused letting his eyes take in her body then move up to capture her gaze.

"Are you sure about this?" he asked again, his voice rumbling low in his chest. She didn't speak and he searched her lust filled gaze. He was prepared to back away. Knowing what she'd been through recently, and the fact that they hadn't known each other very long, it was probably a big mistake. Although backing away was the last thing his body wanted.

Her answer came on a breathy "yes" and her lips met his in a kiss so hungry it left no doubt. He had never felt lips so soft, so sensual and there was no way he could hold back any longer.

His hand skimmed down her hip pushing her shorts and panties down her legs while his lips trailed down her neck over her shoulder.

Her fingers skated along the top of his briefs pushing at them until he took over. His body sank down on top of hers and his fingers brushed her brown curls away from her face before he smoothed his hand down her hip. Then his head dropped. It had been so long. He nearly made a huge mistake. Trying to calm his intense need for her that had already ramped up his breaths, he said, "I don't have a condom."

"I'm on the pill. I'm clean."

His eyes lifted to hers. "I haven't done this in a long time."

"I'm fine, if you are."

"You sure?" Her hand wrapped his neck and she

pulled him down in another hungry kiss letting her fingers thread through his hair. When her eyes met his, he knew. His whole body lit up with tingles like he'd been jolted with electricity, and he could barely breathe. He dusted her lips with light pecks and gently pulled his fingers through her hair. A moan swept up the back of his throat as his lips continued down her cheek, brushing kisses against her neck. His hand slid down her hip and he pushed inside her. The sensation made his body shudder. *Shit.* It was too much, and he stilled.

Her eyes closed and he drank her in. God, she was absolute perfection. His fingers laced in hers and he slowly began to move. Her body responded in perfect sync, giving and taking. Their mouths melded together. She wrapped her legs around him and let out a whimper when he plunged deeper. He was quickly unraveling. Every touch of her fingers, every gasp from her lips pushed him dangerously close to that precipice, and he was trying to hold on for dear life. He didn't know if it was because he hadn't been with anyone for so long, or if it was Jessi, but something almost inhuman within him had been unleashed. His senses were heightened. He felt like a wild animal needing to mark every inch of her soft skin, possess every piece of her. She was so beautiful with her hazel eyes, long lashes and her plush lips.

She suddenly stilled, and a low moan erupted from deep within her. Her body trembled and her nails dug into the sheets, gripping them as she came apart. Watching her surrender to the spasms ripped the breath from his body. Plunging deep inside her, a surge of electricity roared through him, and his body shuddered sending him over the edge with her. His head dropped to the crook of her neck trying to steady his breath as he chased the surges pulsing through him.

Minutes passed. His heartbeat slowly settled. Raising his head, he tilted her chin up until he could claim her lips in a tender kiss, then rolled to his side. A million thoughts crowded his mind. What was she thinking? She was being too quiet. For the briefest moment a wave of worry hit him. He barely knew her. But even though he couldn't read how she felt, something about her felt right. Did she feel the same?

Glancing at her, her eyes were locked on him. She skimmed her bottom lip with her teeth then a slow smile emerged on her face. Mitch's brows lifted, questioning. Her smile increased and he smiled back at her. She snuggled into him, and he leaned down and kissed the top of her head. His eyes closed and as his fingers played in her hair, he was thankful his concern was unfounded.

"I'm going to run to the bathroom then do you want to take a shower while I get breakfast started?"

Mitch sat up a little. "Sure." He checked the alarm clock on the nightstand. Eight thirty. "Then I probably need to go." Jessi's face immediately winced. "I need to pick up my kids at ten."

"I know. I just don't want you to go." He leaned down and gave her a quick kiss. She scooted off the bed and he watched her stroll into the bathroom. Finding his boxers, he slid them on and stood. His body felt relaxed, and a smile crossed his face as he headed up the hallway. His clothes lay at the corner of the sectional. Picking up the blankets and bedding, he tried to fold them then placed them back on the cushion before picking up his clothes and trekking back down the hall to wait for her to come out of the bathroom.

After showering, he opened the bathroom door and

was hit with a delicious scent coming from the kitchen. He shrugged on his shirt without buttoning it and headed into the living room. His eyes scanned the area for his phone, finding it in his shoes next to the sectional. There was a message. Making sure it wasn't from the babysitter, he shoved it into his pocket and walked to the kitchen buttoning his shirt. "Something smells amazing."

Jessi stepped up next to him and gently ran her hands inside the opening in his shirt. "Are you hungry, because it's almost done."

"Yeah, I kind of worked up an appetite." A wolfish grin crossed his face and Jessi's cheeks garnered a tinge of pink. He leaned in and kissed her.

"Coffee is there." She pointed. "Cups are in the cupboard above it. Milk is in the fridge." Mitch reached in the cupboard, grabbed a cup, and poured.

Jessi handed a plate to him, and he took it to the table and sat down. He retrieved his phone remembering the message. Jessi sat down across from him.

"Everything okay?"

He peeked up and noticed her eyes on his phone. "Oh, yeah. I got a message from my buddy Cody." He clicked on the message and a photo popped up. A chuckle burst from Mitch's belly.

"What is it?" Jessi questioned.

"Cody and his wife Jenna had a baby boy last night." He flipped the screen to her revealing a red cherub faced sleeping baby wrapped in a printed blanket.

She took the phone. Her face softened. "Aw he's beautiful. He's got quite a bit of hair." She handed the phone back to him. "What's his name?"

He typed a congratulations and sent it on, then

glanced back at the information Cody sent with the photo. "Alexander Joseph Spencer. He said they are going to call him AJ." Mitch's thoughts flashed back to the day Brandon was born. He remembered the feeling he had holding his wife's hand while she brought their first child into the world. He was so proud of her. The pain that she went through was obviously more than anything he had ever endured, and she stayed so strong. Guilt washed through him thinking about the way their marriage ended. But he decided to let it go. It was time for a change. The conflicting feelings still lingered though, not sure what to make of the woman sitting across from him. He pushed his fork into his omelet and shoved a bite into his mouth. His eyes tipped up, peering up at Jessi from under his brow. Everything happened so fast between them, and he wasn't sure what it meant. The last thing he wanted to do was hurt someone else. He wasn't necessarily ready to give up his career but after fifteen years on the force, he knew it wasn't as important as his family.

"Mitch?" His eyes raised to hers. Her voice broke the dark cloud that had drifted over him. "Are you okay?"

He squeezed his lips together. "Yeah." His response was obviously unconvincing.

"Are you sure?" Her voice softened. "You aren't regretting what we —"

"No. No," he said emphatically. He didn't. "That was…" He didn't even know how to describe it, but a smile snuck onto his face as he let out a long sigh, and Jessi giggled.

"Good."

His chest pinched. "I have to be honest though.

This," he moved his finger between the two of them, "is so foreign to me. I have been out of the dating scene for nearly twenty years. I was married for almost fifteen years and buried myself in my work for the past four so I think it will take me a little bit to navigate everything. It's happened so fast that I'm having a hard time wrapping my head around what I'm supposed to be doing."

"I understand." Her eyes dropped to her plate and Mitch could see her lips purse.

His hand moved across the table gently caressing hers. "If you will be patient with me, I would really like to see where this goes."

Jessi raised her brows and quirked her mouth to the side. She picked up her plate, then his and leaned down. "I've been with Dante for four years and before him I was still getting my career going, so I'm kind of trying to figure things out too. I had fun last night, and this morning was…a very nice way to wake up. That is another skill you definitely haven't lost. And I'd very much like to do all of it again." Her lips met his for a quick kiss before taking the plates into the kitchen but there was a pain in her eyes that left him wondering what else was going on in her head.

Mitch stood, picked up his coffee mug and followed her. "Is there anything I can help with?"

"No." The sadness in that one little word made him decide to push just a little more.

"Are you sure you are okay with all of this?" he said slowly. "I know you have been through a lot, and I don't want to push you into—"

"Yeah. You aren't pushing me. If anything, it's the other way around. I mean I'm the one who invited you over." The hint of a smile she pasted on her face didn't fool Mitch. He could see something else was going on, and he was determined to find out what it was. His arms crossed over his chest, and he leaned back against the counter. From the look in her eyes, she knew he wasn't moving. "It's not so much us." She paused and tucked her hair behind her ear. "I was thinking about my relationship with Dante. I knew the end was coming, I couldn't stay with him with the path the relationship had taken, however it's ending was kind of abrupt. My life flipped upside down, and I honestly don't know what's going to come of it."

"Can I ask you something?"

Jessi shut the dishwasher then lifted her eyes to him. "Sure."

"What was your plan?" He moved his hips away from the counter. "I mean when you ran, what did you think was going to happen?"

"Well, when Dante started drinking heavily, I had talked to my mom about it. I guess she mentioned it to one of her friends and about a month ago she came to me with the possibility of working at the vineyard. At first, I wasn't even considering it. I mean let's be honest, Arkansas is a far cry from Pennsylvania and Dalton is not the metropolitan mecca that Philadelphia is." She walked past him to the table, picked up her coffee mug and headed into the living room. "I just didn't think I would like living the country life again. When things deteriorated between Dante and me, I decided I needed a change of scenery. At least for a while. So, I called the winery and spoke to Vicki. She basically offered me the job over the phone, but I told her I wanted to come for a visit before I agreed to anything." She sat down on the sectional and Mitch followed. "Then she called me again and upped the ante by telling me she had spoken with the Valentis, the owners of Lake Village restaurant, who wanted me sight unseen just from my reputation. Honestly, at the time, a job was my only thought. I needed to have a way of making a living and then I would figure everything else out."

"So, now that you are here, what are you thinking?"

"I like it here. People are different. I don't know how to describe it. More relaxed maybe? People up north have a different sense of humor." Mitch wrinkled his forehead. "Okay, who am I kidding, let's just say people up north don't necessarily have as much patience as people down here."

"Oh. So that's why you tried to run over me."

She snickered. "I didn't try to run over you." Mitch raised one brow. "I tried to run over your grocery cart."

"Are you planning on staying?" He had to put it out there because he didn't want to pursue a relationship and have his kids get attached to someone if they didn't plan on sticking around.

She took a deep breath. "It's too early to tell. I haven't started work yet. I liked what I saw yesterday, and right now, there is a whole lot more holding me here than making me want to go home."

"Are you okay with being so far away from home?"

"You mean from family? Sure. Would I like to be closer? Yes. I was less than two hours from my family though, and I hardly ever saw them. My parents are basically retired, and they plan to do many more RV trips, so who knows, I might see them more often. My mom loves to travel, and I think she would enjoy coming down for visits."

"I just—"

"I know, Mitch. You have kids. When someone dates you, they date your kids. And this is happening fast. I get it. There are several things that factor into whatever we decide to do, and I will understand if you decide it's not worth it. I won't be happy because I kind of have a wee bit of a crush on you. But I will understand." Mitch bit his cheek trying not to smile at her confession. She took a sip of her coffee. "Now, can I ask you something?"

He shrugged.

"I mean since we are having this…talk."

"Sure."

She averted her eyes momentarily and he wondered what question was coming. She obviously was trying to find the right words.

"You talked about being married for nearly fifteen years and working four years since your divorce so—"

"Am I an old man? Is that's what you are asking?"

"How old are—"

"I'm thirty-seven." He took a sip of his coffee watching her expression. "Is that going to be a problem?"

Tilting her head, she stared at him and smirked. "I think you still have some good years left in you." A soft giggle escaped, and she added, "I was just curious since," she glanced at his hair, "you have some silver."

"Some? You make it sound like I have a few wayward hairs." He chuckled. "I started going gray in high school. You know what that's like?"

"Was it bad?"

"I got teased quite a bit when it really started coming in. Called 'old man' by my teammates. It's inherited. My grandpa was white headed by forty."

She scooted in closer and ran her fingers through his hair. "I happen to think your silver hair is sexy."

"But seriously. My age isn't a problem for you?"

"No. Why?"

"How old are you?"

Her eyes twinkle and she leaned in. "Guess."

"Oh no. I won't be doing that? That is the most dangerous thing you can do to a woman other than being asked to guess their weight."

"Well, then I guess you won't find out." She leaned back.

"Come on. I told you."

"Nope. Guess." She tucked her lips between her teeth.

Letting out a huff, he stared at her. "Twenty-eight?" He grimaced hoping he wasn't about to get slapped.

She stared back at him completely still for a long moment and Mitch felt panic settling in his chest. Then a smile slowly tugged at her lips. "Good job. My birthday is in a few of weeks, and I will be thirty."

A relieved breath escaped then he sat gazing at her. "What has kept you from getting married?"

She squinted her eyes. "Two things." Her finger shot up. "One, I've never been asked." She added her second finger. "And two, I'm basically married to my work." Her voice became airy as she spoke. "I traveled quite a bit when I lived in Philadelphia and that was not conducive for a lasting relationship. The only reason Dante and I worked was because he traveled as much as I did."

He could hear the pain rise in her voice, so he decided that was enough discussion about Dante and changed the subject. "When's your birthday?"

"It's June twenty-fifth." She tapped him with her foot. "And if we are going to do this thing where you and I see each other, I expect a huge blowout party." Anxiety shot through Mitch's body once again. That was one thing he wasn't, was a party planner. He had only had to plan a couple of his kids' birthday parties and they were small get-togethers. His ex-wife usually handled that stuff. "That's something else about us city girls. Some of us are what you call 'high maintenance.' "

"What do you expect?" he asked wondering if she was serious.

Her eyes locked on him so long it made him squirm, then she bit her cheek trying to stifle a smile. "You know you are so adorable when you get flustered."

"I don't think I have ever been called adorable. Not even when I was four when I really was adorable."

"No? That's what sucked me in, in the first place. When Georgia pointed out the bruises on my face. The grimace you had on your face was priceless."

"Don't remind me. That little girl doesn't have a filter. Nothing is off limits."

"I was the same way when I was her age. I think that's what made me want to defend her. I had so many of those same moments when my parents tried to rein me in." She stared down at her cup—"I need some more coffee,"—then stood and pointed to his cup. "Do you need some more?"

"No. I am going to have to get going." He stood. "But I need to know what your expectations are for your birthday first." She grabbed his cup and strolled into the kitchen with him behind her.

"I expect for you to have flowers and balloons and banners. Take me to a really swanky restaurant. Feed me the finest wine and chocolate, then…"

"Okay," he said slowly.

She rinsed the cups out and set them in the sink then stepped in close. "Do you really want to know what I expect?"

Now he was confused. "Yes. Please."

"I expect you to remember, wrap your arms around me, give me a kiss, and tell me happy birthday. That's all."

His hands lightly brushed up and down her arms. "That's it?"

"That's it." She snaked her arms around him and pressed her body into his. "I'm not big on celebrating anymore."

"Why is that?"

"Layla died on my birthday."

"Your dog? You gotta be kidding me." His heart squeezed imagining how hard it had to have been.

"Yeah. It was easily the worse day of my life. And that's saying a lot considering what has happened recently. My family was always big on celebrating birthdays, and until then, I was all about it. Now, it will always be associated with that awful day." Her eyes lifted to the shadowbox. "Like I said, she was my world. My best friend."

Chapter Nine

Jessi smoothed her T-shirt and checked to make sure there wasn't any dirt on it. She'd barely gotten any sleep and was almost late for the herb festival. The minute she arrived Burt put her to work setting up the stand. Even though it was early, she felt beads of sweat on the back of her neck. The day was supposed to be warm, so she fixed her hair in a high ponytail. Reaching up, she slicked her hands over her hair hoping it wasn't too messy. She would pay good money for a mirror.

Burt had given her ten different wines to critique during the week. Some, they were planning to serve at the festival, although she had no idea which ones. When she met with Burt later in the week with the critique, she gave him the five she felt would best represent the winery at the festival and why. As she unloaded the boxes of wine, Jessi realized every one of the wines she had chosen were there, and a satisfied smile crept across her face. After a week of working at the winery, she was still feeling a little disoriented though. Even though she really liked Burt and Vicki, and she loved the fact she was learning the art of making wine, she realized there was a lot to learn. As opposed to her first day at Lake Village. Anson gave her a few directions then basically let her take the reins, and it didn't take her long before she felt right at home. Halfway through the evening rush, Jim and Peggy Valenti made an appearance and she was finally, officially, introduced, albeit a very short introduction. Overall, it had been an interesting week.

She had texted back and forth with Mitch throughout the week and was even able to squeeze in a couple of lunches with him. The more she was around him the more she realized how different he was from anyone she had ever dated. She always seemed drawn to the pretty boys. Those who dressed in the expensive clothes, had their hair perfectly groomed, and drove the expensive cars. She could spot them a mile away. Mitch wasn't that at all. He was clean cut, yet rugged. He wore no name blue jeans and basic button downs. His hair was cropped short, and he had a bit of a five o'clock stubble that fit him. His thick southern accent caught her off guard at first and made her heart stumble every time he spoke. And there was no denying he had an air of confidence about him. Except, of course, when his little girl was around. Nothing could fluster him faster than Georgia Gallagher. Jessi shook her head and snickered remembering his expression when little Georgia commented about his divorce. She needed to remember to make time to take Georgia for a girl's day.

With one last check of the booth to make sure everything was in place, she scooted up the stool and had a seat. It looked good. Burt had purchased a custom tent that was a light purple with the Purple Skies Winery logo printed across the top and a large mural of the winery with the lavender and grapevines filling the back. Empty barrels were stacked against the mural which gave it a 3D effect. In front of the booth were a couple of tables made from the wine barrels.

She watched as people started strolling by and wondered how busy they would be. It was still early for their booth. Even though they had items other than wine for sale from the winery, like wine and lavender infused soap and crazy cork screws and decorative items, she knew they wouldn't be visited much until later in the day. She smiled at an older couple who passed by and watched a couple of teenagers playing corn hole in the middle of the green space.

"Hello." The sound of the deep voice behind her made her jump. She hadn't noticed the man walk up. He wore a pressed navy-blue button-down shirt with heavily starched and pressed gray chinos. His dark wavy hair was slicked back with a pair of sunglasses propped on the top of his head. A large watch sat on his left wrist. He obviously had money. Something about him seemed familiar and made her uncomfortable.

Her eyes met his. "Hello."

He showed his bright white teeth, tipped his brow quizzically, then perused the merchandise.

"If you would like a sample of any of the wines let me know. My name is Je," she cleared her throat remembering she needed to use her alias, "Michelle."

His fingers brushed over different items in the booth, though his eyes never left Jessi. Picking up each bottle displayed, he examined them carefully. As he set the last one back in place, he gazed at Jessi from below his brow and studied her. A sudden quiet melody had him reaching in his pocket and walking away with his phone pressed to his ear. She watched him walk across the green space and something in her gut told her he wasn't there to buy the wine. The way he kept glancing at her made the hair on the back of her neck stand on end. She grabbed her phone and took a photo of him as he spoke on his phone. Was he part of Dante's uncle's associates? Was that why he seemed familiar? What if he was talking to Dante? Her gut soured the more she watched him. He kept looking back at her. Was she just being paranoid? There was no way Dante could know where she was. Could he? How would he? The man peered back at her and then turned away again still talking on his phone. With her heart thumping wildly in her chest, she quickly sent a text.

—*Hey Mitch. I know you said you and the kids would be coming to the herb festival later, but a guy came by the booth and made me terribly uncomfortable. He didn't do anything wrong it was just the way he looked at me—*

—*We are heading up there now. I will notify Shawn, the officer working the festival—*

—*I have a strange feeling I've met the guy before. I know I'm probably being paranoid. I'm sorry—*

—*No. Don't apologize. You absolutely need to tell me if something makes you feel uncomfortable. We are leaving now. Be there in a few minutes—*

—*Okay—*

She shoved her phone in her back pocket about the time a younger guy approached the booth. His eyes darted around for a moment then examined the bottles of wine. He peered up at her and asked, "Can I have a sample of the Cab and the Chardonnay?

Jessi blinked slowly at him and smirked. "Can I have a look at your I.D.?" The young man rolled his eyes then gave her a pleading expression. Jessi just shook her head.

"Are you going to card me too?" The man's voice startled her. Jessi felt more protected with the younger man there, but he soon walked away, and her heart began beating out of her chest again.

She swallowed trying to steady her nerves. "Back so soon."

"I'd like a sample of the cab."

"I.D. please."

"Seriously?" he huffed.

She hoped that looking at his name might help her figure out who he was. "I'm sorry I have to check everyone."

"Jessi. Are you really going to pretend you don't know me?"

Her breath disappeared like someone popping a balloon. He knew her. But how? She skimmed the information on the license and let out a sigh of relief. She did know him. Todd McDonald. He was one of the wholesale wine distributors for the Philadelphia restaurant. They stopped using him because they found out he was up-charging them. What was he doing here? She wanted to know. Still, she couldn't let him know it was her. She needed to throw him off somehow.

She handed the license back. "You are good to go. Did you say you wanted the cab?"

His head tilted, obviously a bit miffed that she didn't pay attention to his comment. "Yeah, the cab." She poured him a sample and pushed it to him. "You really don't remember me?"

She tried to put on a little southern accent. "I think you've got me mixed up with someone else."

"I know exactly who you are. You're Jessica Maddox, award winning sommelier. The one thing I don't know is what you are doing down here in Podunk, Arkansas."

"Where do you expect me to be?"

"Philadelphia?"

"Tell me again who you think I am?"

"Jessica Maddox. Worked at Austere Nouveau Restaurant. The leading sommelier probably in the U.S."

"Psssh. I wish." She smirked. "No. my name is Michelle not Jessi." She pointed to the nametag attached to her T-shirt." Out of the corner of her eye she caught Mitch jogging up.

"Hey, baby." He winked and leaned over the counter. Jessi leaned in for a kiss. "The kids are playing corn hole. I was going to go get us some lunch. Do you want some?"

Todd glanced out to the green space then to Mitch then back at Jessi.

"Yeah. Get me whatever you get. I'm starving."

"Can you keep an eye on the kids? I shouldn't be too long."

"Sure, but don't leave me hangin, I'm the only one here right now."

Mitch's attention was pulled away for a brief second and Jessi noticed a young police office wander by. Mitch tapped the counter, caught her attention, and winked at her, then walked away.

She smiled shyly then set her attention on Todd. "What do you think of the cab?"

His forehead creased in confusion. He stared deep into her eyes and studied her face. "It's really nice."

"Let me get you a taste of the Chardonnay."

His hand wrapped his mouth and he chuckled. "I guess I owe you an apology. I seriously thought you were Jessi. It's strange how much you resemble her, and you work in the wine industry."

"I wouldn't say I work in the wine industry, just our

little winery here in Podunk, Arkansas." She gave him a wink feeling a little better about him buying her story. "So, I'm taking a wild swing at this. I'm guessing you aren't from Arkansas."

"No. I'm actually from Pennsylvania.

"And what brought you to Podunk, Arkansas?" Continuing to poke at his not so subtle jab at the southern lifestyle.

"I'm with Swig Wholesale Distribution. My distribution area takes in Pennsylvania as well as some of the surrounding states." He dug in his wallet and handed her his card. "There have been several really nice wines that have come out of this area in the last few years, and we thought we would try to capitalize on it. I get a monthly newsletter that provides information on wine events around the U.S. I noticed there were going to be several wineries from all over northwest Arkansas at this herb festival so I thought I would come check them out and see if we could add some to our product distribution."

"Ah. Well, we have been producing wine for several years and got into selling on a commercial basis a couple of years ago. We only brought out a small variety for today's event. However, if you would like to come out to the winery, I would be happy to set up a tour for you."

"No. That's not necessary. Both of the samples you gave me are excellent. Why don't you give me those, and any others you think I should consider. I will take them back to Philadelphia and see what the rest of my team thinks, and if they like them then I will get back in contact with you. Do you have a card?"

Crap! Her pulse escalated. No business cards yet. Where did Burt put his cards? Her eyes scanned the counter. "Oh." She reached into the plastic tray on the counter and pulled one of the cards out. "I forgot where I put them for a second. The owners are listed on the card."

He flipped the card over. "You aren't the owner?"

"Oh. No. Just a hired hand." She bagged up the bottles and handed them to him, then charged his card and asked, "Is there anything else I can get you?"

He studied her face again. "No. I guess not. I'm sorry for the mistake earlier."

She waved her hand at him. "No big deal. I wish I was her. Sounds like I would be making a whole lot more money." She chuckled. He laughed and nodded.

"Well, thanks for the wine. I'm sure we will be getting back in touch." He tapped the card on the counter.

"Great." As Todd walked away Jessi let out a long breath. Her focus landed on the young officer standing across the courtyard and she nodded. What were the odds of Todd showing up like that?

"Everything okay?" Jessi jumped again. Her eyes darted to Mitch walking up to the stand.

"Geez you scared me." She put her hand to her heart to steady it. "Yeah. Well, sort of. The guy was one of the distributors for the restaurant I worked for. I didn't recognize him at first because we cancelled our contract with them right after I started."

"What's he doing down here?" He handed her a bag then his eyes drifted out across the greenspace and nodded to Shawn who waved and walked away.

"He said this area has produced some very good wines in the past few years so he's here to take some samples back."

"Do you feel good about it?"

"Yeah, I think so. It seemed like he believed my story." She opened the bag and pulled out a soft taco. "Thanks for the support though, Hubby. I think it helped sell the story."

"I think it was your southern accent." He winked at her.

"You caught that, huh?"

"Not too shabby. Might turn you into a southern girl yet."

She took a bite of the taco and closed her eyes. "Tia Luna?"

"Yep."

"Vicki told me about that place last week and I got a breakfast taco from there Thursday. Oh my gosh. It was delicious."

"Yeah. They have the best tacos in town." His gaze drifted to the green space. "I let Shawn know to keep an eye on you. I would myself except it's kind of hard with the kids."

"I appreciate it. He didn't let me out of his sight while Todd was talking to me." She took another bite of the taco. "I'm sorry. I am just paranoid. I don't think Todd was any way connected with Dante. It was just a strange coincidence."

"Still, I'm glad you called. Any time you get worried, call me."

"I don't want to waste your time with me being overly cautious though."

"You aren't wasting my time. Trust me. I've checked into the Angenelli family, and they *are* dangerous."

She knew. Even though she had no firsthand accounts. She knew. Hearing it come out of Mitch's mouth though, set her on edge. She hoped she was safe, but deep down in her heart she knew she never would be, until something or someone took them out of the picture.

"How much have you found out?" she asked, taking another bite of her taco.

"I really don't think it's a good idea to discuss it here."

She quirked her mouth trying to hold back a smile. "Could you maybe come by tomorrow? I'm off."

Mitch gave her a wolfish grin. "Let me see if my babysitter is available and I will give you a call."

"Okay."

Mitch patted the counter. "I better get back over to the kids. When will you be off?"

"I'm leaving here at four because I have to be at the restaurant at five." She leaned on the counter with her elbows.

Mitch leaned on the counter in front of her. "Okay. I'll text if I can make it tomorrow." He was so close his nose brushed against her. Then he stole a kiss.

"Daddy? Brandon got all six bags in the hole on corn hole." Mitch backed away quickly. Jessi discreetly wiped her mouth with her finger and peeked down at Georgia with a smile spreading across her face.

"Really?" Mitch tried to be excited, although Jessi could see a flare of frustration on his face. Brandon walked up and rolled his eyes.

"I told her to leave you guys alone."

Jessi met Mitch's eyes wondering if Brandon was onto them.

"It's okay. We need to finish our rounds and get you ready for your baseball game.

"Do you play baseball?" Jessi asked.

"Yes ma'am. Dad got me on the competitive team."

"Their babysitter's husband coaches. Brandon's been playing off and on since he was in t-ball. I asked Scott if he would let him tryout even though it was in the middle of the season, and he made the team."

"That is awesome. I would love to come to one of your games."

"They play at least once a week so there are plenty of opportunities," Mitch said with a hint of annoyance. Jessi shot him a "don't be rude" glare.

Georgia bounced up and down. "Daddy used to play too."

Jessi leaned over the counter so she could see her. "Did he?"

"Yes. And he was really good."

Jessi smiled. "I bet he was."

"He used to play with the other policemen."

"Oh. He doesn't now?"

Mitch broke in. "I decided not to since I was getting the kids full time. I figured I would miss too much."

"Ah."

"I told them if they needed an emergency fill in, I might be available—"

"It's kind of hard to know what your schedule will be like."

"Exactly."

"So, you're pretty good, huh?"

Georgia piped up again. "He's great. He can run all the bases."

"As in homeruns?"

Mitch slowly blinked his eyes and sighed loudly. She could see the pink filling his cheeks. "I've had a few."

"Man, I would love to see that. I am a huge Phillies fan."

"Oh, that might be a problem."

"Why?" Jessi asked curious as to what the problem would be.

"Seriously? You have to ask?" He pointed to the cap on Brandon's head. "St. Louis all the way."

She rolled her eyes. "I guess I could have two favorites."

Mitch chuckled. "I'll text you later."

"Okay." He gave her a wink and walked away with the kids in tow.

****

The restaurant was full, and it had barely opened for the evening. Saturdays were always busy days for restaurants. Staring through the kitchen doors at the crowd, she felt tired from her already long day, and also a little excited. Anson gave her a heads up. "Be prepared." Wait staff were at the tables greeting guests. She made her way around the room helping with wine orders. Things felt comfortable. She felt strangely at home even though she'd worked there less than a week. She noticed an older gentleman sitting alone at one of the tables that overlooked the lake and approached his table.

"Hello. My name is Michelle. I am the sommelier for Lake Village. Can I interest you in some wine this evening?"

The man lifted his head from the wine list and smiled at her. The hairs on the back of her neck prickled. There was nothing suspicious about him. She didn't feel like she recognized him. It was the way he smiled at her. Something about his eyes. A look of possible recognition. Breathing deep, she slowly let out the breath

140

trying to still the growing panic in her gut. *For Pete's sake. I can't be paranoid of someone smiling at me.* She tried to return the smile but felt like it probably looked like she smelled something bad.

"How is the Purple Skies Cabernet?"

"It's very good. Pairs well with our ribeye. Starts out very smooth with a little bit of smoke. Has just enough bite on the tongue and it finishes with a hint of berry."

"Sounds good. I will take that." He smiled again and his eyes lingered on her face a moment too long. Goosebumps ran up and down her back. She took the menu and nodded before walking away. When she got to the kitchen she stopped and leaned against the wall. Her eyes met Anson's.

He continued to chop a colorful vegetable medley. "Everything okay?"

His concern gave her comfort. She had explained everything to him when she filled out her paperwork. He was the only one other than the owners who knew her true identity.

"Yeah. I'm fine." She walked through the kitchen to the bar and grabbed the cabernet, pouring a generous amount into the glass, then made her way out to the patio where the gentleman sat. As she approached the table, she noticed him looking at something, then he tucked it away in his pocket when she approached. "Your wine, sir. May I get you anything else?"

"I don't think so. What is your name again?"

"Michelle."

He smiled and nodded then turned his attention to his glass.

As the evening wore on, Jessi kept her eye on the gentleman. He made no ill moves or comments to make her suspect he was anything other than a gentleman having dinner. She saw him staring at his phone once, but so were half the other guests in the establishment. Nothing new there. *Geez I have to quit being paranoid.* The man paid his bill when he'd finished his meal and left. One of the staff said he left a fairly large tip. *Probably just some lonely old man.* The rest of the evening seemed to go by without any other issues. Mitch texted her letting her know he was available after lunch if they wanted to get together. Her heart thrummed thinking about him. She thought about saying something about the evening but figured it could wait until tomorrow.

When the last customer made their way out the door, she spoke to Anson for a moment then headed to her car. Driving up the highway, her mind drifted to Mitch. She couldn't wait to see him again. He looked so handsome at the herb festival dressed in his blue jeans and red Henley shirt. Heck everything looked good on him. Lights reflecting in her rearview mirror caught her attention. She took her exit and the car followed. *I'm not going to be paranoid.* Taking a left onto her street, she noticed the car still behind her, and she could feel the panic tightening her chest. In a split-second decision, she passed her driveway just to be safe, and continued up the road to a small convenience store. She pulled to the front and went inside. The car continued on, and she waited a few more minutes before making her way back to her car and headed back to her house. When she pulled up into her driveway, she scanned the area, but all was quiet. She took a deep breath and went inside.

Chapter Ten

Mitch had raised his voice for the thirty-second time trying to shut down the kids' bickering. He hoped feeding them from their favorite sub place would at least get rid of some of their crankiness. If nothing else, shut them up while their mouths were full. He was more than ready to drop them off and head to Jessi's. A warm rush of blood flooded his body just thinking about what the night might bring. Although his head and body were still at war with each other, he couldn't deny the way she made him feel. He was happy. Happier than he had felt in a very long time. Yes, he knew he was taking a huge chance. He knew the consequences he might face. But after the night he spent with her, he was willing to face them head on.

Dipping his French dip sandwich in the au jus, he savored the salty flavor of the meat and let out a chuckle when he wondered what wine would go well with it. She had definitely gotten under his skin and captured his thoughts. His phone played a distinct melody, and in unison, both kids screamed, "Mom." Mitch handed the phone to Brandon and Georgia stood next to him. He had started out letting the kids take turns as far as who held the phone until Georgia disconnected several calls. Mitch decided to give Brandon the responsibility after that. He was thankful for the fact that they had technology now where the kids could video chat with their mom daily, even if she was half-way around the world.

They gave her updates about what they had been doing. Brandon told her about getting two doubles in the baseball game and scored once. Then Georgia got on the phone. Mitch held his breath every time Georgia took over. So far, she hadn't mentioned Jessi, but he knew it was coming.

"Hey, Mom. We went to the herb festival yesterday. Brandon got six corn holes in a row. He got mine and his. Dad let us eat cotton candy and then we went and talked to Miss Jessi, and she is going to come to one of Brandon's games."

And there it was. He ran his hand through his hair. There was no doubt his ex-wife would be asking about Jessi. Unless she didn't hear what Georgia said. She did have a tendency to talk fast. Who was he kidding? He knew it was coming. What would she think? What would he say? In the four years they had been divorced she knew he'd never seriously dated. He heard her say, "Let me talk to Dad," and Brandon held his phone out to him. He took it and pointed at the food. "You guys finish your sandwiches and then get your stuff together." Walking into the bedroom, he pushed the door closed. "Hi, Lorrie. How's Poland?" He really hadn't talked to her much since she left, allowing the kids to take most of the phone calls.

"It's beautiful, a little chilly. So how is everything going? Are the kids doing okay?"

"We're doing fine. I won't lie. There has been an adjustment. I am exhausted."

A smile crossed her face and Mitch stared at his phone. Waiting.

"So, talk to me about this new lady."

He let out a long breath. "Do we really have to do this? She's a woman I met. I barely know her."

"Mitch?"

He let out another sigh. "Fine. Her name is Jessi. She works at Purple Skies Winery and is a sommelier at Lake Village restaurant."

"How did you meet her?"

"Lost some stuff on the highway while she was moving here. It was my last late shift and I got called out to pick it up. She came by the police station to get it and we wound up having dinner with her."

Mitch recalled the conversation Georgia had with her and he fought the smile trying to form on his lips.

Silence drifted between them for a moment. "I saw that. You like her," she teased.

Heat coursed through his veins, warming his cheeks but he figured he might as well not fight it. "Yeah, I do. We are taking it slow though." He thought about their night together. *Well kind of slow.* "I don't want to start something and then have my job get in the way again. And plus, I have the kids to consider. They seem to like her, Lorrie."

He watched Lorrie's expression become somber. "Mitch I'm going to tell you something and I want you to hear me, so listen very carefully."

Lorrie had a tendency to talk to him that way, and when she did it made him feel like one of the kids. He sighed. "Okay?"

"I know I said your job was a factor in the break-up of our marriage, and for a long time I believed it, because I didn't want to accept what the real reason was."

"And what was that?"

"That we were too young. We didn't know what we wanted out of life. Or at least, I didn't. When you got your job, I admit, I was jealous. You seemed to be moving forward and I wasn't. By the time I realized what I wanted, I had to come to terms with the fact that I might not ever have it because we had two kids. As much as I loved them, I wanted something more than to be a small-town housewife. I wanted to see what the world had to offer and see what I could contribute.

"I became resentful because you seemed like you were happy and as much as I loved you, I wasn't. It had very little to do with your job other than the fact that you had something you were passionate about, and I didn't. And it didn't have to do with me not loving you either. It had to do with me not loving me, and what I was doing with my life. I hated myself for not being happy with what I had been given. You were amazing, a great husband, a fantastic daddy and I hated the fact that it wasn't enough for me."

"You know I would have supported you—"

"There was no doubt in my mind that you would have. I just needed to figure myself out and I couldn't do that with you. I'm sorry. I know it sounds harsh—"

"No, I get it actually. Why are you telling me all this now though?"

"Because you obviously have opened yourself up to someone, and you need to stop beating yourself up over what happened with us. It wasn't your fault and I know you shut yourself off because you thought it was. You're a good guy, and you deserve to be happy."

Her words played through his head. Was she telling him the truth? He wasn't to blame after all? It felt like a boulder had suddenly been lifted off him. "Thanks

Lorrie."

"Anyway, anyone who is willing to sit through a little league baseball game, who isn't a parent of one of the players, has my vote."

"She says she likes baseball."

"If she really does, then go after her, because she is one of the few."

"I thought you liked baseball."

"I liked the player, not the game. I know it's exciting to some, but in all honesty, it bored me to tears." Mitch was at a loss for words and chuckled at the thought of how many games she sat through rain or shine for him. "Anyway, I need to get going."

"Yeah, me too. Thanks again for talking to me."

"You deserve the best, Mitch."

"Thanks. Talk to you soon."

He disconnected the call and stared at his phone thinking about the conversation, then shoved it into his pocket and went back into the dining room with the kids. Brandon had picked up his and Georgia's plates and cleaned the table. Mitch was so proud at how his son seemed to be stepping up to responsibility and remembered Lorrie's comment about him being a good dad. He took a couple of more bites of his sandwich and threw away the rest.

"Do you guys have all the stuff you want to take to Kathy's?"

"I think so." Brandon responded.

"Okay then, let's head out."

****

Merging onto the highway once he dropped the kids off, his mind was flooded with thoughts of Jessi and the night they had spent together. Even though he had only

147

known her for a few weeks, it had felt natural to be with her. There was no question. They both wanted it, but afterward he battled with his feelings.

Was Lorrie telling the truth or just letting him off the hook? Yes, they were young when they got married, and in some ways naïve to what the world had to offer. He hated what happened to their marriage and often felt like he failed. Maybe he hadn't. Maybe it wasn't all his fault after all. And maybe it was time he stopped punishing himself and shutting everyone out.

Jessi had made him smile, a genuine smile. Not something he slapped on in front of the kids so they wouldn't see how much he hurt. There was so much that drew him to her. She had an easy laugh, yet an edge about her. Was it wrong for him to want to pursue a relationship with her? The only thing really holding him back was her, and her reason for being in Dalton in the first place. His thoughts were interrupted when his phone rang.

"Hello?"

"Mitch. Hey this is Randy."

"Whatever it is, the answer is no."

"We need you tomorrow, man."

"Still no."

"George is out. He threw his back out."

"What about Bruce?"

"He's out of town."

"Seriously?"

"I know you are busy, and I wouldn't ask if it wasn't an emergency."

"All right. I'll be there." He hung up. Maybe he could talk Jessi into keeping an eye on the kids. His finger grazed the screen.

"Hey, Kathy, it's Mitch."

"Hey, Mitch."

"Can you drop the kids off at Taylor Park tomorrow night? I've got a game and I'm going to have to go straight to the park from work."

"Sure. I've got to drop off Robby there also. He's working at the concession stand, so it works out perfectly."

"Great. I appreciate it." He hung up and pulled into Jessi's driveway. His phone dinged. The front door opened. There she was. His whole body tightened as his eyes committed her to memory. It wasn't just that he wanted her, his entire being needed her like it needed air and she somehow always knew exactly how to provide it. Her hair was loose wavy curls tossed to one shoulder over a hot pink spaghetti strapped tank that said, "wine is bottled poetry." A pair of cut off white jean shorts hugged her perfectly. Her tan legs appeared a mile long all the way down to her bare feet.

Her eyes locked on him, when he stepped out of his car, and worked their way up to his face. A huge smile spread across her face. "I couldn't wait for you to get here." Running her fingers through her hair, she shyly added, "You look very nice." He smoothed his hands down his teal striped polo. She stepped out of the doorway to meet him. Her arms wrapped around his neck and his hands immediately pushed up her tank and danced against the soft bare skin of her back. He'd never get tired of how she felt. "You have no idea how bad I've needed to kiss you." He leaned in until their lips met. Fire coursed through his body as he slowly savored her. Backing away, he spun her around, and putting his hand in the small of her back, pushed her into the house.

"Didn't want Dale and Betty to get an eyeful in case they were working on the house," he said, shutting the door behind him and dragging her back into his arms. Her fingers laced through his hair as his mouth pressed against hers again. Their tongues collided with the parting of her lips. He pressed her into him letting her feel what she did to his body. The ding of his phone a second time had him pulling back with a frustrated sigh. He gave her three quick pecks and held up his finger. "Give me one second. I need to make sure this isn't the babysitter." He dug his phone from his pocket. "Shit." Stephen.

—*Call me. I got something*—

His eyes darted to Jessi. "I need to make a call. I had a guy in cyber security up in Little Rock keep an eye on the web for anything related to your ex-boyfriend and he got a hit." His finger punched the button.

"Hey, Mitch." The voice on the other end answered.

Mitch rubbed the back of his neck, walked over to the dining room table, and sat down. "What's up?" Jessi followed him to the table and Mitch caught her eye. He lifted the phone from his ear. "Can you get me a pen and some paper?" She nodded and walked into the kitchen.

"We screwed up." That was the one thing Mitch didn't want to hear. He rolled his eyes as Stephen kept talking. "We lasered in on Dante Angenelli putting the word out for Miss Maddox and didn't get much of anything there, so I decided to do a reverse search, using a facial recognition for Miss Maddox and I immediately got a hit. I found a photo of her being shared all over social media. It looks like some local guy found a photo of her outside of Dalton and is trying to find out who she is."

"Dammit. When did it post?" Jessi returned with the paper and pen. Mitch nodded his appreciation.

"You aren't going to like this." He already didn't like any of it but there was nothing he could do about it now. "It posted over three weeks ago, so I'm guessing right after she got there. It's gotten eighty-two thousand hits on the original post as of this morning and has been shared over two thousand times so it's ramping up quickly. I was able to take the original down and I am chasing the others as fast as I can. I just don't know if I'm going to be able to keep up."

"Okay. Is there anything tying the photo to Dalton?"

"Hell yeah. The guy said he found the photo outside of Dalton and his locator says he is in Collinsville. Plus, those who first shared of course were his friends so most of those were probably located somewhere around there."

Mitch let out a heavy sign. "But you haven't gotten any indicators that Dante Angenelli has picked up on it?"

"No. Nothing yet. So far on him all we know is he was released on bail. He has been in contact with a few shady people but no direct hits on Miss Maddox. I went back to see if I could trace a connection with him and the photo that was being shared, and so far, I couldn't find anything, but that doesn't mean much. Just means he is being smart. It wouldn't take much, possibly using some high-tech equipment, or hiring a private detective to research."

"Do you think there could have been?"

"Like I said, it's possible. Especially if they are working through the dark web. If he is connected with the Mafia, then that's a high possibility. I've got people checking that direction. They haven't gotten back to me yet. I sent you what we have so far."

"Okay." Mitch pinched the bridge of his nose and closed his eyes. "Well, let me know if you find out anything else."

"I will."

"Thanks." He punched the button on his phone, dropped the phone on the table, then lifted his head leveling his eyes at Jessi who was sitting across from him. Fear filling her eyes.

"He's going to find me, isn't he?" Jessi's voice was low and thick with pain. The last thing Mitch wanted was to see that look of terror in her eyes. He felt like somehow it was his fault.

"We don't know. Someone found one of your photos and put it out on social media wanting to find you. It's had eighty thousand views and two thousand shares. I thought I got all the photos but evidently not, or someone just happened to come across one before I got to the site. Anyway, they've taken the post down and are working on all the shares, but it's virtually impossible to take down all the shares because it multiplies."

Jessi sat silent. Mitch knew she was trying to hold back tears. Her eyes darted away, and her lips pursed. She stood and wrapped her arms around herself. Mitch stood and grasped her elbows, pulling her into him. Tears slid down her cheeks. "I don't want him to find me," she whispered.

"Do you think he would come after you? I mean a smart man with an assault charge pending would not go after the person he assaulted.

She shook her head and shrugged. "I don't know. He has changed so much."

"You said when he was sober, he treated you okay?"

"Yes. But the last couple of months he wasn't ever completely sober."

Tipping his head to the living room, Mitch guided Jessi over to the sectional and lowered her to the seat, then sat next to her. "If he was sober, do you think he would try to find you? Maybe to apologize and get you back?"

"I don't know. Maybe. The thing is, he did share with me that his family was part of the Mafia so I don't know if that is common knowledge or information that could get me killed."

"No. When I did my search, I found that the Angenelli family name runs pretty deep in the Mafia rings across the nation. I think it is fairly common knowledge, so I don't think that alone would cause them to come after you."

"I got Dante arrested though. So, I am sure they aren't happy with me. I mean I'm sure the police are sniffing around now."

"Yeah. But again, the police know full well who they are. Is there anything else?"

"No. It's just this feeling. I know he was up to something shady and if the family thought I somehow figured it out they might come after me."

Her comment made the hair on the back of his neck stand on end. "Do you have any information? Did you overhear any conversations? Find anything written down? Catch anything when he was on the phone? Anything like that?" Mitch's gaze landed on her. She stayed silent and chewed the side of her lip. His gut tightened. "You did. Didn't you?" Mitch pulled her against him hoping it would give her the comfort she needed to confide in him. She remained silent for a moment, then began to relax.

"When Dante took the job with his uncle, I started finding random things hidden around the house. At first it didn't register what exactly he was doing. I found a couple of things, papers in an envelope, and a notebook in odd spots and just figured he was distracted. When I approached him about it, he took them and acted like it was no big deal, so I let it go. Then one night, after he'd come home and had gone to take a shower, I heard a ding in the entryway by the door, which was odd. It wasn't like the doorbell rang, it was a single ding, so I went to check it out. I found a phone taped to the underside of our wine bar."

"Okay."

"I'm guessing he was hiding things he thought might be incriminating if the police were to ever show up at our door with a search warrant." Jessi took a shaky breath and continued. "It wasn't his regular phone. On the screen was a reminder to meet John at PSBT for key at twelve thirty." She paused. "He was always a stickler for being on time, so he had reminders set for everything. I guess he just forgot to silence the phone before he hid it."

"Are you sure that's what it said?"

"Yeah. Pretty sure. Meet John at PSBT. It could be PBST maybe, but it was definitely at twelve thirty."

"Do you think this was a job he had to do?"

She nodded. "I'm sure of it. I mean why would he hide the phone if it wasn't?"

"Does he know you saw his reminder?"

"No. It was on the home screen, so I didn't click on it, and I put the phone back where I found it."

"Then I don't think he would be coming after you

for that."

"Maybe not, but…I don't know…I'm paranoid that he will, or his family will. They knew we dated. His family has seen me. What if they think he told me about what he has done?"

"I guess that's a possibility. It's also possible that nothing will come of this."

"So, do you think I'm crazy for being this scared?"

"Hell no. He beat you. Whether you left because of his mob ties or not, you needed to get as far away from him as possible. It doesn't matter that he is connected to the Mafia. He abused you. If that was your only reason for leaving, it was a good one."

"I hate being paranoid of everyone and everything." She shifted and curled her body into him. His arm wrapped around her, tightening his grip, as her words resonated in his thoughts and something about the way she spoke set off more alarms in his head.

He leaned her up to face him. "Jessi? Did something else happen?"

Her focus shifted and he already knew the answer. "You're going to think I'm crazy."

"No. I won't. I've told you that I want you to tell me when things make you uncomfortable. What happened?"

"When I was at work last night there was a man sitting alone. I spoke to him about the wine list." She bobbled her head and stared up at the ceiling. "I don't know, there was something about the way he stared at me and smiled. It was like he knew me. Like Todd did. But I definitely didn't know this guy. It gave me the creeps. Then I caught him looking at a piece of paper and when I approached the table, he quickly shoved it back in his pocket when he saw me."

155

"Could you tell what it was?"

"Not really. Just a piece of paper."

"Did he do anything else?"

"No. Everything was normal. He paid his bill, left a hefty tip for the staff and was gone." She cut her eyes to him. "Again. I am probably being paranoid."

"No. You need to tell me when things make you scared or worried. It could be important."

"There's one more thing."

The whole situation had Mitch feeling sick to his stomach. He was already pissed about the photo being shared and not catching it until now. It was obvious how much it scared her. Now, to find out she was holding back on other information, because she didn't want to seem paranoid, it had him nearly crawling out of his skin. He could see the scenarios playing out in his head of why that man might have been there. Maybe it was all completely innocent. What if it wasn't?

"On the way home last night a car pulled out onto the highway and stayed behind me all the way home. It freaked me out, so I drove past my driveway and pulled into Bare Necessities convenience store and waited for a few minutes before I went home."

Everything was raising red flags for Mitch. There was too much falling together. The photo, the man, the car following her.

"And you are sure it wasn't the guy from the restaurant?"

"No, not really. It looked like there were two people in the car behind me."

"And you're sure you didn't get tailed when you left the convenience store?"

"I don't think so."

"Are you sure?"

"Yeah, pretty sure. I looked around for a car when I got home and didn't see any."

He didn't want to scare her any more than she was already, but he needed to make sure she was safe.

"You know what? I think we should go to my house until I can get a little more information on all of this. Just to be on the safe side." If someone was keeping an eye on her, they probably already made his car. It was not an easy car to miss. He would have to make sure they weren't followed. "Pack some clothes and stuff for overnight and I will get to work on it tomorrow."

"Mitch I can't do that. I can't put you and your family in danger."

Her words set a bomb off in his gut. How could he protect his kids and protect Jessi? Until now, he was more worried about having time with the kids and being a good dad. She was right though. If someone did come after her, he had to make sure his kids were out of the line of fire. "I will call the babysitter and have Brandon and Georgia stay there."

"No. I can't ask you to do that. I am sure they would rather stay with you."

"Are you kidding me. They will be ecstatic to have another sleepover. I just need to make sure Kathy is good with it." He pulled out his phone and hit the button. "Kathy. Hey, it's Mitch. Hey, I hate to ask, but do you think Brandon and Georgia can stay with you guys tonight? I have a situation with work I need to tend to."

"Sure. You know any time you need them to sleep over it's fine. I will bring them to Taylor Park tomorrow."

"That works for me. Thanks Kathy. I owe you." He

disconnected and shoved his phone back in his pocket. "See. It's all good. Grab your gear and let's go." The expression on her face told Mitch he hadn't avoided scaring her. He followed her back to her bedroom and watched as she filled a suitcase.

"I'll stay tonight, Mitch. But I am not putting your family in danger."

"Let's just focus on tonight."

Chapter Eleven

Jessi stared out the window. Her heart pounded. The scowl on Mitch's face was unmistakable when she told him about the man at the restaurant and possibly being followed home. He tried to sound calm, but his expression gave him away. When he told her to grab her gear, all the calm had left his voice. He had barely said a word to her since then. She glanced over at him wondering what was going through his head. His eyes were trained to the road in front of him and his mouth was set in a straight line. This man. He could be so serious at times, but when his vulnerability accidentally made an appearance, he was irresistible.

They traveled up into an area filled with pine trees above the center of town. She rolled her window down and breathed in deep. Heading up a street filled with older homes, they pulled into the driveway of a pretty, gray and white craftsman house with a huge porch that was split in half by a large dark stained wooden door with a dormer above. Around the side was a double car garage. Probably an add-on. Still, it fit in with the house well. The hum of the garage door echoed as they drove in. Mitch grabbed her bag and led her into the house still not saying a word. Was he angry with her for not telling him sooner about the gentleman and the car? Or was he just worried?

The inside of the house was painted a gray green

tone with a natural stained trim. In the living room was a large beige tiled fireplace surrounded by a massive stained wooden mantle with bookcases on each side. A comfortable leather sofa sat facing the fireplace with a printed beige rug on the floor, and a matching leather chair with a soft blanket sat off to one side in front of a big picture window.

The living room led into a dining room that fed into a large wrap-around kitchen with natural stained cabinets. Dark gray granite counter tops were accented with a glass backsplash. A large island sat in the middle. The ceiling in the kitchen had a steep pitch with exposed beams. Everything about the house had a sturdy masculine feel to it, yet it still felt very comfortable.

Mitch motioned her to follow him. He led her past the kitchen into a good-sized master bedroom. The king sized four poster bed sat in the middle of the wall facing another large fireplace trimmed in beige tile and surrounded by more stained hardwood. An oversized striped fabric chair with an ottoman sat next to a picture window with a small side table and lamp. "The bathroom is right through that door."

She stopped in her tracks as he continued to walk out of the bedroom. "Did I do something wrong?" Her voice wavered more than she expected, and he stopped and spun on his heels. "You haven't said a word since we left the cottage." All the memories of her and Dante and his erratic behavior flooded back, and tears stung her eyes. Her mouth quivered and her hands wrapped around her waist trying to steady her heartbeat and hold back the tears. He stared at her, the muscles of his jaw ticking as he inhaled deeply. The longer he stayed silent the more her panic ramped up. The tears trickled down her cheeks, and she quickly wiped them away.

Narrowing the distance between them with two strides, he cupped her chin. "No. I'm not mad at you." His face softened. "I'm trying to figure out how to keep you safe." He slowly pushed her hair out of her face, and wiped away more tears, then pulled her to him. His eyes filled with concern. "Shit, Jessi, you're shaking." His arms pressed her against his chest. "I'm sorry if I was quiet. It's how I process things."

Pushing her away from him, he caressed her hair as he gazed into her eyes. *Holy cow, those eyes.* The way he studied her with such intensity made every hair on her body stand on end. Something about him made her feel alive and it wasn't just the way he looked at her or touched her.

Dante had always been so agreeable with everything she did that sometimes she felt like he really didn't care about her at all. The last few months proved he didn't. Mitch, on the other hand, challenged her. Made her think. When she spoke, he listened and made her feel like every word she had to say was important. And, when she told him about her job, he seemed genuinely impressed. The calming, matter of fact, way he spoke to her, made her feel like a precious gem.

"It's okay. I was just worried that you were mad because I didn't tell you what was going on."

"God no, babe. I'm not mad at all and I'm sorry I made you feel that way," he said as his hands gently moved up and down her arms. "You do need to tell me though when something doesn't feel right. Don't worry about being paranoid. Okay? Tell me. It's the best way for me to make sure you are safe." He drew her into a hug and kissed the top of her head. "I think, for right now, we've got that taken care of. I didn't see any signs we were being followed." His hand wrapped around the back of her neck and began massaging the area under her hair. She closed her eyes and leaned her head on his chest then slowly brought her hands to his sides. Her fingers followed the creases of his muscles through his shirt. Mitch lifted her chin and brought his mouth to hers. Her fingers gripped his shirt and pulled herself into him.

Lifting her head slightly, she whispered on his lips. "How did you do that?"

"Do what?" he whispered back.

"A second ago I felt like I was about to spin out of control and your magic hands calmed everything."

"It's my superpower." He captured her mouth again gently sucking her bottom lip, then her top and setting off a shiver through her body. As her lips parted his fingers dove into her hair and he took control letting his mouth feast on her. Her legs trembled at his attack, although it wasn't from being scared, it was from an overwhelming desire. She needed him. Her body was starved for him. The low growl from the back of his throat only managed to stoke the inferno already engulfing her. Her hand slowly made its way around his neck and threaded his short hair through her fingers. He already had her gasping for air as his hot breath seared his kisses to her neck. "What do you need baby?" he whispered in her ear as he took her lobe between his teeth and pressed his body to hers letting his fingers skate down her side while he continued to kiss and nip at her neck.

"I…" she couldn't put together a coherent thought. Her body filled with tingles with every brush of his lips. She loved the way his whole body went rigid, like he was

162

desperately trying to hold himself back with her.

"Do you know what I want Jessi?" he asked as he lifted her shirt and buried his face in her stomach. His eyes focused on her, waiting for her answer but she still was unable to push words from her brain to her mouth. A low animalistic moan rumbled in his chest. "I want to claim every part of you. Taste every inch of your skin." His fingers tightened on her hips. "I want to ruin you for any other man." His teeth sank into her bottom lip and her eyes closed drinking in the feel of his lips. Each kiss was like a torch lighting darkened places in her soul. Each touch reminded her that she could be cherished. Her breath caught as his fingers ran along the edge of the fringe of her shorts. "Do you like that?" She nodded in response. Had he rendered her completely speechless? His mouth found hers again and her hands drifted down to where his shirt tucked into his jeans. Tugging until the shirt was free, she pushed it up and let her hands freely roam his hot bare skin and her lips meet his bare chest. She was rewarded with a strained groan. Finally, she was given free reign when he yanked the shirt over his head. Flames ignited in her core and her body was engulfed.

Mitch lifted her and laid her back onto the soft white comforter then crawled on top, straddling her. His eyes darkened as he asked his question again. "What do you need, Jessi?" There was no question what he wanted, and her body begged for it.

"I want to feel you inside me." Gently pushing up her tank top, he let his hands drift across her smooth stomach.

"God you are so beautiful, Jessi." His lips followed behind his hand, kissing his way up to her mouth. A whimper escaped from the back of her throat as his mouth danced over her body driving her insane. Her gaze locked on him, and her heart stumbled from the hunger in his eyes. The angry glare he could possess was nowhere to be found. His eyes smiled and his mouth quirked like a little boy successfully sneaking a cookie. Mercy, her heart could not take much more. A pang of fear hit her. This didn't feel like a simple lust- filled crush or hook up. Could she really be falling for him? Was that even possible? She hadn't known him that long. How reckless did she want to be with her heart? How much more could she take? What if it didn't work out?

He grasped her top and gently tugged it over her head. Reckless or not, she couldn't stop herself if she tried. God. The way he touched her, kissed her. It was like she was quenching his thirst on a hot day. And it made her want to lay back and let him devour her. She let her head drift back against the pillow as he unclasped her bra and then cast it aside. They were skin to skin, and the tufts of his peppered chest hair had her fingers itching to run through it.

He continued slowly undressing her in between kisses, without saying a word. Then it was her turn. First the snap, then the zipper. Her fingers ghosted the ridges of his muscles while she removed the rest of his clothes and left them in a pile on the floor.

She could feel his chest rise and fall as he dragged her to him grabbing her hip and wrapping her legs around him. Their bodies converged like the melody and rhythm of a song, fitting together perfectly, filling each other's needs. His hands tenderly gripped her hips and he slowly moved with her. Whimpers of pleasure escaped. He knew exactly how to move, where to kiss, and where to touch her, to elicit sounds that she never knew she could make. And he loved it. She knew that because she loved to make him moan. Like when she rocked her hips taking him deeper. She loved knowing she could make him feel good. His mouth found hers and she moaned in a desperate need for him. No. this definitely wasn't a simple hook up. There was so much more involved than just physical need. He made her smile and laugh and feel like she was beautiful.

He knew instinctively how to make her feel desired and how to bring her body pleasure.

She could feel the hunger taking over, pushing her toward the edge and Mitch took control. Touching her, kissing her, meeting every need, letting her lose herself completely. With every caress of his warm breath against her skin, and every brush of his lips, she lost herself further to him.

Her breaths came in short gasps. Tremors gripped her and she cried out as her body exploded with pleasure. Everything blurred around her, and her fingers dug into Mitch's back while he continued to skillfully provoke spasm after spasm through her body. He played her body like a well-rehearsed symphony. And just as she felt her body begin to relax, Mitch's gaze locked on her, and his body tensed. He lowered his head against her shoulder as a low growl rumbled from his chest. Her body responded like it had been waiting for the moment. Her eyes slammed shut and her soul felt like it had completely disconnected. She could hear herself moaning, feel her arms wrapped tightly around Mitch yet everything within her felt light, like she was floating.

They lay still in each other's arms letting the minutes tick by while they regained their ability to breathe. Mitch chuckled, pressed gentle kisses along her neck, and pulled her against him as he rolled over, fluffing the covers around them. "Damn." His eyes danced and he smirked.

"Yeah. I kind of think I had an out of body experience."

"You too?" His fingers played in her hair. "I thought I might have died there for a second." Jessi's stomach growled and she suddenly realized she hadn't eaten any lunch and it was now dinner time. She could feel the tingle of embarrassment creep up her neck. "Are you getting hungry?"

"Maybe a little, although I like lying in this soft comfy bed next to you right now. You're nice and warm. We worked up a sweat." She brushed her hand against her forehead wiping away the moisture.

Mitch adjusted his body so he could be face to face with her. "I love the way you look right now all relaxed and sweaty."

"I probably have mascara smudged under my eyes."

He continued to absentmindedly run his fingers along her back. "You're beautiful, Jessi." The sincerity in his tone sent a shiver down her spine and the pesky little twinge of fear sent an ache to her chest. She wondered how he felt about her. Even though he basically told her he wanted to date her, she knew he had to be careful since he had kids, and dating was a far cry from making any real relationship commitments. And what if Dante did come after her? What would happen then? She would never want to put Mitch or his kids in danger.

"Hey. Where'd you go?" His voice called her back to reality. "You okay?"

Not wanting to delve into exactly what was going on

in her brain, she rolled into him. "Yeah. Just very, very relaxed."

"Okay. Well, before we both fall asleep, we should probably get something to eat. So, do you want to find something here, or would you like to go somewhere?"

"I don't know too many places around here yet."

His fingers brushed up and down her shoulder. "Let me take you to Arnie's. Have you been there yet?"

"No. What kind of food do they have?"

"A little bit of everything. It's a town favorite."

Jessi rolled over onto her back and stared at the ceiling. She would much rather stay right where she was completely and utterly content. Her stomach growled again, and Mitch shot her a playful glare.

"Okay. Let's go, tiger."

Heat spread from her chest up her neck to her face. "I guess I am hungry."

****

Mitch pointed to the sign that read "Congratulations! You made it out of bed." They glanced at each other, and both doubled over in laughter.

"Their signs change about every other day. I think it's one of the ways they keep people coming in."

The bell dinged when they opened the glass door. A young waitress wearing a T-shirt with Arnie's on the front and "Have you seen the sign" on the back, walked past them.

"Sit wherever you like."

Lacing his fingers in Jessi's, Mitch motioned to a green vinyl booth, and they took a seat. The waitress dropped off a couple of menus and waters and quickly disappeared. Jessi scanned the menu and chuckled at the strange names of their offerings. Glancing at the drink offerings, she stopped. "They have Purple Skies wines." Her eyes tipped up above the menu. "You have to try the red blend. It is amazing."

"Was it one of your fifteen bottles?"

"Yes, it was."

"What would you have with it?"

"It's got a little bit of sweetness, a little bit of oak so a roast beef with horseradish or a blue cheese would pair well."

"I'm not a big blue cheese fan. Tastes like sweaty feet."

"And you've tasted that?" she questioned with a smirk.

"No. Smelled it though. Be around Brandon for any length of time and you will understand. That kid has some stinky feet."

"What about this Cowabunga? Roast beef with horseradish aioli, provolone cheese, butter lettuce, tomato and fried shoestring purple onions."

"That's one of my favorites."

"Is it?"

"It's really good."

"Sarge?" A deep voice called behind Jessi. She turned to see a large man with sandy blond hair holding a baby with a full head of dark brown hair wrapped with a tie-dyed headband.

"Hey, Cap. Where's Bekah?"

"She's on her way. Had a late client. Just me and Maizy right now."

"Well, have a seat. You're welcome to join us."

"You want to introduce me before we barge in."

"Good idea."

"Brant, Jessi Maddox." He motioned. "Jessi, Brant

168

Ellington…oh, and Maizy." A twinge of panic shot through her with the mention of her real name, but she figured it probably was safe for his friends to know who she was, so she smiled, and Maizy gave her a toothless grin. "Brant is about to be one of our newest paramedics."

"About to be?" Jessi asked.

"The graduation is next Saturday. I'm hoping to get certified as a flight medic after that. It's what I did in the military."

"That sounds exciting."

"He's also our resident actor."

"Oh yeah?"

"They just finished a movie at an old hotel up the road about the gangsters back in the twenties and thirties." Mitch nodded to Brant. "Who did you play?"

"John Dillinger."

"Wow! How did you land that?"

"My mom was one of the executive producers."

"Oh?"

Mitch leaned over and whispered in Jessi's ear. "His mom is Sandra Gerard."

"No way." Jessi's eyes cut to Brant.

Brant nodded.

"Now that you say that. I do see a resemblance, through the eyes."

Maizy latched onto a paper napkin and tried to get it to her mouth. "No, baby girl." Brant said in a soft voice. The door dinged and Brant leaned out to see who it was, then smiled back at Maizy. "Here comes Momma." He stood and motioned her back. A woman, dressed in a flowy printed skirt, white tank, and sheer peach cover, appeared. Her hair was piled on her head and wrapped with a peach and white scarf tied at the nape of her neck and draped over her shoulder. She tipped up on her toes and gave Brant a kiss, then Maizy.

"That's Bekah. Brant's better half and Dale's granddaughter."

Bekah held out her hand to Jessi. "Are you the one who moved into grandpa's cottage?" Jessi nodded. "It's nice to meet you."

"Jessi Maddox. You too."

"I probably should come over and pick up all my furniture. I'm sure it's in your way."

The waitress stopped by and dropped off two more menus and waters. "No actually, I didn't bring much with me, so I was glad to have it."

"Oh, if you need it, then great. You are more than welcome to use it." Brant sat back down, and Bekah followed. She clapped her hands together and Maizy leaned toward her. Bekah grabbed her and gave her a big smile. "There's my sweet girl."

Brant looked at Mitch. "We actually got some more good news this week."

"What's that?"

"Her ex relinquished all his rights. Our issues are finally getting resolved."

"That's fantastic news." Mitch responded. "So are you—"

"I filed for adoption the minute we got the news. They said it would take a while. I'm hoping it comes through before our belated honeymoon trip."

"When is that?"

"We pushed it out to September after Joe and April's wedding."

"That's right. April and Joe are—"

"August." He tipped his head to Bekah. "Yeah. She wouldn't let me use the trip to the Maldives for their wedding as our belated honeymoon." Bekah elbowed him. "I thought it was a great idea."

"The Maldives sounds amazing don't get me wrong, but you already had me sold on Australia."

Jessi smiled. "Oh, you will love Australia. I've been there a few times on business. They are well known for their wines. If you need any tips, let me know."

"Really? What do you do?"

"I'm a sommelier. Australia is a large producer of wines, so I've made a few trips over there to check out some of their vineyards and products."

"What an interesting job. Do you like it?"

"I really do."

"You are going to have to come to our girl's night and teach us about the wines we should be drinking. Of course, Jenna and I are sidelined right now but we still have fun with our non-alcoholic stuff."

"I would love to."

"I guess you heard Jenna had the baby," Bekah said tapping the table in front of Mitch.

"Yeah. Cody sent me a photo."

Jessi loved knowing Mitch had such a tightly woven group of friends.

The waitress returned. "My name is Felicity, and I will be your server. Are you ready to order?"

Everyone eyed each other and nodded. Mitch nodded to Jessi. "Um…okay. I'll have the Cowabunga with a glass of your Purple Skies blend."

"White, wheat, or rye bread?"

"Rye please."

The girl's attention moved to Mitch. "I think I will

have the same, extra crispy onions."

The waitress laughed. "Do you want added crispy onions or do you want them extra crispy?"

"Oh, added. Good catch."

"And for you?" She focused on Bekah. "I want my usual." She lifted her eyes to the girl and smiled, and the girl smiled back.

"Blue Whale with ginger ale?"

Bekah nodded and handed her the menu. "You are good."

The waitress took the menu and gave Brant a contemplative look and he lifted a brow. "The Collective on rye with a ginger ale?"

"Perfect." He handed her his menu. She picked up the other two and disappeared.

"Wow! I guess you guys come here quite a bit."

"I told you. This place is a town favorite," Mitch said. "I usually stop by here at least once a week at lunch. They have some great specials.

Jessi's focus drifted to Bekah. "So, what do you do? Brant said you had a late client today."

"I'm a psychologist."

"Forensic psychologist," Mitch added. "She has helped me with a few cases."

"What does a forensic psychologist do?"

"Well, I predominantly work as a clinical psychologist, however on occasion I will help with crimes. I examine videos of suspects, read body language and facial expression to see if there are tells on what the person is thinking. I listen to testimonies and statements for voice inflections. Sometimes they'll accidentally say something. I even check crime scenes for tells."

"That's fascinating."

"Yeah. I might need you doc, for Jessi's case."

Bekah's eyes opened wide. She handed Maizy back to Brant. "Oh?"

Mitch turned to Jessi. "I won't share if you don't want me to."

"No. I'm fine with it. The more eyes looking out for me the more protected I will be."

"We're not sure about any of it yet. She has an ex that is a nephew to a Philadelphia crime boss. She left and came here to get away from him. We're trying to figure out if he is searching for her."

"Well. Let me know if I can help in any way—" she said to Mitch and then turned to Jessi, "—or if you need to talk."

Jessi nodded. She appreciated the offer and was glad to have found someone her age she could possibly confide in. "Give me your information before we leave." Bekah reached in her bag and retrieved her card and slid it to Jessi.

"Call me."

The food arrived. Bekah put Maizy in the highchair the waitress provided and dropped a teether on the tray for her to chew on while everyone started in on their meals. The hint of pepper flavor in the wine paired perfectly with her sandwich and Jessi caught Mitch sniffing the glass before tasting it. She pinched her lips together trying hide her smile. Maizy let out a shriek and banged her toy on her tray and everyone's attention moved to her.

"How old is she?"

"She's a little over four months." Bekah added a colorful ball to the mix on the tray in front of Maizy. "We have just started adding some organic vegetables and fruit to her diet. She does not like blueberries."

"No. She loves blueberries. They don't love her." Brant corrected. "And we don't love her diaper explosions."

Bekah swatted him. "Excuse me, I'm eating." She lifted her eyes and motioned. "We're eating." Jessi chuckled, followed by Mitch. And, as if on cue, Maizy's diaper rumbled.

"Not it." Brant said quickly. Bekah gave him a side eye. "What? I've had her all day. Do you know how many diapers I've changed?"

Bekah stood, lifted Maizy out of the highchair, and checked her pants. A smile crossed her face. "Hehe, just gas."

Jessi couldn't help wondering what it would be like to have a baby of her own. She had never considered it with Dante. They always were too busy with their jet set lives to even consider it. Her eyes drifted to Mitch. She wondered what Mitch would think since he already had two kids. *Why am I even thinking about this? Our relationship is so new.*

"Do you like yoga?" Bekah blurted.

Jessi's wandering mind was brought back to the conversation. "Come again?"

"I was wondering if you liked yoga."

"Yes. I took some yoga classes at my gym in Philadelphia. My mom was actually the one who got me interested."

"Great. I teach some yoga classes at 24 to Life. I have three different classes that cover every level. You should come try it out. We have a good group in Flow Yoga."

"I think Mitch mentioned that you taught some

classes. I am definitely interested."

Maizy started grunting and whimpering. Bekah motioned to Jessi. "I'm going to take her outside while the guys pay out. Wanna come?"

"Sure." Mitch let her out of the booth, and she followed Bekah out the door. The evening was warm with a slight breeze. They sat on the metal bench outside the door. Maizy was bouncing on Bekah's lap. Jessi rubbed her finger against the baby's cheek.

"Wanna hold her?" Bekah asked.

"Are you sure?" Bekah leaned Maizy to Jessi, and she took her in her arms. Maizy's eyes opened wide as Jessi lowered her on her lap. "You are a beautiful little girl. Aren't you?" She stared at the little girl and Maizy smiled big and cooed back at her. Two teeth came into view. "Look at those pretty teeth."

"Yeah. She has been chewing on everything and drooling." The boys pushed through the door of the restaurant. Jessi snuggled Maizy close and breathed her baby scent in before handing her back to Bekah, then rubbed her hand over the little girl's dark brown curls.

"Are you ready to go?" Mitch asked Jessi as he approached.

"Yeah." She stood, then turned to Bekah and Brant. "It was nice to meet you." Her eyes met Bekah's. "Let me know when you guys have the next girl's night out."

"Absolutely. And call me," she said with a nod. "Let's do lunch soon."

"Okay."

Mitch put his hand in the middle of her back and escorted her to the car. As they merged onto the highway, Jessi glanced over at Mitch and said, "That was fun."

"Yeah. They are good people." He eyed the road

then his focus returned to her. "Bekah had issues with an ex-boyfriend too."

"Really?"

"That's what Brant was talking about. Her ex was trying to blackmail her. He tried to frame Brant with rape while he was working on the movie and attacked Bekah when everything started unraveling."

"Seriously?"

Mitch nodded. "And as far as your case is concerned, we need to go over everything we have so far." He pulled into the driveway and opened the garage. "It would be good to come up with a plan." Mitch flipped on the lights of the darkened house then retrieved his computer off the side table and sat down at the dining room table. Jessi scooted out the chair next to him and sat down. He opened his e-mail from Stephen. The photo that was taking over the internet was one similar to the one of Jessi with the tray of pizza. "Oh geez. That's what is posted all over the Internet?"

"Yep. I get why it got so much of a response."

"I was like nineteen in that photo."

"You haven't changed much." The sincerity in Mitch's voice made Jessi smile.

"So, if Dante saw this post somehow, he could have easily sent someone out to find you. We have to commit to the idea that he may know where you are." Mitch tented his fingers against his mouth. "What I think we should do is, first thing tomorrow, get you a rental car. If the guy at the restaurant was tailing you, he knows the Jaguar, so you are too easy to spot driving it. He may not know about your job at the vineyard, and you don't go back to Lake Village until Wednesday, right?"

"Right. But do you think a rental is necessary? I

mean if you can drop me off and pick me up, we can save time."

"I thought about that, but I actually have a game tomorrow night and I'm probably going to have to go straight from work to the game and I don't want to leave you stranded."

Jessi's face brightened. "Where's the game?"

"It's over at Taylor Field off Thirteenth Street. Would you want to come? I mean, you don't have to. I just—"

"Are you kidding me? I wouldn't miss it. I get a chance to see your skills."

"I don't know what skills I will be displaying. I haven't played in a while. I'm a little rusty."

"I can't wait. It will be fun."

"Anyway, I think it would probably work out better if we got you a rental for the time being until we know what's going on."

"Okay. If you think that is what's best."

"It will keep you from having to rely on others to get around and will buy us some time." He tapped on his computer. "Now tell me again about what you found on the burner phone?"

"Burner? Oh. Dante's other phone. It was a reminder that popped up to meet John at PSBT at twelve thirty to get the key."

"And when was this?"

"It was about a month before I left. That's when things really started getting bad. Most nights he would come home drunk, go take a shower, and sit silently watching TV or playing on his computer. About the time I found the message he started coming home and it was almost more like he was drugged than wasted. He was loopy but jittery and would go off on anything. I could look at him wrong and he would jump all over me."

"Do you think he knew you were planning on leaving him?"

"I think he knew our relationship was falling apart but I don't think it was why he was acting that way, because I didn't start thinking about leaving until after he started verbally abusing me."

"You said he was meeting John to get a key. Right?"

"Yes." She nodded.

"And this would have been around six or seven weeks ago?"

"Right."

"Did he leave town around then?"

"No. Not that I can remember. He didn't travel much after he was laid off."

"I'm just trying to get an idea of what PSBT might stand for."

"I have no idea."

"Okay. I'm going to do some digging around to see if I can link anything together."

Chapter Twelve

Mitch felt oddly comfortable having Jessi sitting next to him in his police cruiser as they drove to Fayetteville. They picked up a black Camry, something that wouldn't stand out like her Jaguar. Once Mitch made sure the car was in good shape, he gave Jessi a quick kiss and they parted ways.

At the office he contacted a few of his connections and started trying to piece together what Dante might have been involved in. He had three questions he needed answered. One. What did PSBT stand for? Two. What was the key for? And three. Was there anything major that happened crime wise six to eight weeks ago? He booted up his computer to find a page full of emails and other items that needed his attention before he could even get started with his search.

About halfway through the day, He was finally able to get started on the case. Traveling down a rabbit hole on his computer, he found he was getting nowhere on his questions, then it hit him. He'd found a key at Jessi's house that she didn't recognize. What if that was the key? What if it was something he'd hidden, and it accidently got into her stuff. It was a long shot. He wasn't even sure if "the key" in the message, meant a physical key. It could mean a key code.

The one he found on the floor was definitely not a house key. More like a locker key. He shut down his computer and drove over to the cottage. Scanning the area for anyone possibly keeping eyes on her place, he moved up the driveway when he didn't see anything out of the ordinary. The front door was locked when he tried it and so were the French doors off the back. He walked back around front about to knock on Dale's back door when he noticed the open window. *She didn't learn her lesson the first time.* Silently saying a prayer that the squirrel was not around, he tugged at the screen until it was free, shoved the window the rest of the way open, and crawled in. Slowly, he walked from the bedroom up the hall to the kitchen. Nothing seemed out of place. Everything was quiet. No squirrels. He couldn't help the feeling though that something wasn't right. She wasn't being paranoid.

He opened the drawer she had dropped the key in and rummaged around until he found it. Holding it up, he tried to decide what it would go to. Flipping the key over, he noticed at the base of the handle it said PSBT. It was the key. His heart raced as the realization hit that not only was she not paranoid, but she was also probably in real danger. A moment passed. He stared at the key trying to formulate a plan. Trying to figure out how to keep her safe as well as his family. Wondering what evil had already invaded the town. He inhaled deeply trying to steady his pulse then dropped the key into his pocket. Walking back into the bedroom, he locked the window, and exited through the front door replacing the screen before he left.

Back at the station, he scrolled through different types of keys on the Internet trying to figure out what the key might go to. It was long and flat and had an odd set of teeth on it. He had seen one before but couldn't place where. His eyes scanned through rows and rows of keys. Nothing resembled the key in his hand.

Now, more than ever, he needed to solve the mystery. The quicker he got answers the more likely he could keep Jessi and his kids safe.

An hour of searching brought him no closer to an answer than when he started so he decided to try a different route. His gut said they were storing something. Probably drugs. Maybe weapons. An alarm chimed, startling him. His reminder. He was running out of time. He had an hour before he needed to be at the game. What did PSBT stand for? He tapped the letters into the Internet and scrolled through the possibilities. One listing was Premier State Bank and Trust. *A bank?* Since Jessi said Dante didn't do any traveling, he tapped in PSBT in Philadelphia and scrolled through the list. There it was. Philadelphia Security Bank and Trust. *Okay. Now we are getting somewhere.* He twirled the key in his hand. *A safety deposit box.* The alarm sounded again. And again, Mitch was startled. *I need to change that damn alarm noise.* He glanced at his phone. Fifteen minutes until the start of the game. "Dammit. I need more time." He leaned back in his chair, flipped his computer off, and headed to the parking lot.

****

Mitch crawled out of his car and snatched his gear from the back. He let out a sigh as he approached the dugout. Peering up in the stands he didn't see Jessi or the kids. It was still early. His gear dropped off his shoulder onto the bench. The air was thick. A storm was brewing to the west. He grabbed a bat and started stretching, twisting back and forth. Randy came up and slapped him on the shoulder. "Thanks for filling in."

"About that. Umm…I saw Bruce today. I thought you said he was out of town."

"Well…" Randy averted his eyes and rubbed the back of his neck then slowly let his eyes drift back to Mitch, "it's just—"

"I didn't even ask who we are playing."

"Brookside."

"Say no more."

"You know how cocky they are and to be honest you were one of our best players."

"And George?" Mitch put his hands on his hips.

"Truth?" Mitch cocked his brow up. "He put me up to this."

"I'm the ringer?"

"Not technically. I mean you were on the team the last time we played them, and we lost by one."

"They were so damn smug."

"Yeah, and they won because Garcia got called out and we all know he was safe."

"So, I'm guessing I'm on first?"

"Yeah."

"Got it." His attention moved to the stands. There was still no sign of Jessi or the kids. The glow of the concession stand called him, and his stomach growled. He figured he would get a hotdog to tide him over. Jogging over, he stood behind a round balding player from Brookside. The guy glared back at him but didn't speak. He ordered, then gave him a scowl as he carried his order away. Mitch narrowed his eyes to let him know he wasn't intimidated. He ordered his hotdog, clasped his hands behind his back and waited. A hand reached in and laced their fingers with his.

"Is that the best thing to be eating right before a

game?" A sultry voice whispered in his ear then he felt soft wet lips on his cheek and his body heated. His chin dropped and he glanced at her from the corner of his eye. Jessi's dark brown hair draped like satin over her shoulder.

"It's better than trying to play on an empty stomach." He shot back still watching the lady retrieve his hotdog. Jessi's fingers gently raked up and down his back. His voice lowered to an amused whisper. "And if you keep doing that, I'm going to forgo the game all together and take you behind the concession stand and have my way with you."

She leaned in and whispered back. "Promise?"

His eyes met hers. "Woman. Don't be doing that to me in these pants. It will be highly embarrassing." Her eyes twitched to his pants and a wicked smile let him know he just stoked the fire. "I missed you." He leaned down and took her mouth in a chaste kiss, but it wasn't enough. It was never enough. Wrapping his hand around her neck, he deepened the kiss, letting his tongue roam until he heard someone clearing their throat. When he backed away, he noticed the lady at the concession stand eyeballing the people who were lined up behind him. She pushed his hotdog to him. Jessi licked her lip and smirked.

Quickly grabbing the plate, he put his hand on her hip and guided her away from the line. His hand slipped down to her bottom, and he gave her a swat for her antics, then helped her into the stands.

"Did you have a good day?" he asked as she sat and snuggled up beside him on the aluminum seat.

"I did. How about you?"

His thoughts went back to the case, and he wondered

if he should say anything. The last thing he wanted to do was scare her, and he didn't have anything definitive. There was still so much left unanswered. "It was pretty good," he finally said taking a bite of his hotdog. "I think I might have found something."

Jessi's expression filled with surprise. "Oh? What?"

"I'm not sure yet. I need to make some phone calls." Taking another bite, he noticed her staring at him. "Wanna bite?" Her eyes bounced between him and the hotdog, and she leaned in. He held it out to let her take a bite. Her eyes met his as she bit into the dog, and his body immediately heated. She held her hand to her mouth as she chewed. "Lord woman. You took half my dog."

She chuckled. "Stop. Don't make me laugh or I'll choke."

His eyes widened and he motioned with his hand. "You took half my dog."

"I did not," she said still covering her mouth and chewing.

"Gallagher. Are you playing?" Came a voice from the dugout."

Mitch's attention swung to a white-headed man standing by the fence. "Give me a minute. I'm getting something to eat," he said around a bite.

"Sure you are."

Mitch glared at Randy. "I'll be there in a minute." He stuffed the rest of his hotdog in his mouth. "Do you want me to get you a hotdog?"

"No. I might get one later."

"The kids should be showing up soon. I don't know if Kathy will have them fed or not."

"I will make sure they get something if they're

hungry."

He leaned in and gave her a soft kiss then stared into her eyes. "Thanks for being here."

"I told you, I wouldn't miss it." She leaned her head to his. "Go out there and kick their butts!" Her lips met his and sparks shot through his body igniting the hunger inside him. He backed away and gave her a peck on her nose then stood and headed to the dugout.

The first inning ended with the score two to one in Brookside's favor. Mitch headed to home plate, ready to bat. With two runners on, he needed a hit. He flipped his hat backwards and shoved the plastic helmet on his head as he glanced into the stands. Jessi sat with Georgia in her lap and Brandon a space away. Brandon was sitting forward with his arms resting on his knees. Mitch waved at them and heard his son call back "Go, Dad!"

He approached the plate and dug in. His bat swung back and forth over the plate before he hoisted it above his head. Glancing at the tall skinny guy at the pitching mound he wondered if the kid was even out of high school. The ball came in hard and fast, and he barely saw it as it hit the catcher's glove. Strike one.

Holy cow. Wasn't expecting that. Okay. I'm not going to just stand here for the next two. He toed his cleats into the dirt, swung his bat over home plate then lifted it above his head. His eyes zeroed in on the pitcher and the noises around him stilled. As if in slow motion, he watched as the pitcher wound up and released the ball like a bullet aimed at him. He felt the vibration in his arm when the bat connected, then it fell from his hands. His heart ticked up and with a hop, his legs began to move. He had no idea where the ball went. He was laser focused on first base, then second. There was a vague realization that his teammate Craig had crossed home plate and Shawn was racing toward it.

"Run, Mitch!" He heard a sweet voice yell from the stands. His lungs burned and legs felt like they were gaining weight by the second, but he kept moving. He dove for third when he saw the baseman lean out. "Safe," he heard the Umpire say and he laid there for a second trying to catch his breath. When he stood, his gaze immediately went to the stands. Jessi, Brandon and Georgia were all cheering. He snickered and shook his head. *I'm getting too old for this*.

Twisting back and forth trying to loosen his back, he watched the next batter. When he heard the whack, he took off running again. His eyes caught the outfielder slinging the ball into the air from the corner of his eye and dove for his life over home plate, skidding to a stop. "Safe." The sound of the cheers filled his ears. He could hear Jessi's voice above them all, like a cool breeze covering his body on a hot day. His eyes lifted to the stands as he continued taking in ragged breaths.

Dusting his hands against his legs, he glanced down and realized it probably didn't do any good, he was covered in dirt. His eyes locked on Jessi again. She stared at him and licked her lips and smiled. God, he loved when she did that. He sent up a wink and headed for the dugout. Hands went up in high fives as he traipsed over to a spot on the bench and collapsed. His elbow stung and he noticed most of the skin was gone and blood was dripping from it when he checked. He got up and searched the bag in the corner of the dugout. The plastic container that normally housed the first aid supplies was nowhere to be found.

Stepping out of the dugout he caught Jessi's

attention and motioned with his hand. She stepped down the bleachers to him. "Would you mind going to the concession stand and getting the first aid kit?" He held up his arm and Jessi's nose wrinkled. She eyed Brandon and Georgia. "They'll be fine," Mitch assured, seeing the concerned expression on her face. He wasn't going to let them out of his sight.

Without a word she stepped off the bleachers and jogged over to the concession stand. When she returned, she carried a large red box and motioned to Mitch. He sat down beside her as she opened the box. She carefully grasped his arm and poured some water from a water bottle over the scrape then wiped it with a square of gauze. He hissed and let out a pained grunt when she dabbed it with an antiseptic wipe but watching her purse her lips and blow on it gave him a pain of a different kind. One that had his whole body prickling with electricity. She was so gentle. After applying some antibiotic ointment, she wrapped it with gauze and taped it up.

Her hand went to his cheek and dusted off some dirt. "You are doing awesome."

He followed her lead and dusted his shirt. "I'm getting too old to be doing this."

"Well, it might not hurt so badly if you wouldn't slide into all the bases." Mitch glared at her playfully then leaned in for a kiss without thinking. His eyes caught both of his kids staring down at him from their seats and a flutter of anxiety hit. He stood and quickly headed back into the dugout.

By the top of the eighth inning, Dalton was behind by one. Mitch had tagged two out at first and gotten on base two other times without scoring. He was up to bat again and as he checked the stands, he saw Jessi and Georgia clapping, and Brandon, with his elbows on his knees again, looking serious. He popped the batter's helmet on and lifted the bat with both hands over his head stretching as he walked to home plate. A different pitcher was on the mound. This one was thicker and not quite as tall. Tattoos dotted his arms.

Bases were loaded and there were two outs. He needed a hit. Really needed to get some runs in even if he was sacrificed in the process. His body ached. He was ready for the game to be over, and they still had an inning to go. His eyes locked on the pitcher as his cleats ground in the dirt. Swinging the bat above his head, he let his shoulders settle.

The ball whistled past him below his waist. Too low. The catcher trapped it at the plate. Ball one. Mitch glared at the pitcher again. The thought crossed his mind that the pitcher would make him walk. He didn't want that. He wanted to bring his teammates in. He wanted the points.

Scraping the dirt, the pitcher straightened, reared back, and let the ball fly. Mitch leaned into it and swung with no connection. Strike one. He couldn't let that happen again. He needed a hit. His eyes narrowed. Zeroed in. Watched the movements. Watched the release. His muscles stung as the bat cracked against the ball. His cleats dug into the dirt as his legs churned. He could hear the crowd's screams including Brandon screaming, "Run!" His foot hit first, and he continued. *Runner one should be in.* He rounded second and the roar increased. Jessi was screaming, "Keep going," so he did.

He glanced up to see another runner hit home, then felt the ball whiz by him and watched it skip across the field. He hit third and hesitated for a millisecond. *Can I make it?* His lungs were shutting down and his legs felt like they had fifty-pound weights tied to each. He pushed on, running for his life. The final stop was in his view. *Where's the ball? Should I dive?* He pushed harder, touched the plate, and watched the umpire's hands spread. "Safe."

Gasping for breath, he leaned over, gripped his knees, trying in vain to push air in and out. Players surrounded him, patting him on the back and giving him high fives. His eyes tipped up, peering from below his brow to see Jessi, Brandon, and Georgia jumping up and down in the stands. He stood and waved weakly. "Hell yeah," he said satisfied. "Let's see them catch up to that."

The game ended with a victory for Dalton, and Mitch couldn't keep the smile from his face watching Jessi, Brandon and Georgia descend the bleachers to greet him. Jessi smirked. "Show off," she said in a playful tone.

"I got lucky."

Brandon piped up. "Yeah, you did. That ball hit the ground then popped up and I knew you were out, except the outfielders both went after it, and it dropped between them. Left fielder tried to throw it to the third baseman, who wasn't paying attention, and it went right past him."

"It doesn't matter how it happened. It was fantastic!"

"I told you my daddy could run around the bases."

"You sure did, and he definitely proved it tonight."

Georgia patted Mitch. "Daddy, can we go get some ice cream."

Jessi raised her brows, staring at Mitch. "I think that is a great idea. We need to celebrate."

"Then I'm sending these two home with you, because they will be bouncing off the walls."

"That's fine with me. We can get some blankets and pillows, build us a pillow fort, and camp out in the living room."

Georgia jumped up and down. "Can we daddy?"

He studied Jessi then his focus dropped to Georgia. "I wouldn't do that to Miss Jessi. She has no idea what you two can get into. We'll go get ice cream though."

Jessi rubbed Georgia's hair, noticing she was starting to pout, and squatted in front of her. "We are going to have a girl's day soon. We'll go get our nails done and go shopping. Okay?" Georgia rubbed her eyes and sniffed but nodded. Jessi gave her a hug. "Now, let's go get some ice cream." She gently clasped Georgia's hand in hers and helped her down the rest of the bleachers.

Mitch glanced at Jessi. "Do you know where you are going?"

Jessi gave him a sidelong glance. "I haven't the foggiest."

"Follow us."

Chapter Thirteen

Chilly Dips Ice Cream Parlor was everything Jessi thought an old-fashioned ice cream parlor should be, with black and white vinyl floors, metal counters and blue and pink glittery vinyl bar stools. Blue and pink vinyl booths with Formica tables lined the wall that held photos of fifties movie stars. It looked like they stepped back in time. The wait staff even wore white aprons and paper hats.

Glass display cases were filled with homemade candies, cakes, and cookies. They sat next to metal containers that held different flavors of ice cream and assorted toppings.

"What do you guys want?" Mitch asked, scanning the menu that hung behind the counter. Silence took over both kids. Their eyes glazed over while they tried to decide.

Jessi leaned in and lowered her voice. "What do you think about getting a 'Brain Freeze'?"

"How much can you put away? That thing is huge."

"You know how you said brownies are your weakness?" Her eyes tipped to the ice cream case.

Mitch's mouth lifted into a smile, and he shook his head. Turning to the person at the counter, he said, "We'll have one 'Brain Freeze.' "

When it came to the table, Jessi stared at the large bowl filled with eight scoops of various flavors of ice cream, several toppings including fudge and strawberry, brownie bites, chunks of pineapples, cherries, sprinkles, and of course whipped cream. Both kid's eyes grew to the size of saucers. Mitch doled out the spoons and everyone dug in.

"Now this is a celebration," Jessi said as she dipped her spoon in for another bite. "That was such a great game."

"Miss Jessi, will you come to my game tomorrow?" Jessi smiled at Brandon who stared into the ice cream and wouldn't meet her gaze.

"What time?"

"It's at six," he said quietly.

"At Taylor Field?"

"Yeah."

"I will be there. I wouldn't miss it." She caught a slight smile creep across his face. He resembled his dad so much when he smiled like that. She cut her eyes to Mitch who had the same expression.

Georgia whimpered beside her. "You said we could have a girl's day." Jessi knew she was going to have to handle this situation with care, or the youngest at the table was not going to last long without a meltdown. It was getting late, close to her bedtime, so they were on borrowed time.

"Well, if Brandon's game isn't until six then there is nothing stopping us from having our girl's day before that...unless your dad—" Her eyes glanced at Mitch.

"Far be it for me to stand in the way of a day of pampering."

Jessi smiled at Georgia and gave her a high five. "I will make the appointment tomorrow morning to get our nails done. Can you let Kathy know I am going to be picking her up a little after three?" Jessi asked noticing Mitch looking a little green when her attention was back on him.

Mitch slowly looked up and dragged the spoon from his mouth. "Let's work out the logistics when we get home."

"Wait. I—"

"We'll figure it out when we get home." He dropped his spoon in the nearly empty dish. "I have officially celebrated myself sick."

****

"I can't put your family in danger, Mitch. I will be fine at my house. You have patrol coming around and I promise I will keep my gun by my bed and will call you if I hear anything," Jessi said when Mitch came down the stairs after putting the kids to bed. He'd asked her to stay.

"I don't like that plan. Take my bed and I can sleep out here."

"No. I told you I won't put you and your kids in danger."

"Why did you show up at the baseball field then?"

"Well, considering it was two teams of cops, I kind of hoped we were pretty safe."

"True. Good point."

"How are you feeling, by the way?"

"Like an old, bloated toad." He did a quick check of his bandaged elbow and plopped down on the sofa. She patted his leg that he had propped up. "I don't think I'm going to be able to sleep tonight with all the sugar I consumed."

"No more than the brownies the other day."

"I need more of those."

"Not until you learn to share." Mitch rolled his eyes

making Jessi giggle. "Now, I appreciate what you have done, but I am heading home." She stood and he followed.

"Jessi. Please?"

"No, Mitch. I will be fine. I promise, I will lock all the doors—"

"And windows."

"If it makes you happy, I will make sure I lock the windows."

"I'm going to call my buddy to meet you and do a walk through."

"I don't think that is necessary, but if it makes you feel better, okay." Did he really think it was that important? Was he really that worried something was going on? When she asked about the lead he had in the case, he acted evasive and just said he couldn't really say much until he made some phone calls. She tried not to be too concerned. Deep down inside though, she was glad he was taking the precautions. She would have stayed in a heartbeat if the thought of putting them in danger didn't completely overwhelm her. She would never forgive herself if something happened to them.

On the drive home she tried to take her mind off the rising anxiety filling her gut with a little music. She tapped the screen and flipped through the channels until she heard the familiar tune "Thinking out Loud." The weather was warm, it looked like it was about to start raining so she rolled her window down and let the smell of the impending rain fill the car.

At the stoplight she watched a car in the other lane pass, and her body tightened. The man behind the wheel looked like Dante. She swallowed hard. It can't be. It wasn't his car. He drove a red Audi. That car was silver.

Her head was spinning. Was it the same car from the night before? *I am being paranoid. Mitch has got me scared.* She continued to her house and waited for the officer to show up. After doing a thorough search and making sure her window was down and locked in her bedroom, he left. She sat on the sectional and retrieved her phone.

—*I'm home. All is well. Your buddy Garrett stopped by and checked everything out—*

—*Okay. Keep your phone with you and make sure your gun is close by. I'm really not comfortable with you being there, but it's your decision—*

—*I know—*

She let out a breath. *I'm really not comfortable with the situation either.* Her mind went back to the car at the light. It couldn't have been Dante. She got up and gazed out her window. Everything was quiet. *It wasn't Dante. I am just making myself scared.*

****

Jessi knocked on the door of the house down the street from Mitch. A pretty brunette with ivory skin pulled the door open. She pushed her glasses up on her nose and brushed her hair back from her face. Jessi could hear the chaos coming from inside.

"Hi. Are you Kathy?" Jessi asked through the storm door.

"I am," the woman said, pushing the storm door open. "You must be Jessi. Mitch said you would be stopping by to pick up Georgia. Come on in." She pushed the door wide, and Jessi stepped inside. "Let me go get her." Kathy walked away and ruffled the hair of a blond headed little boy as she passed. Jessi stood by the door letting her eyes wander.

Toys littered the floor everywhere her eyes landed. Glasses of milk and juice were scattered about. Still, past the toy clutter, the house seemed well kept. Kathy's attitude seemed laid back and easy going. Jessi heard Georgia's voice before she saw her come around the corner. Her smile widened when the little girl ran up and wrapped her arms around her making her heart twinge. She had never really been around young kids that much. The more time she spent with Mitch's kids though, the more attached she grew, and a sigh escaped wondering if it was a mistake. Jessi ran her fingers through Georgia's curls letting the thought go.

"Are you ready to go get pampered, Little Miss?" Georgia nodded. Jessi glanced up at Kathy. "It was nice meeting you and thanks for letting me steal her."

"It was good to meet you too. Mitch spoke very highly of you. He wouldn't let his kids go with just anybody. You know, the law enforcement side of him is suspicious about everything."

"He is very protective, and I don't blame him. There are a bunch of crazy people out there. He's a good guy and a good daddy."

Georgia decided it was time to go and yanked on Jessi's arm. "Let's get this girl day started," she said.

Jessi stumbled and gave Kathy a wave. "I guess we will be going now."

"I will see you at the game this evening."

"Oh. Does your son play too?"

"Yeah. He and Brandon are on the same team and my husband Scott is the coach."

"Oh. That's right Mitch mentioned that. I can't wait. Should be fun." Georgia tugged Jessi to the door and pushed it open.

Chunking her backpack in the back seat, Georgia climbed in the passenger seat and strapped in. "Daddy doesn't let me sit in the passenger seat. He says I'm too little. Brandon gets to though. He always gets to do the fun stuff."

"Well, I will drive very carefully. I am sure it's hard sometimes when your brother gets to do stuff you can't. Your day will come though. You just have to be patient."

"I'm not good at being patient."

"Really? I wouldn't have thought that," Jessi said sarcastically even though she knew Georgia probably wouldn't understand.

"Daddy says I don't have any."

"Well, when you are seven, I don't think that is one of the things you have developed quite yet."

They drove up the road and headed into the downtown area. "We have a little time before we are scheduled for our nail appointment so I thought we would stop for a snack and then go shopping." She pulled into a parking spot and helped Georgia unbuckle her seat belt. They walked up to a bright yellow storefront with a multicolored sign that read "When I was a Kid" above the door. Jingle bells sounded as the door opened. Georgia's head darted back and forth as she took in all the unique toys and books. "Have you been in here before?"

"No."

Jessi had found the store online when she was searching for fun things they could do. It had only been open a short time so she was hoping it would be something she and Georgia could experience together. Georgia ran to a table filled with wooden puzzles in different stages of completion. Jessi took in the array of toys that were obviously displayed for the kids to play with.

Several bookshelves were filled with children's books. Jessi picked one up. Thumbing through the pages, she noticed the vibrant colors and intricate artwork. It was about a girl who lost her mittens and the creatures that found them. She clutched the book in her arms and moved on. Another book had more of an abstract feel. The people had harder edges like caricatures. It was about a high-end restaurant. She held onto that one too.

Glancing over at Georgia who had put on a sparkly rainbow tutu and had a beautiful baby doll propped up on her shoulder, Jessi remembered her favorite baby doll that she carried everywhere with her when she was little. She wondered if her mom still had it. Georgia cradled the doll in her arms and gently let her tiny fingers comb through the doll's hair. Finding a blanket in a nearby doll stroller, she wrapped her in it.

Once the doll was wrapped up, Georgia began to sway back and forth. She moved to another area of toys, still cradling the doll in her arms and Jessi sat back and watched Georgia create an imaginary life. She knew Mitch could easily get flustered with his little girl, but what Jessi saw was a smart, loving, curious little girl, and it made her heart ache for her, wondering if she missed her mom.

In the back of the store was a small café area. Jessi ordered two teas and two orders of cake bites. They sat at a bistro table and waited. The waitress arrived with a teapot, two cups and saucers with rose patterns and two plates filled with small cubes of cake bites. Jessi showed Georgia how to dunk her teabag and squeeze it with a spoon against her cup. They sat and had their tea and snacks and then Jessi paid for her books and Georgia's tutu and doll that she had yet to put down.

Their next stop was the nail salon. They picked out their colors for their fingers and toes, then Jessi helped Georgia get up in the chair for their pedicures and even turned on the seat warmer and back massager. Georgia sat back and closed her eyes. "Have you ever had a pedicure?" Jessi asked after she got settled.

"Yes. My mom took me and the other girls in her wedding party to get them before the wedding. The place wasn't like this though."

A young lady with long blond hair sat down in front of Georgia, poured some lotion in her hands, and rubbed it on Georgia's foot. Georgia jerked away and giggled. "It tickles."

"It does a little. Doesn't it?"

They lowered their feet into the warm water and Georgia let out a little moan. "That feels good." The girl picked Georgia's feet up one at a time, dried them off and filed her nails. Jessi's girl, a brunette with glasses, let her dip her feet in paraffin. "What is that?"

"It's wax. It's a little too warm for your delicate skin so they suggested we not do that for you.

"Does it burn?"

"A little. But once you take it off it makes your skin really soft. Your skin is already soft. So, you don't need it." Georgia seemed to agree, and she nodded. Her attendant grabbed the polish, a hot pink with sparkles, and started shaking it.

"Oh, now the good part." Georgia clapped and smiled. Her two front teeth were missing but one tooth was starting to come in. Georgia sat up and watched as the girl began to apply the polish with light short strokes.

Jessi's attendant carefully removed the paraffin from her feet and legs and gently scraped her heels with a pumice stone before grabbing her polish in the shade of a dusty rose.

They carefully got up, once their toes were done, and moved to a table where their attendants started working on their hands. Georgia again got the hot pink glitter polish, but her mouth dropped open when the attendant took a small brush and drew tiny white flowers on her two ring fingers. "Daddy is going to be so surprised." She showed Jessi then fanned herself.

"I know. You look very pretty Georgia."

"Thank you, Miss Jessi. So do you."

They left the nail salon and strolled down the sidewalk for a while checking some of the other stores. Popping into a bakery, they got some cookies to take to the ballpark along with some lemonade. Jessi checked her phone and realized they only had about thirty minutes to get out to the baseball field, so they started heading toward the car. Georgia chatted about what she thought about living with her dad full time. Jessi was happy to hear that she didn't mind it and she liked going to Miss Kathy's. Ashley was her best friend even though she could be kind of bossy. Somehow Jessi felt it was probably a mutual feeling. She told her she did miss her mom but knew she would get to see her sometimes.

Jessi stared off thinking about her mom and dad. She hadn't talked to them in a while and probably needed to check in. Several people chatted at the outside café tables, as they passed. The day was perfect even though rain was supposed to be coming in. It would be a nice night for the game.

Her eyes drifted to the passing cars. An older man

passed by in a cherry red Thunderbird. His windows were down, and "Sweet Emotion" was playing loud enough for those on the sidewalk to hear and Jessi immediately started humming along. A silver car appeared, and Jessi froze when the man in the passenger seat leaned forward and stared in her direction. Even though he had on sunglasses she could swear it was Dante. Panic gripped her and the man quickly sat back. She grasped Georgia's arm and raced to the car.

"What's wrong Miss Jessi?" Georgia asked.

Prickles formed all over Jessi's skin and she tried to steady her voice as she spoke. "Nothing, sweetie. I just realized we are going to be late if we don't get going. We need to get to the baseball field, or your daddy will be worried."

"He likes you." The words from the little girl made Jessi's cheeks heat momentarily although the sight of the man had already made a rush of panic flood her veins. Dropping their packages in the seat, and making sure Georgia was buckled in, she took another deep breath and steadied her voice.

"Why do you say that?" Jessi asked as she eased out on the road, checking her rearview mirror to see if anyone was behind her.

"He kissed you, and he looks at you, and smiles. He doesn't smile a lot."

"Really? Why not?" Her foot pressed the gas and her eyes continued to dart to the mirrors. So far no one was behind her.

"I don't know. But he smiles more when you are around."

"Well, I'm glad I make him smile." Her mind was drawn away to their conversations, and how much he made her laugh. His kisses consumed her body. Even thinking about them sent fire to her blood. How could he have taken over her thoughts so quickly? She had only known him a few weeks. He had something she needed desperately. Her body craved him. She loved how protective he was and how safe she felt with him.

Safe. Something she didn't feel at the moment. She checked her rearview again. There were cars behind her now, though she couldn't tell if any of them was the silver car she had seen. Her pulse pumped harder. She would feel better once she was at the baseball field with Mitch.

Her eyes darted to Georgia who was staring out the window holding her new doll. She had a sweet smile on her face, completely unaware of the panic Jessi had wracking her body. She was so cute with her rainbow tutu. Jessi wondered what Mitch would say. She let her mind drift again for a minute, letting her imagination wonder. What would it be like to be married to Mitch and be Georgia's and Brandon's stepmom? A sigh escaped and she glanced at Georgia again who was now staring at her.

"Did you have a good day, Georgia?"

"The best."

The gravel crunched under the tires as Jessi drove into the lot at the baseball field. From where they parked, she could see Mitch, in his police uniform, sitting in the stands, talking on his phone. She sat and stared for a moment. He was so handsome. He caused her heart to stumble every time she saw him. She helped Georgia unbuckle her belt. "Stay with me, sweetie." Grabbing Georgia's hand, she scanned all the cars around her. No silver cars in sight. She smiled at Georgia, and they walked to the bleachers.

Chapter Fourteen

Sitting in the bleachers, Mitch watched the players warm up and shoved his phone back in his pocket after discussing Jessi's case with one of his colleagues. The information he had been given didn't sit well with him, and Georgia and Jessi hadn't arrived yet. He still wasn't sure of anything, although more and more pieces seemed to be fitting together and the likelihood of Jessi being in danger continued to ramp up. If Dante was out there, mixed up in what he was putting together in his head, he would be coming after Jessi. No question.

Scott and Kathy were bringing Brandon along with their son. He would feel a whole lot better when his family was with him. It made him chuckle at the thought he already included Jessi in his family. His mind drifted to the night with Jessi. Just thinking about her made a surge of heat spread through his core.

"Anyone sitting next to you?" The sound of her voice sent his body into hyper drive, and he released a relieved breath. She was here. Her hair was in a ponytail and her face glowed from the heat of the day. The sight of her made the words catch in his throat, so he just patted the bleacher next to him. She stepped up and scooted in.

"Daddy!" Mitch spied Georgia crawling up the bleachers in a rainbow tutu, her face beaming. The doll held tightly in one arm, made it harder for her to get to him.

"What do you have there?"

"Miss Jessi and I went to this store. It had all these toys everywhere. We had tea and these tiny cakes, then we went and got polish." She held up her fingers on her free hand and one foot.

"That is very pretty, Baby. Did you remember to tell Miss Jessi thank you for all the stuff?" She tapped her mouth with her finger and didn't respond. "Georgia, you best tell her thank you."

She stepped over to Jessi and put her arms around her and nuzzled into her neck. "Thank you." When she stepped back, she gave Jessi a kiss on the cheek. Jessi tightened her arms around her and gave her another hug.

"I had the best time with you Georgia. We will have to do it again soon. Okay?" Georgia nodded. Jessi gave her a kiss in her hair then lifted her eyes to Mitch. He tried to swallow but a lump had formed in his throat. Georgia sat down beside Jessi. Mitch's mouth dropped open in disbelief. Jessi eyes twinkled as she shrugged. Mitch could only chuckle. He'd been replaced.

He put his hand on Jessi's knee then peeked at her from the corner of his eye. "How was your day?"

She leaned over and grabbed his full attention. "Work was pretty good. Still learning the ropes. Way different than I'm used to, but I honestly enjoyed it. And Georgia was wonderful. We had a great time." Mitch's brow lifted in surprise. Jessi's fingers laced with his and he lifted her knuckles to his lips. "How was yours?"

"Actually. I think I've got some more information on the lead you gave me on Dante." Mitch felt Jessi's hand tighten around his.

"Do I want to know?"

"I can't exactly say anything. Besides, I'm still figuring out what is going on."

"Still?"

"One step at a time. I don't want to give you half the information and it turn out to be wrong."

"Is it bad?"

"I don't know."

Kathy stopped on the bleacher below them with her hand wrapped around her daughter Ashley's. "Hey Mitch." Kathy's eyes glanced at Jessi, and she smiled. "How was your girls outing?"

"We had a great time."

"Miss Kathy, look." Georgia stood up and held up her doll, then showed off her fingernails and toenails.

"Very pretty."

"How was the rest of your afternoon?" Jessi questioned.

"Oh, you know, constant chaos. That's how I roll."

"Did my two give you any trouble?" Mitch quickly added.

"Are you kidding me? You don't know how much you have helped me by letting your kiddos come over to entertain the two of mine. I should pay you."

"I'm willing to let you borrow them to help you out any time you need me to, free of charge," Mitch said with a chuckle. Then added, "I do appreciate it though."

"Happy to help." Kathy took in the team warming up.

Mitch followed her gaze. "Do you think we have a shot at these guys?"

"I don't know. Scott said they have a few more wins on us, although their schedule hasn't been that hard."

"Well, if our guys play like they did the last game, I

think we have a decent shot."

"Mine's playing with a hurt hand compliments of his sister."

"What happened?"

"He took something from her, and she picked up one of wooden logs from the building set and nailed him across the back of his hand with it." Mitch and Jessi both grimaced.

"Hopefully it won't affect him too much."

Kathy continued up the stairs with Ashley.

Jessi rubbed Georgia's back. "You never told me. Did you have fun at Miss Kathy's?"

Georgia shook her head. "Miss Kathy got on to me because she said I was being disruptive."

Mitch rolled his eyes and Jessi glanced at him with a glare. "What were you doing, Georgia?" He wondered why Kathy hadn't mentioned it.

"Nothing."

"Georgia. I don't think Miss Kathy would say that if you were doing nothing."

"Daddy." She took on a no-nonsense tone. "She put on music while we were supposed to be resting. What did she expect? You are supposed to dance to music. Not sleep."

Mitch blinked, slowly shaking his head. Jessi clamped her lips shut and he quickly put his hand to his mouth to try to hide his smirk, then gently grasped Georgia's arms. "We'll talk about this later."

Her brows pinched. "Okay. But I know I'm right. When they put music on in school you are supposed to dance." She stared up the bleachers then whipped back around. "Can I go sit with Ashley?"

"Yeah, As long as you do what Miss Kathy tells

you."

"Yes, sir." She scurried up the bleachers. Mitch's focus was back on Jessi, and he shook his head again. His hand returned to her knee. "Did she behave for you?"

"Yes. I told you. She was absolutely perfect. We had a great time." Jessi stared out at the team. "Georgia said you like me."

"Oh, she did, did she?"

"She said she saw us kiss and that I make you smile."

The corner of Mitch's mouth lifted. "She is very observant."

"Yes, she is."

He glanced back over his shoulder at the curly headed little girl. "You really didn't have to buy her all that stuff today. I know how persuasive she can be."

"She didn't ask for anything." Mitch's gaze returned to Jessi and his brows squeezed together. "I wish you could have been there to see her. She was so sweet. The way she held that baby doll and rocked her, I couldn't make her leave her behind."

His focus returned up the bleachers where Georgia and Ashley sat. Georgia was letting Ashley hold her doll and rock her. He knew today had been good for her.

The announcer came over the intercom for the start of the game announcing the lineup for each team. Mitch stood and yelled, and Jessi whistled when Brandon's name was announced. Brandon lifted his gaze to the stands and smiled. Jessi sat down on the edge of the bleacher intently watching the field. Looking around, Mitch smiled, suddenly realizing how genuinely happy he was.

At the bottom of the second inning the score stayed

zero to zero. Brandon hadn't been up to bat yet, and Mitch's mind drifted wondering what he might have found out if he would have stayed at the office a little longer. His eyes quickly landed back on Jessi who now had Georgia and her baby doll sitting in her lap. A peaceful smile played on her lips and the setting sun had the golds and greens of Jessi's eyes shimmering. He couldn't take his eyes off her. If anything were to happen to her…

A breeze blew small pieces of her hair that had fallen from her ponytail across her face. Her delicate finger reached up and pushed them back. Seeing her, sitting with her arms around his little girl, so comfortable, made his heart thud in his chest. She handled his kids so easily. Things that would normally have him yelling at the kids, didn't rile her in the least, and now he found himself being a little slower to react with his temper.

Brandon's team, the Hurricanes, was up to bat. Mitch shifted in his seat as the first batter stepped up to the plate. He carefully watched the batter get settled in his stance. The first ball was outside. The second was also. Mitch shifted nervously again and glanced at Jessi. She was all in, completely engrossed in the game. *She wasn't lying that she loved the game.* The third ball connected with the bat and the batter took off running. He touched first and headed for second but turned back.

Next up was a tall lanky kid. Mitch pointed. "This kid is good," Jessi leaned in a little. The batter swung at the first ball. It didn't connect. The second was way outside. The batter tapped his shoes with the bat then lifted it ready for the next pitch. Mitch zeroed in trying to will the bat to connect with the ball. The pitcher eyed first base, lifted his leg, reared back and hurled the ball at the batter, hitting him in the side. Immediately, the batter dropped to the ground. Mitch glanced at Jessi who had her hand over her mouth. The coach and manager ran out of the dugout to check on the boy. Mitch scanned the stands to see the batter's mom and dad standing together, obviously worried. Within a minute though, the batter was jogging to first base.

"Tough kid. That's going to leave a mark," Jessi commented.

"Yeah."

Brandon was up next. He stared up at Mitch as he walked to the plate. Digging his cleats in, he settled in his stance and lifted the bat above his head. First pitch was inside nearly clipping Brandon in the side.

"This pitcher is dangerous," Mitch said, keeping his gaze locked on his son.

"I hope they take him out before he hurts another kid." Jessi responded quietly to Mitch then cupped her hands around her mouth. "You've got this Brandon." Mitch chuckled at her change in volume. He loved watching how excited she was getting.

The second pitch was wide, and Brandon glanced back up into the stands before twirling his bat above his head and settling back into his stance again. The next ball connected solidly with his bat sending the ball into a line drive. The outfielder took off running but the ball disappeared over the fence. Brandon ran past first.

Mitch jumped to his feet. Jessi sat Georgia on the bleacher seat and stood.

Mitch cupped his hands around his mouth. "Bring it home, Brandon!" He watched Brandon round second and head to third as the player in front of him hit home.

"Way to go Brandon!" Jessi screamed her fist

pumping in the air.

"Brandon Gallagher with the homerun. That puts the hurricanes up three to nothing with no outs at the top of the third inning." The announcer rang through the intercom. Mitch grabbed Jessi and gave her a hug.

"Wow, someone takes after their daddy."

"Oh, no, I'm sure he will surpass my skills by the time he's twelve."

"I don't know so much about that after what I saw last night." She paused. "Are you ready for another brain freeze?"

"Oh geez, no. I was up half the night burping pineapple." He smiled at her. "How did you sleep by the way?"

"Fine. You had me a little skittish, but everything was fine."

"Well, again, until we are sure you are safe, I don't want to take any chances." For a brief second Mitch thought he caught something in Jessi's expression but then it was gone. Had something else happened?

"I know, and I do appreciate you checking into everything and…" He waited for her to continue but she didn't.

"You okay?" he finally prodded hoping she wouldn't shut down. His thoughts went back to the earlier phone call. There was no way she would be sleeping at the cottage tonight.

The smile she gave him didn't reach her eyes and he knew something wasn't right. Although now wasn't the time to delve into the case. "I'm fine…I…" the whack from the bat connecting jerked both of their attention back into the game.

At the top of the eighth inning, the Hurricanes were

up six to two. Brandon played short stop and had thrown two players out and tagged one.

"Georgia, are you getting hungry?" Mitch asked.

Georgia nodded energetically.

"I'll go get it. What do you want?" Jessi said patting his leg.

"Are you sure?"

"Absolutely. Brandon might be batting, and I don't want you to miss it."

"Can I go too?" Georgia asked, and Jessi glanced at Mitch who nodded.

Jessi held out her hand to Georgia. "Of course, you can." She stood. "Hot dog?" Mitch nodded. "Mustard, relish, onions?"

"Mustard, ketchup, relish, no onions."

Jessi wrinkled her nose "Ketchup?"

"You ate it last night."

She tipped her head in agreement. "Chips? Drink?"

"Plain and…just water."

"Got it. We'll be back in a few minutes." Georgia placed her hand in Jessi's, and they disappeared around the corner of the bleachers.

Minutes passed. Mitch sat up when Brandon walked out to the plate. A runner was on first and there were two outs. Brandon scuffed the dirt, swung the bat back and forth and leaned into the plate. "You got this son," Mitch yelled. The first pitch sailed inside. Brandon hopped back, tipped his head from side to side, swung the bat and settled into his stance again. Mitch sat up. The second pitch popped in the glove of the catcher directly over the plate. Strike one. Mitch twitched on the bleacher and clapped his hand. "That's okay. That's okay. Settle down."

"Georgia?" Mitch jerked, hearing Jessi's distressed voice. He stood and walked to the side of the bleachers. "Georgia?" Mitch's eyes locked onto Jessi holding a cardboard tray of food, her head darting back and forth. His chest tightened. He took the bleachers two at a time, swung around the rail and ran to Jessi's side. The sound of a ball hitting the bat rang through the air. Mitch glanced at the field, then turned to Jessi and grabbed her arm. "What happened?"

"Georgia said she had to go to the restroom." She pointed; her voice filled with panic. "It's right there, so I told her to go and come right back. I kept an eye on the door, but I got to the front and had to order." Mitch scanned the area. "It couldn't have been more than two minutes. When she didn't come out, I went to check, and she wasn't in there." Her hand clutched her chest.

His stomach churned. He had done the same thing with her a thousand times, although it wasn't him this time, it was Jessi, and the fear inside him boiled. "Why didn't you get out of line?" he said sharply.

"I'm sorry. I should have, but the bathroom is right there." She motioned again. "And she said you let her go by herself all the time."

He let out a huff and spun around. "Georgia?" Mitch called as he jogged under the bleachers searching, hoping that Georgia would pop out. "Jessi, check behind the concession stand." He called out.

She set the drinks and food down and took off behind the building.

Mitch ran up the stands to the top to get a better view. He watched as Jessi searched the area around the concession stand then ran out into the parking lot screaming for Georgia. In a split second a man was on her, covering her mouth. She kicked and flailed as he dragged her across the lot to a silver car. Mitch's heart stopped when the car door opened, and he heard his baby girl's cry.

It happened so fast. His legs couldn't carry him fast enough down the bleachers and he stumbled on the last step. Before he could make it out to the parking lot they were gone. All he could see was the rear lights disappearing. His hands hit his knees as he gasped for breath but not from him running. Tears filled his eyes. "Dammit!" His lips pursed and his hand wrapped around his mouth. They had his baby girl. And they had Jessi.

He yanked out his phone and notified the station although from where he was standing, he couldn't even give them a good description of the car. Units were dispatched. He knew the protocol. This time though, he was the victim. He desperately wanted to do something, but he knew he had to wait. His fingers slid through his hair as thoughts spiraled in his head and tears seeped from the corners of his eyes.

He had been on the other side of similar situations many times, taking statements from victim's families, and now he knew how the families felt, wondering if they were okay. Wondering where they were taking them. Wondering if that would be the last time they would see them alive. Most of the time, things worked out, but he knew who had Jessi and Georgia, and he knew what the Angenellis were capable of. A feeling of hopelessness wrapped around him. He took a shaky breath. *This can't be happening.*

Police cruisers raced into the parking lot with their lights flashing and sirens blaring, and a crowd quickly formed. His thoughts swayed wondering why he had let this woman complicate his life and put his family in harm's way then remembered she didn't ask for this. She was a victim. He found Kathy and filled her in, asking her to keep Brandon for the night so he would be safe.

The game ended and people started making their way to their cars. The crowd grew. Mitch felt like a caged animal. His entire world was spinning out of control and the last thing he wanted was an audience.

Hurricanes won. Mitch couldn't even congratulate his son because he was still talking to the officers. His coworkers. His friends. He knew the only way for him to get any peace was to head to the station and figure this out himself.

Angry tears spilled from Brandon's eyes when Mitch filled him in on what happened. And it took everything within him not to break down when he had to physically force his son into Kathy's car. He wanted to stay with Mitch and help him find the scum who took his sister and Jessi. Mitch could see so much of himself in him. He kissed him goodbye and watched the car drive away.

His body quaked as he climbed the bleachers to grab Jessi's purse and Georgia's doll and he sat. His legs refused to hold him up. He couldn't breathe. Tears wet his cheeks. Rage consumed him and he let out a guttural scream that echoed through the stands. Running his hands down his face, he then rubbed them together and growled, "I'm coming for you."

Mitch picked up the baby doll and Jessi's purse and stormed to the car. By the time he got to the station his stomach was in knots and he felt like he was going to be sick. Throwing his keys on his desk, he dropped into his chair and booted up his computer. The screen glowed in the darkness of his office, and he realized he neglected to flip on the light. He didn't care.

An email caught his attention. It was from the cyber security guys in Little Rock. When he clicked on the link, a news report, out of Florida, dated March sixteenth, appeared. The story was about an armored car that went missing after receiving a shipment of rhodium, worth close to ten million dollars. The armored car was found empty in Philadelphia. As he read through the information, it became clear that the key he held would be the key to getting Georgia and Jessi back.

Chapter Fifteen

Jessi sat in the back seat of car; her hands tied, heart racing. When they threw her in the car, Georgia was curled up in the floorboard wailing loudly. Luckily, they hadn't tied her up and she crawled up in Jessi's lap. She managed to get her arms around the little girl even though the zip ties were tight around her wrists. Georgia's tears were coming hard and fast and it broke Jessi's heart. She leaned her head down and kissed the mess of strawberry blond curls trying to calm her. This was all her fault. Mitch would never forgive her. It might not matter though. She probably wouldn't make it out alive.

Scenarios flashed before her eyes and none of them ended well for her. She didn't care as long as Georgia survived. She had to make sure the little girl wasn't hurt. She kissed her again on the forehead. Georgia's arms wrapped tight around her. Her head was sweaty against Jessi's neck.

When Georgia disappeared, she was so frantic, she didn't notice Dante until he had his arm wrapped around her waist and hand over her mouth. She fought him trying to get away then he whispered, "I have something you want, and you have something I need. Don't fight me and maybe, just maybe, we can each get what we want without anyone getting hurt."

Panic filled her as she realized what he was

meaning. She stopped fighting. A howling noise hit her ears as they made their way to the waiting car. She knew that cry well. Her high-pitched screeching wails were unnerving to say the least, and she figured it was probably the last thing these thugs figured they would have to deal with. The car door opened. The ear-piercing howl grew. A giant beast of a man stepped from the car. Tattoos filled his arms. He slipped zip ties on her wrists while Dante continued to hold her, then shoved her into car. Everything happened so fast she didn't even know if Mitch realized she was gone. For all she knew he was still searching for Georgia.

The panic on Mitch's face when he asked what happened made her stomach burn. She could barely speak. She wanted, so badly, for Georgia to appear from under the bleachers giggling from scaring them. But she didn't, and the more she searched the more she knew something horrible had happened. Still, for some reason, she never suspected it was Dante who had her. Not until she felt his hands on her. Not until she made eye contact. Not until her mouth was covered so she couldn't scream.

Her mind drifted. The menacing look in Dante's eyes bore no resemblance to the man she knew. He was almost unrecognizable. Her eyes landed on the man in the front seat. His dark brown hair, which used to be filled with soft tousled curls, now was slicked back with some greasy goo. His beautiful brown eyes that would gaze at her with a twinkle of adoration, now were more like those of a wild animal. He appeared gaunt even though his strength, when he held her, was overpowering. What the hell had happened to him? How had he gone from such a sweet soul to this, this monster? Their eyes met in the rearview mirror. Something flashed in his for a second then it was gone. What was that? Fear? Concern?

She cleared her throat. "What do I have of yours, Dante?" she questioned softly, on purpose, trying to see if he would crack again. He glanced in the mirror again then turned away quickly. He knew she saw his vulnerability. He wouldn't make eye contact with her now. "Tell me, Dante."

Instead, he growled, "Show us where you live."

She hesitated, but Georgia's small frame shifted in her lap, and she knew she had to protect her at all costs, so she guided them to the cottage. The car pulled up in her driveway. Dante and the tattooed beast got out. Jessi tried to scoot out when they opened the door, but Georgia's body was too heavy. She had cried herself to sleep.

Dante reached in and grabbed Jessi's upper arm and tugged her. Georgia stirred and started whimpering again. Jessi yanked her arm away from Dante and glared at him then focused on Georgia. "Georgia, look at me." She zeroed in on the child's eyes. "You need to do as I say. Okay?" Georgia rubbed her eyes and whimpered again. Jessi knew she was on the cusp of wailing again. "You need to be a big girl. Can you do that for me?" Georgia nodded her head still rubbing her eyes. "Get out of the car and I will be right behind you. I will keep you safe." Georgia climbed out and Dante grabbed her arm. Jessi slid out behind her. Her attention was drawn to Dale's place, and she wondered if he was there. The light in the kitchen was on although she didn't see any movement.

"Where's your key?" Dante asked in an even tone. He pushed her forward toward the door.

"It's in my pocket." She moved her hands to the right and Dante reached into her pocket to retrieve the key. He unlocked the door, pushed it open, and dropped the keys on the table next to the door. Walking into the kitchen, he opened the refrigerator. Jessi couldn't believe he was just making himself at home like they were old friends. He pulled out a beer and waved it at Jessi.

"Tell me Jessi, who's the new guy?" He dug in the drawer and found the bottle opener and popped the top. "Didn't even take you a month." He tipped the bottle to his lips and guzzled some down.

Jessi's heart pounded wondering when he would go off. Would he hit her in front of Georgia? "I don't have a new guy, Dante."

"Oh, no?" He took another swallow then his eyes cut to the silent beast man and held up his beer. The tattooed henchman nodded. Dante reached into the refrigerator again, retrieving another beer. He popped the top and set it on the bar. The man stepped forward and took the bottle. "See, Jessi, I don't believe you. You know why?" His eyes bore through her. "You hate beer. Told me you couldn't stand the flavor. So why would you have beer in your refrigerator?"

"I do have friends Dante."

"Like the one who is the daddy to that little urchin?" He nodded to Georgia. "The one you were snuggled up with at the game? Is he your *friend,* Jessi?" A sinister smile crossed his face. Jessi could feel herself trembling. Tears filled her eyes. She had no answer. Dante walked over to Georgia who was latched onto Jessi's legs. He put his hand on Georgia's head. "Wonder what he's doing right now, Jessi." His hand twirled a few her curls then gently combed his fingers through them. "It would be a pity if she didn't make it home."

"Dante, please, I beg you. Let her go. All you need is me. Tell me what it is you want. I will give it to you."

Jessi watched him as he scanned the room then his eyes seemed to land on something, and he moved across the room to the shadowbox of Layla. He yanked the photo box off the wall and smashed it on his knee. Digging inside the jagged glass, his face suddenly paled. He held up the dog collar and shook the box, twisting it from side to side. "Where is it, Jessi?" Examining the box closer, he shook it again, then threw it on the floor and stormed over to Jessi gripping her face hard. "Where did you put it, Jessi?"

She leaned back jerking her face from his grip. "Put what? I don't know what you are talking about."

"The key, Jessi. Where did you put the key?" Spit flew into Jessi's face as he spoke.

Panic coursed through her veins. "What key?"

"There was a key inside the shadowbox. I put it there. It's not there now."

"Dante, I swear, I don't know what you are talking about. I don't know anything about a key." Her mind drifted back to the night Mitch helped her unpack and her eyes jerked back to Dante. "Wait. I did find a key on the carpet when I was unpacking. I thought it might have been the previous tenants. She hurried to the kitchen and pulled out her junk drawer scanning each item. When she didn't see it, she moved the items in the drawer around thinking it had to be underneath something. "It's gotta be here. I swear I put it in here." Her heart felt like it was going to explode. *Where the hell is the key?* Tears filled her eyes. What would Dante do if she couldn't find it?

Dante walked up next to her. "Where is it, Jessi? I

got to have that key." Jessi continued to feel around in the drawer hoping the key would magically appear. Dante joined in. Jessi noticed he was sweating.

"I swear I put it in this drawer." He pulled the drawer out and set it on top of the counter so they could get a better look. Dumping everything out in the cabinet below and still not finding it, he started searching the other drawers. The tattooed man stepped up to the bar joining in the search. Dante peeked up quickly then continued his search.

"Where's the kid."

Jessi's gaze went to the front door standing open. Dante jerked his head to the beast man who took off out the door.

"He won't hurt her, will he?"

"No. I don't think so." Dante leaned over the counter, checking the door. "I'm a dead man if we don't find the key, Jessi."

"What?" Jessi's head jerked, unsure she heard right. The raging monster from moments before was gone. His voice had softened and was laced with fear.

"I was forced to work for my uncle, Jessi. I had no choice if I wanted to stay alive. I screwed up royally."

"What do you mean?"

"I was hemorrhaging money searching for a job, and the last thing I wanted to do was to work for my uncle. So, I used what I had left in my savings to place a bet that I thought was a sure thing. I was told it was a sure thing. It would at least give me enough to get by for a few more months until I found another job. Only it didn't happen the way I had hoped. Not even close."

"Shit, Dante. Why didn't you tell me?"

"I didn't want you taking care of me."

"But we were together." Even as the words spilled out of her mouth something became overwhelmingly evident. They were never truly together. No matter how good he treated her during the good times, there was no bond. Though they lived together, their lives were separate. They were merely playing house.

"It was a mess, Jessi. The minute I lost the bet, I found out just how far my uncle's *business dealings* reached. I was set up. Marked. These guys had a vendetta against something my uncle did years ago, and they decided to use me as their pawn. They were part of a Cuban mob, and they set me up. I owe them a shitload of money from the bet, and because of that, they have my uncle right where they want him. Indebted to them. That's why I had to go to work for him. He's making me dig us out of this hell. And that key is literally the key to do that. If I don't get that key, I'm as good as dead. If he doesn't kill me, the Cuban mob will."

"What is it for?"

"It's a security vault key." He leaned over the bar again making sure the beast man was still out of earshot. "There is a deal going down Friday that is worth millions of dollars. Tens of millions. Once that deal is done, the debt will be washed. I will be given a part of the take and will have the money I need to make it through until I can get a new job."

"So, your uncle is just going to let you walk away? No questions asked?"

"He said it was for my dad, his brother. Payment for another debt he owed. He wouldn't go into any explanation. I think he was responsible for my parents' deaths." He stared at her and she could see the regret in his eyes.

Jessi's head was spinning. Within a split second the Dante she knew from before, was back. His body language shifted. Was it all an act to get her to comply? She was so confused.

"Dante, I hope you aren't thinking—"

"Jessi, I am truly sorry for what I did to you. I was messed up. It's no excuse, I know. You pressing charges was the right thing to do. It helped me get my head on straight. I knew the minute I took the job with my uncle I would lose you, and I wouldn't have tried to find you at all if it weren't for the damn key. Now that my uncle has dragged me into his world, I'm not dumb enough to believe that I will ever be truly rid of him, and I would never knowingly make you a part of it."

"Why don't you go to the police?"

"My uncle has them in his pocket. It would get back to him."

"Not here."

He glanced over the bar once more. "I can't get away from Lou. He's not here to help me. He's here to make sure I get that key and follow my uncle's orders."

Jessi felt her phone buzz in her back pocket. Dante jerked his gaze to her then pulled the phone out. She felt her stomach bottom out knowing who might be on the other end.

Dante's expression hardened. "Who's Mitch?"

Jessi dropped her head. "He's my friend. Georgia's daddy."

Dante turned the phone to her.

—*I have the key*—

"You need to take me to him," he said through gritted teeth.

"It's not that easy."

"Yes, it is. You know where he is. Right?"

"Maybe—"

A loud shriek came from outside. "I guess Lou found her."

Jessi's voice dropped to a whisper. "Dante. Mitch is a cop. You need to let him help you. How many of your uncle's henchmen are here?"

"Just me and Lou. He's my uncle's eyes. I can't shake him."

Jessi studied Dante. She could see pieces of the hardened exterior he had pasted on, falling away. It quickly returned when the shrill screams of the six-year-old let them know Lou was back with Georgia. He walked through the door with her tucked under his arm like a football. Her hair and tutu were filled with sticks and leaves, and she was kicking and flailing, and screaming at the top of her lungs. Lou kept trying to adjust her where her little fists and feet were not in range of any vital parts, but her foot nailed him square in the crotch. His face grimaced and he doubled over losing his grip on the little girl. His knees hit the floor and she bolted for the door. Lou glared up at Dante in obvious pain. "I'm not going after her again. She can just keep running."

"I've got my own problem. Go get her."

"Taking her was your idea. Not mine," he said through clenched teeth.

"Shit Lou, she's our leverage. Her da—"

Jessi stomped on his foot. He groaned as his eyes whipped to her and she shook her head slightly and he took the hint. With clinched teeth, he grasped Jessi's arm and dragged her out the door yelling. "Call for her dammit. Make her come to you."

"Georgia?" She hollered, then whispered. "Let me help you."

Dante ushered her farther away. His eyes darted back to the door, then he responded. "I can't do that Jessi. They will kill you. I just need to get the key and get as far away from you as possible. It's the only way to keep you safe."

"Will I be safe? I mean, I did put you in jail. I can't imagine your uncle is happy about that."

"It wasn't a big deal. He's got most of the police force on his payroll. He wasn't too happy when I told him you left with the key though."

"How did you find me anyway?"

"Again, my uncle has people in his pocket. It didn't take long with some facial recognition software to find you. Some guy on the internet posted your photo from around here. We flew down with a private detective and set up a search. Had the detective check higher end restaurants. Once he found you, he called."

She searched his face and turned his words over in her head. "If you won't let me help you, let Mitch. Please."

Dante stopped walking. His shoulders slumped as defeat took over his body. He handed Jessi her phone. "Text him. Tell him to meet us," he said in a low voice and pointed, prodding her.

"Georgia."

Dante swung a glance behind them then continued. "He can't be in uniform." He prodded her again.

"Georgia." Rustling leaves caused Jessi to run up to some bushes in front of Dale's house. "Georgia?" She took her phone and flipped on the flashlight. She could see Georgia's brightly colored tutu. "Georgia. We are going to go see your daddy." The little girl stepped out from behind the bush and ran up to Jessi wrapping her hands around her.

"I want my daddy," she whined, her voice cracking.

Jessi pleaded with Dante. "You have to let her go."

"He's got to give me the key."

"What do you want him to do?"

"Meet us. If he gives me the key, I will let you both go."

"Where?"

"That gas station off the highway at the Meridian exit. Twenty minutes."

—Mitch, Dante wants to meet at the gas station off fifty-one and Meridian in twenty. Bring the key. No one else. No uniform. Silver Toyota—

—Got it. Are you and Georgia okay? —

—Yes—

Dante grabbed her arm and leaned into her ear. "Is he good to you?" His question caught her off guard.

Her mind immediately conjured a picture of how panicked he probably was. He tried so hard to protect her. "Yes," she said softly.

"Then you have to trust me." Her head jerked. She was prepared to offer a snide response but when her eyes met his she knew what his words meant. It was the only way to keep Mitch safe.

Shoving her phone in her pocket, they walked back through the open door. Dante tightened his grip on her and hitched his thumb at Lou. "Let's go. I got the information I need. Her new boyfriend has the key." His voice held a low angry tone that sent a wave of shivers down her spine, but she now knew it was an act.

She knew the man he was before, and saw a glimpse

of him, so she had to trust that he wasn't going to hurt her or Georgia. He pushed Jessi and Georgia back out the door to the car. Dante crawled into the driver side while Lou rode shotgun.

Jessi held on to Georgia and hoped her instincts weren't off. He seemed sober, which was a change since the last time she saw him. His whole disposition changed once Lou was out of sight.

They traveled up the highway and Jessi wondered what Dante had planned. When they pulled into the gas station her heart nearly leaped out of her chest when she saw Mitch's car. Dante drove around the side of the building into the darkness and parked. He tugged on her hard dragging her and Georgia from the car and directing them to the back of the building where it was dark. Lou took out across the parking lot. Jessi noticed he had taken a position where he had a good view of everything going on, then she saw something flash. A reflection. *He has a gun.*

Jessi stood trembling; her arms wrapped around Georgia who had gone completely quiet. It all felt like a horrible nightmare. Dante leaned into Jessi again. "Please Jessi. Trust me." His voice held no anger and as it stood, she had no other choice. She had to trust him.

Jessi watched the corner of the building and Mitch appeared wearing an untucked dark blue T-shirt and blue jeans. She let out a relieved breath. He wasn't wearing his uniform. The remnants of his baseball injury were still visible on his arm. Her eyes fixed on him and then, for a brief second, she closed them, praying that they made it out alive. A jerk on her arms and Georgia was gone. "Daddy," Georgia screamed. Mitch dropped to his knees and his arms wrapped around her. He pushed her back and cupped her cheeks with both hands.

"Georgia. Go to the car. Shut the doors and lock them, then lie down in the seat. Got it?" Jessi could see his eyes glistening and hear the catch in his voice. It about shattered her to pieces. She'd caused all of this.

"Got it."

Jessi watched Lou, making sure his gun didn't trail her as Georgia took off running. Mitch waited until Georgia was safe and continued down the side of the building. Jessi felt her pulse kick up and the tears burn. She couldn't stop them from coming. Dante's hand gripped her arm harder, and she felt something cold press against her side as he pushed her forward.

"Stop," Dante barked. Mitch followed the instructions. Dante pushed Jessi forward enough for a dim light on the side of the building to shine on her, while he stayed in the shadow. Mitch met her gaze for a brief second then let his eyes lock on Dante.

"Just throw the key and I will let her go."

"You know I can't do that, Dante. I saw your goon with his gun trained on me. The only leverage I have is this key. Why don't you meet me in the middle? You have a gun on her so there is nothing I can do that won't get me or her shot. Right? One wrong move and I die, or she does. Right?"

"Right."

"Then we meet in the middle. I hand you the key. You get your rhodium, and I get Jessi."

Rhodium? What the hell is rhodium? Dante squeezed her arm then loosened his hold and rubbed his thumb across her skin. Was he giving her a sign?

"What do you know about rhodium?" His voice dipped.

"Just a hunch. Am I right?"

"Meet in the middle. You step, I step." Jessi bumped against Dante's arm and that's when she felt it. He was trembling. He leaned down enough for her to hear him. "Do what I say, no questions." She nodded once. His head raised. "Step forward," he growled. And Mitch obeyed. Dante pushed Jessi forward one step. They were both now visible. "Again." Mitch followed the command. One more and they would be close enough for the exchange.

Jessi could feel Dante shaking but his voice didn't give him away. "Again." Mitch stepped forward, grasped Jessi's arm, and extended his hand with the key. Dante snatched it and, as if in slow motion, Jessi watched as Dante stepped back, raised the gun and pointed it at her head. She closed her eyes, not wanting to see what came next, then heard him scream, "Get down!" Mitch threw her to the ground.

Pain vibrated through her body as shots rang out. Jessi didn't know where they came from but felt Mitch's body jerk. It all happened in a split second. Then everything went quiet, and she felt Mitch's weight lift off her. His hand grabbed her arm and pulled her to him. "You okay?" It took a moment to register that it wasn't Mitch asking. Dante was staring at them with his hands on his knees still holding his pistol. Jessi's focus bounced to Mitch who was staring back at Dante.

"Jessi. Go to the car and make sure Georgia is okay." Mitch's voice was harsh and strained. She stood and he threw her the keys, then pulled his gun and aimed it at Dante.

"Lou was going to kill her if I didn't. That was the order. Get the key and get rid of her." Dante flipped his gun over to give it to Mitch. Mitch took it and tucked it in his belt then motioned for Jessi to leave. She noticed strobes of lights out on the road moving in fast.

Opening the door to the car she saw Georgia in the floorboard of the car with her hands over her ears. She slid into the seat and rubbed her hand over Georgia's hair. Georgia immediately crawled into Jessi's lap. She didn't make a sound other than a sniffle. It still was enough to send Jessi over the edge. She couldn't hug her close with her wrists tied but the fact she had her in her arms and they were finally safe caused her to release the flood of emotions that she had held back since Dante took her.

Staring out the window she saw Mitch and Dante hunkered over Lou's lifeless body giving him chest compressions. Flashing lights surrounded them now. Several cruisers had shown up as well as an ambulance. The EMTs took over for Mitch and she watched him walk over to the ambulance. Jessi couldn't help wondering if Lou was still alive. She closed her eyes and sobbed thinking about everything that had occurred. Thinking about what she had put Mitch's family through. The driver's side door opened and made Jessi jump.

Mitch leaned in. His eyes went to Georgia. "Is she okay? Did they hurt her?"

Jessi shook her head. "Her gaze dropped to the little girl who had fallen asleep pressed up against her. "Other than being terrified I think she's fine." Her attention was drawn to some white gauze wrapped around Mitch's bicep. "What happened?"

"Nothing. Just got grazed."

Jessi gasped. "You got shot?"

"I'm fine. Don't worry about me. Are you okay?"

"I'm fine now, but you—"

"Jessi, I'm okay. If you are good, I'm going to send the EMTs on their way."

"I'm not hurt, and I think Georgia is okay, but I do need to ask a favor."

"What's that?" Mitch's brow tipped up and Jessi held up her hands to show the zip ties around her wrists.

"Oh! Gotcha." He returned within a minute and clipped the zip ties. Jessi snuggled Georgia to her and kissed her on her head. Mitch crawled into the driver seat and Jessi's attention was drawn to him. "We still need to go up to the station to give our statements but it's almost over."

Tears streamed down Jessi's face. "I'm so sorry I got your family involved with this Mitch. I can't—"

"Jessi, stop." His words were hard, and her immediate reaction was to shrink away, and it was obvious Mitch noticed. His face softened and he took a deep breath. "I told you before, I took this job knowing what the risks were, knowing how stressful it might be, and knowing that I might someday encounter a case that quite possibly could put my family in jeopardy. Unfortunately, it's the nature of the job. Do I like it? Hell no. I was petrified when I realized what was happening. But it's over now."

"It's my fault though."

"No Jessi, It's not. You are a victim. Remember that. You did not cause this to happen. Dante did."

Chapter Sixteen

"You didn't answer my question." Mitch walked into the drab lifeless room devoid of anything other than a heavy metal table and a few chairs. He was tired. Make that exhausted. He had been drained of every ounce of strength he had from the sheer terror he'd felt just a few hours before. However, he was the only person the man seated in front of him would talk to. The man who'd been responsible for causing that terror, and he wasn't going to pass up the opportunity to get information from him. Mitch didn't quite know what to make of Dante Angenelli. With a folder in his hand, Mitch leveled his eyes on Dante who had a look of trepidation on his face.

Jessi had given her statement earlier, and he had one of the officers take her and Georgia back to her car at the baseball field. Dante had reassured him that there were no others associated with the Angenelli family in town and they were safe. It was well past midnight, and he was ready to be home and even more ready to slip into his warm bed with someone to snuggle up to. Ordinarily he would have left the interrogation to someone else, except Dante waived his right to counsel and requested to talk to him; only him. So, here he was.

Dante's elbows rested on the table with his hands cupped behind his neck. He peered up from below his brow when he heard Mitch's voice. "What question's that?"

"Does this key have to do with the rhodium that was stolen when the armored truck went missing in Florida a few weeks back?"

Mitch tossed the folder on the table and scooted out the chair across from Dante. "How in the hell did you make that connection?"

"I'll get to that. Where's it going?"

"Cuban Mafia. The drop is Friday."

Mitch opened the folder and shared a photo of Dante in an expensive suit entering the bank carrying a large black duffel bag.

"That could have been anything, how did you know?"

"Observant, I guess. The timing fit. What do you put in a security vault? Valuables. What kind of valuables does your family deal in? Money? That doesn't go in a security box. That goes in an offshore bank account. Arms? Nope. Too big, and bulky. That goes in some nondescript storage unit. Drugs? Nope. Again, too big, too bulky, and you need to keep your hands on it. It's not something you lock away. Now, a metal more precious than gold that can be used in making bombs? That needs to be kept secure. Kept under lock and key until just the right time."

"Still, that was a reach to get all of that off some random key."

"Jessi saw a reminder on your burner phone about meeting someone to get the key right around the time the armored van was found abandoned in Philadelphia. I found the key when she was moving in and put the pieces together." He sat back and scratched his head. "Tell me about this drop."

"I don't know anything other than it's supposed to

go down after I've turned the stuff over to my uncle." Mitch was ready to push him, but he continued. "My part was to get the rhodium to him and then I'm done."

"Done done?"

Dante nodded.

"You really think he's going to just let you walk away from the organization?"

"He claims he's repaying a debt owed to his dead brother. My father."

"He had connections to his deaths?"

"Nothing was ever proven. Always ruled a car accident due to slick roads."

"And what was your plan then? If you got away with it?"

"I'm supposed to get a cut from the payment for the rhodium and I planned to get as far away from Philly as possible."

"So you wouldn't get implicated?"

"Well, that's kind of a moot point now. But, no. I wanted to be as far away from the organization as possible. I traveled some with the company I worked for before shit hit the fan, and I got laid off. I enjoyed it. So, I thought about just doing that for a bit until I found a place I liked."

Mitch was a bit surprised at how open and candid Dante was. He'd almost forgotten that this was an interrogation and not just a chat, when Dante's voice pulled him from his thought.

"How did you and Jessi meet?"

"I'm supposed to be the one asking the questions." Dante leaned back in his chair and stretched his arms across the table. Mitch waited for a moment then answered. "Box of photos fell off the trailer when she was moving down here. I got called out to get it out of the road. She came into the station hunting for it." His mind flashed to the loose photos he found and the bruises on Jessi's face when he met her. He leaned forward. "I saw what you did to her."

Dante winced. "I wasn't in my right mind."

"Not an excuse. No one deserves to be beaten like that. You damn near killed her. I don't know how she was still moving from the marks she had on her in those photos. I'm still not sure she wasn't lying when she said nothing was broken."

Dante's face filled with shame. "You're right. She didn't deserve any of it. I don't know what she told you, but I didn't want this life. The last thing I wanted to do was go into business with my uncle. I screwed up. I admit it. And I am paying dearly for it. Trust me. If she hadn't taken the key, I would have let her walk out of my life forever to make sure she was safe from my family and from me. And I'm sorry for dragging your family into it."

"You know you are in some deep shit here, right?"

"Oh. You think? From both sides. If I don't do what they want, I'm dead. If I don't cut a deal with the law, I'm in jail for probably life. Hell, I just about killed a guy not, what, two hours ago."

"Your first." Mitch stated.

"You could tell?"

"The expression on your face and the fact you were shaking like it was thirty below when you handed me the gun kind of gave it away."

"I have had a gun for ages and shot it at the gun range regularly. Still, pointing it at a target is a hell of a lot different than pointing it at someone knowing you are about to kill them."

"Well, look. I don't like you and I never will. You beat the hell out of Jessi and kidnapped her and my daughter. And to be perfectly honest, it's hard for me to even sit here with you without wanting to reach over and choke the life out of you. However, you did shoot the guy to save Jessi and me, and that bodes well for you especially if you are willing to work with us. Well, with this side of the law."

"It depends on who you want me to work with. There are plenty of people in my area who are not exactly on the good side of the law even though they wear a badge. They are on the take."

"You know this for sure?"

"Absolutely. I've overheard conversations. The only problem is, I have no idea who it is."

"All I can do is use my resources to try to give you as much protection as I can. I can't guarantee anything though."

"I get it." Dante sat forward and blew out a long breath. "I brought this on myself, and I've known all along I might have to pay a hefty price for it."

"I'll do what I can. I'll make a few calls, but after tonight I'm more or less a bystander."

"I know." Dante leaned back in the chair and his focus drifted. "Jessi told me you were good to her." His eyes moved back to Mitch's. "That's all that's important. There's no way out for me, so I'm going to trust you'll do what's best. Let's do this."

"Okay. Be right back." Mitch stood and left the room. When he returned, he carried a small device and sat it in front of Dante. "Start with your name and give as much detail as you can about your uncle's operation and Friday's drop. I may stop you and ask some questions. Once you have given your recorded statement, we will take your written statement."

****

Two hours later, with Dante bedded down for the night, Mitch quietly slid into his bed. His arm wrapped around Jessi and snuggled her close. He tried to clear his thoughts of the day. Tried to steady his breath and settle down. Still, his mind wouldn't quiet. Thoughts of Georgia running to him, and Jessi's terror filled eyes kept playing over and over. His job had him taking fear out of the equation when he was on a call. He had been in situations where he felt an inkling of fear, but for the most part, he could keep it at bay and stay calm. But this? This was different. This was his baby and someone he cared about, and he had never been so scared in all his life.

Then there was the thought of telling Lorrie. He hadn't even had the kids a month and Georgia had nearly gotten killed. Would Lorrie demand custody? He wouldn't blame her if she did. He knew part of the reason she wanted him to have the kids was so the kids' lives wouldn't be disrupted, but it also had to do with her needing time to adjust to married life again. He hoped she would understand and not immediately request them be flown to Poland to live with her. His heart ached. Even though having the kids full time could be exhausting, he'd already gotten used to them being there. They'd already gotten into a routine.

He pulled Jessi closer, and she rolled over, snuggled in, kissed him in the center of his chest, then laid her cheek against him. Something about that kiss went straight to his heart. It calmed him. Made all the things swirling in his head, hush. He kissed the top of her head and drifted off to sleep.

The following morning Jessi was up with breakfast made when he strolled into the kitchen with his navy uniform shirt draped over the shoulder of his T-shirt. The smell of bacon and fresh coffee hit his nose and went straight to his stomach making it roll with hunger. He realized he never did get to eat at the ballpark the night before. Georgia sat at the table shoveling pancakes in her mouth. His heart tumbled, thankful to have her safe again. Her eyes locked on his. Scenarios played out in his thoughts of what could have happened to her the night before and stole his breath from him. He could have easily lost her and Jessi.

"Daddy!" She hopped up nearly flipping her plate and ran into his arms. She was one to try his patience on a regular basis, but he couldn't imagine what his life would be like without her. He wondered if the events from the previous night would have a lasting effect on her and made him want to squeeze her a little tighter and hold her a little longer than usual. "Miss Jessi made me Minnie Mouse pancakes, Daddy."

"She did?"

"Yeah. see." She grabbed him by the hand escorting him to her chair. "Well, I kind of ate her ears—"

"Were they good ears?"

Georgia nodded.

"Good. Sit back down now, and finish so you can get ready to go to Miss Kathy's." His hand stroked her hair and he kissed her on the top of her head. "I love you, Georgia."

"I love you too, Daddy."

"I'm going to get Miss Jessi to make me a turtle."

He walked back into the kitchen and met Jessi's eyes.

"I have basketball and soccer ball pancakes already made. I can make you a turtle though if you would like?"

"I'll take one basketball and one soccer ball." She gave him a smirk. "How long have you been up?"

Jessi loaded the pancakes on his plate. "Around an hour. Little Miss in there came and got me. She was hungry."

Mitch felt the heat skirt up his neck at her words, and the implication they had. "I'm sorry. Did she say anything about you being in bed with me?"

"No. And don't apologize. I didn't mind a bit."

"Yeah, we didn't get to eat last night." He plucked a strip of bacon from the plate and shoved it in his mouth.

"Go sit down and have some breakfast with your daughter." She kissed him gently on the lips. He loaded some more bacon on his plate before pouring himself a cup of coffee and heading to the table.

Georgia sat up and shoved another bite of pancake in her mouth. Mitch glanced up at her. She was boring holes in him with her gaze. Minutes passed and she finally asked, "Did you get rid of all the bad guys, Daddy?"

Mitch glanced away for a moment. "Yes, I did."

"Did you shoot'em?" she asked matter of fact.

"No. Why?"

"I heard gun shots."

How would she know what gunshots sounded like?

"You did? How did you know they were gunshots?"

Georgia rolled her eyes and flipped her hand. "Duh, Dad. TV?"

Mitch chuckled and nodded. "Of course. I didn't think of that." He was hoping he could steer her away from having to explain the gunshots. "Didn't Miss Kathy say she was taking you swimming today?"

Jessi sat down at the table with a pancake and some bacon.

"Did you get shot last night, Daddy?" She pointed to the gauze wrapped around his arm. Mitch shot a glance at Jessi who met his gaze. "No, baby, I just got a scratch."

Georgia got up from her empty plate and tried to crawl up in Mitch's lap. He pushed away from the table, and she crawled up wrapping one arm around his neck and rubbing her small hand down the gauze on his arm. "I'm glad you didn't get shot, Daddy. I did everything you told me."

A vise suddenly squeezed down on his throat and he wondered if she knew he was lying to her. He fought back the burning in his eyes and forced his voice to work. "Baby, you were perfect," he rasped. "And so brave. I'm really glad you are okay."

"I even got away from the bad men, Daddy. I hid really good. But the big man with all the pictures on his arms was good at Hide and Seek and he found me."

Mitch's eyes again glanced at Jessi whose eyes widened and she bit her lip. He raised a brow wondering what exactly happened and figured he would ask later.

"Well, the bad guys won't be bothering you anymore. Now, go get ready to go to Miss Kathy's."

Georgia disappeared around the corner and Mitch's eyes met Jessi's, questioning.

"She snuck out while we were searching for the key. Lou went after her." Mitch smothered the last bite of pancake in syrup and shoved it in his mouth. "When he found her, she managed to put the beast man on his knees with one well-placed kick.”

Mitch chuckled then choked and grabbed his coffee hoping to remedy the situation. Instead, he managed to burn his mouth. Covering his mouth with his fist, he let out a couple of wheezy coughs. “Are you kidding me?” His coughing fit continued as he tried clearing his throat.

Jessi tipped her head. “Are you surprised?”

“No. No actually, I’m not in the least bit.”

“When she escaped again, he refused to have anything to do with her.”

Mitch shook his head. “Again. Not surprised.”

Jessi got up and picked up her plate then motioned for him to hand her his. “How’s your arm?”

He moved his shoulder. “It’s a little sore but not bad.” Her eyes became glassy, and he knew she was ripping herself to pieces. He stood and wrapped his hands around her cheeks. “Don’t go there, babe. It’s not your fault.” His finger tucked away some loose strands of hair, and he gave her a soft kiss. “I’m fine.”

“It’s—”

“I’m fine Jessi. It’s over.”

“So, what’s going to happen?” Jessi backed away and walked into the kitchen and Mitch followed.

“Dante shared everything that was going on with his uncle. He said there is supposed to be a drop happening Friday. That gives me two days counting today to get things set up. I basically need to get him back to Philadelphia in safe hands, and then hopefully if everything goes well, the feds will have several bad guys behind bars before the day is over on Friday.” Mitch leaned against the counter. “The big guy, Lou, is going to be laid up for a while. Turns out Dante is a pretty good shot. Hit him in the right side of his chest. Once he heals

242

up, he's going to jail for attempted murder. So, he is out of the picture. I've got a call in today to get Dante set up with an FBI team in Philadelphia. He said he was ready to cooperate fully. I guess we shall see."

Jessi rinsed the plates and set them in the dishwasher. "And if he does?"

"He's still going to be facing quite a few charges, although the courts will work with him since he's cooperating."

"Will he be safe? I mean he told me some of the law enforcement officers up there are being paid off."

"I can't guarantee anything. He put himself in a really bad position."

"I know. I just don't want him to—"

"I know and I will do everything I can on this end to make sure he is safe as possible, but my position only goes so far. I'm a police sergeant in a tiny town in Arkansas. That's a blip on the screen compared to what they have up there. I'm just hoping that the people I know, know people who know people—"

She leaned into him. "What exactly is going on? You said something last night to Dante. What did you find out?"

"A few weeks back, a large shipment of rhodium arrived in Florida from South Africa. It's a metal that is commonly used in catalytic converters. The armored truck carrying it was headed to a manufacturing facility that builds heat shields for rockets. It disappeared and was later found empty and abandoned in Philadelphia.

"Why would something used in catalytic converters be such a hot commodity?"

"Rhodium is more precious than gold because of its properties. It's worth anywhere from ten thousand to forty thousand an ounce on the market, so at least ten times the price of gold. This shipment was worth well over five million dollars. Probably upwards of ten.

"Seriously?"

"The metal can withstand high heat and its properties can convert noxious gases into clean air. It's some pretty impressive stuff. Anyway, the key that Dante lost was to a safety vault at Philadelphia Security Bank and Trust. PSBT. I played a hunch that the key I found was connected to the heist because of the date it was stolen and the message you found on his phone. And when I mentioned the rhodium to Dante, his expression told me everything I needed to know."

"He wasn't the one who stole it though."

"No. Dante said the armored car driver had connections with his uncle. He met with a guy who gave him the rhodium and he took it to the bank. They needed someone, who wasn't a well-known part of the family or part of the theft, to rent the security vault in case there were cameras somewhere. I have to hand it to these guys. They are thorough."

"Why did they need a security vault?"

"To store it until the drop on Friday."

"Dante said something about some Cuban mob or something."

"Yeah. From the sound of it, I think they are wanting to get their hands on the rhodium to possibly use it to make bombs."

"What do you think will happen to him?"

"Depends on how far he's willing to go to get his jail time reduced. He could help them take down his uncle and that would definitely score him some brownie points. But I'm not to say. That is up to the group in

Philadelphia. He did contact his uncle. Told him that things didn't go quite as planned and Lou was killed while he was securing the key."

"Lou is dead? I thought you said—"

"No. His uncle needs to think he is until the raid takes place. Otherwise, he might send some more of his men this way."

"And Friday it will be over?"

"Depends on how much Dante cooperates."

"And if he does?"

"If all goes well, yes. It should be over." Mitch swallowed hard. "You will be safe."

Georgia came around the corner dressed in a white T-shirt with a unicorn on it, and denim shorts. A pink backpack with a large-eyed kitty was slung over one shoulder. "Did you pack your bathing suit?"

"Yep."

"All right then, let me get my shoes on and we will head out." Mitch turned to Jessi. "Are you going in to work or taking a day off?"

"I'm going in. I figure working will help me keep my mind off things."

"What time do you need to be there?"

"Not until nine thirty."

"Why don't you follow me, and we can drop off the rental then run and get your car?"

"Don't you have to be at work in like half an hour?"

"Yeah. I'll call and tell them I will be a little late. With everything that went on last night, they know I probably have some loose ends to tie up."

"Whatever works for you. I'm going to run and get my shoes."

****

Mitch sat at his desk staring at the black screen on his phone trying to settle his racing heart. He'd spent the last hour explaining to Lorrie exactly what happened and calm her fears. He hated hearing Lorrie cry. Guilt permeated every pore of his body again realizing he'd chosen his job over his family. He explained that Jessi was a victim. She wasn't the one who was dangerous. She hadn't intended to bring danger to their family. Lorrie peppered him with question after question and he tried to reassure her that everything was over, and everyone was now safe. What seemed like hours of silence passed before Lorrie conceded that it was still best for the kids to be with Mitch. He let out an audible gust of air, closed his eyes, and rubbed his hands down his face.

In the past twenty-four hours he'd run the gamut of his emotions. From the lowest of lows when Georgia and Jessi were taken, to the highest of highs when he knew they were finally safe, then back to the low when he thought about Lorrie taking the kids, and Jessi possibly choosing to return to Philadelphia.

At least Lorrie had seen things his way and the kids were staying with him. Jessi staying was yet to be determined. That answer wouldn't come until the drop went down Friday.

Trying to get his head back into the game, he moved his mouse and his computer lit up. He'd already fired off an e-mail and was waiting to hear back from his contact with the FBI. Knowing that Dante was probably right about some of the law enforcement being on the take, he hoped that the ones he was dealing with, weren't. Once he had his contact in place, they would take the case from there, securing a flight to get him back to Philadelphia and moving forward. His end of the case would basically be done. At least until Lou was healthy enough to be transported. He'd researched the beast man with the gun and found he had a laundry list of crimes under his belt, and Mitch felt damn lucky he was grazed by the bullet and didn't get his head shot off last night.

He was hoping that the plan he and Dante had discussed would work and his uncle wouldn't get suspicious.

His phone chimed. Time to set the next part of the plan in motion.

Chapter Seventeen

She should have taken the day off. Jessi couldn't get her head into her work at the vineyard. The thoughts of the previous day played over and over. Dante's changing personalities both confused her and surprised her.

Saving her and Mitch's life gave her hope that he might be turning his life around. He was more like the old Dante. When he told her what had happened with his money it broke her heart. She felt conflicted because she could see his vulnerability and fear. However, that still didn't take away the bad taste in her mouth of what he did to her or what he did to Georgia. And his confession, albeit well meaning, about not wanting her to be involved in his mess, reinforced everything she had already come to terms with. They were over. Looking back, she could see that even if things hadn't blown up the way they had, they probably would have still gone their separate ways at some point.

Still, when Mitch called earlier telling her he had gotten everything set up for Dante to return to Philadelphia, she couldn't help wondering if he would make it out alive. The way Dante talked, his uncle sounded like a ruthless cold-hearted killer. She definitely was intimidated by him when she met him. She only hoped that he was being honest with Dante about releasing him from his debt as penance for the death of Dante's parents. Dante had told her his dad never got along with his brother and always steered clear of him and told Dante to do the same. She wished he had.

Her shift was over in fifteen minutes, and she needed to do something to take her mind off all that had happened.

—Where did you say that gym was? —

—It's two blocks from your house going east on Main. It's called 24 to Life. When are you going? —

—I'm going to run home and change when I get off, then head over there—

—I can meet you there around five thirty if you want—

—Sounds good. I just need to unwind a little—

Since they weren't going up there for a little bit, it gave her time to run by the store and pick up some things. She thought maybe she could whip up a simple dinner after they were done at the gym.

Once she got the groceries put away, she slipped on some navy shorts, a tie-dyed tank that said, "Save water drink wine" and her hot pink sneakers and headed out the door.

Mitch was right. The gym was only a couple of blocks away. She felt odd driving into the parking lot, thinking she could have walked. She didn't see Mitch's car and figured he would be in soon. The door chimed as she entered. Upbeat pop music played through the speakers. A citrusy smell wafted through the air. Probably one of the automatic air fresheners. The place was bigger than she expected. Plenty of equipment to sufficiently tire out her muscles and hopefully help her unwind. She glanced at the counter that sat in the middle of the entryway of the gym. A very tall, dark-haired, young man with bright blue eyes sat at the counter with a huge smile on his face, vibrating to the music.

"Hi. Can I help you?" the young man asked and stood as she approached.

"I hope so. I'm new here and I'm supposed to be meeting a friend, but he isn't here yet. Would it be okay if I walk around?"

"Sure. Would you like me to give you a quick tour?" He jerked his thumb over his shoulder.

"That would be great."

"My name is Kaleb by the way." He held his hand out and she took it.

"I'm Jessi." She suddenly panicked realizing she had given him her real name then decided maybe it was safe now.

He dropped a brochure in her hand and motioned for her to follow him. "Over here we have our cardio area. There are nine different types of machines to choose from to get your cardio in. So, a pretty good selection to fit your needs, whatever they may be." He pointed at several large windows. "Through there is our CrossFit area in case you are into that. We have three different instructors that hold classes throughout the week. They are listed in the brochure." His eyes locked on hers. "So where did you move from?"

"Pennsylvania."

"Wow. Okay. What brought you to Dalton?"

She followed behind him as he moved quickly to another area. "I'm the new sommelier at Lake Village Restaurant and Purple Skies Vineyards."

"Interesting." He grinned and winked, and Jessi couldn't decide if he was hitting on her, or simply playing with her. Then he continued with the tour motioning with his arms like nothing had happened. "We have between four to six machines for each area of your body, plus a wide assortment of free weights, so you get a good full body workout." He moved on and she had to giggle. His over-the-top gestures made him look like one of the assistants on the Price is Right. He was obviously having fun with it, and she liked that.

"So, when you lived in Pennsylvania, did you go to the gym?"

"Yes. I tried to go at least a couple of times a week."

"Weight training, or did you take classes?"

"Mainly weight training. I took a few yoga classes here and there but liked being able to do my own thing."

"Well, in case you want to try out some of our classes they are held through that door there. We have seven different classes to choose from throughout the week. All of them are also listed in your handy dandy brochure. We have some yoga classes that started up a while back and are pretty popular." He slid it from her hand and flipped it over to the back. "All of our prices are listed here. Classes are separate from the cost of the membership. You can pay monthly or get a discount if you pay for the full year. If you want to do CrossFit classes or one of the other classes, you can pay by the class." He started to stroll back up to the counter. "If you would like to see what it's like today, it's free. All you would need to do is sign a waiver."

"That would be great."

He stepped behind the counter and Jessi heard the door chime. Their attention went to the door just in time to see Mitch. Jessi's insides fluttered from the sensual way he stared at her. Was it wrong for him to be looking at her like that while he was still in uniform?

"You made it." He stepped up to the counter with a

smile.

"This is your *friend?*" Kaleb's voice held good natured sarcasm. "Oh, sweetheart. You could do so much better," he scoffed. Jessi chuckled.

"I guess you met Kaleb our resident comedian." Mitch gave him a fist bump.

"Yes. He already gave me the tour."

"Great. Everybody who works here is usually top notch. This one, they definitely hired for his looks not his brains." He glared at Kaleb.

"I'll have you know I finished high school early."

"Yeah, I'm sure it was because the teachers were tired of your shit and wanted to get rid of you."

Kaleb clutched his chest. "You have wounded me, Mitch. Deeply wounded me."

"Yeah. Yeah. Get over it." Jessi laughed at the barbs they were hurling at each other. "Is your brother and April in town or are they still off exploring?"

"Nah, that was last week. They can't decide where they want to get married. First it was Hawaii. Then it was the Maldives."

"They better get on the ball. Aren't they supposed to get married in August?"

"Yep."

"I never can keep up with all of you. It seems like it's either you or them flying off every other week."

"Hey, I can't help it if I like to be up in the clouds better than keeping my feet on the ground."

"Obviously. You are gone more than you are here."

"I'm working a side job."

"Sure you are. Like you need more money."

"Hey, it takes money to be an A-lister."

"You are so full of shit, Kaleb," Mitch said with a

chuckle. Kaleb shrugged with a suit yourself expression.

Mitch turned back to Jessi. "What do you think?"

"About the gym? I like it. My little gym in Pennsylvania wasn't this nice. It's larger than I thought it would be."

"Well, let me get changed and we can get started."

Jessi nodded and Mitch took off across the gym. She turned back to Kaleb who pushed a piece of paper to her. "This is the waiver form. Any piece of equipment that you are unsure of, let us know and we can show you how to use it safely. We also have professional trainers. Their fees vary depending on the trainer you choose. They are also listed—"

"In the brochure?" Jessi finished, without looking up from the paper until she realized what she had done. Pink filled her cheeks. She held up the brochure. "This brochure holds all the secrets, right?"

Kaleb nodded sheepishly. "It's magic," he said with a wink and Jessi laughed. He definitely knew how to charm the women.

Mitch returned and motioned her to follow him. "What are you used to? You said you work out some?"

She stared out at the equipment. "Yes. I had a trainer for a while, and he had me cross training on the equipment and free weights."

"Did you do a full body workout every time or focused areas?"

"Usually two areas at a time. I tried to go a couple of days a week."

"Why don't we do a little upper and lower body today. Do hips and shoulders?"

"That sounds good. Just warning you, it's been a while so you might have to refresh my memory on some of the stuff."

"I think I can handle that. I'll be easy on you since you are still recovering from your injuries."

She motioned with her hand. "Lead the way oh mighty Captain."

"It's sergeant." She snickered and waved her hand.

****

Jessi finished picking up her living room, waiting for Mitch to arrive. He had helped her take back the rental car and she had returned to the cottage since things had settled down. Her body was a bit sore from the trip to the gym. Still, it felt good to work out some of the tension. Mitch had been a bit quiet at the gym. She was hoping it was because he was still processing everything from the case, although it worried her that he might be upset with her, even though he said she wasn't at fault. He took her through a workout and chatted with Kaleb and when she asked if he would like to come over for dinner he readily accepted. Maybe she was overreacting.

Her mind swirled again with the thoughts of what happened, and Dante. Regardless of what he'd done to her, she didn't want anything to happen to him. His words "they're going to kill me" kept playing over and over in her thoughts.

A knock at the door drew her attention back. Her stomach fluttered with the smile Mitch gave her when she opened the door. And he leaned in for a gentle kiss on the lips.

"There's a few more minutes left on the chicken, would you like a glass of wine?"

"I'm going to pass since I have work tomorrow."

"Tea?"

"Sure."

"Sweetened or unsweetened."

"Lady, by all accounts, Arkansas is considered to be in the south so what do you think?"

"Sweetened it is." She poured him a glass and set it on the bar.

Mitch sat down and Jessi could tell something was still off about him. She didn't know if he was just thinking about the case, or whether she should pry or not, so she let it slide for now. He seemed preoccupied, and she knew he had a lot on his mind with the case. Heaven knows it hadn't been far from her thoughts since Dante abducted her.

Mitch had been up front with her about what was going on, and how much trouble Dante was in, and she knew there was no love lost between him and Dante. Mitch had yet to talk to her about his personal thoughts on the matter though. Which was fine with her. She wasn't sure she was ready to talk to him about it either. Her feelings were so mixed.

Everything had been such a whirlwind of events since she left Philadelphia. She couldn't believe it had only been a few weeks. In those weeks she had met a man that had managed to fill her with feelings she couldn't explain. Feelings that were now confusing her.

The oven dinged and she jumped. Grabbing the oven mitts, she slid out the pan.

Mitch peeked over the counter. "That smells delicious. What is it?"

"Chicken Florentine. And it *is* delicious." Setting the pan on the hot pad, she removed the oven mitts and shoved them back in the drawer. "Grab a plate and get what you want."

He hopped off the stool and rounded the counter. "Is

that spinach?"

Jessi froze. Eyes wide, brows furrowed. "Yes?" Her voice waivered.

Mitch chewed on the corner of his lip.

"You don't like spinach, do you," Jessi stated.

"Honestly? It's not my favorite, no. I've never had this though, so I'll try it."

"If you don't like it, don't worry. Put the fettuccini in the center of your plate then add the chicken and ladle the spinach sauce over it. The spinach is an added flavoring for the dish. Push it aside if you don't like it."

"Okay." He piled the noodles on his plate then added the chicken with a good helping of spinach sauce on top, then scooted by Jessi and sat down at the table.

Jessi couldn't get the feeling that Mitch was hiding something, and she had a feeling it was about Dante. She decided to go straight to the heart of the matter. "So, tell me what is going on with the case."

"Are you sure you want to talk about it? I was trying to steer clear of it until maybe later, since you said you were kind of needing to unwind."

"Yeah. Sure. I want to know what is going on." *Was that all it was? He wasn't talking because he thought it would bother me?*

"I contacted a guy from the FBI who is part of the original case dealing with the theft of the armored truck out of Florida. I feel pretty sure that he has no connections with Dante's uncle. Dante was booked on a flight with an escort for late this evening and should arrive in Philadelphia early tomorrow morning, where he will be handed off to the FBI." Mitch cut a piece of the chicken, added the spinach and sauce then stared at the forkful before taking the bite. He slowly chewed. His eyes lifted to Jessi's. "Disregard everything I said previously about spinach," he said around his bite. "This is delicious."

Jessi's whole face lit up. "You like it?"

"What is this sauce?"

"It's a little white wine, capers, butter, lemon, and cream."

"It's really light and has a great flavor."

Jessi nodded and twirled some fettuccini on her fork. It didn't get past her that he'd changed the subject quickly and the uneasy feeling was still there, so she took another stab at broaching the subject. "Who is escorting him? Someone from here?"

Mitch rocked uneasily in his chair and laid his utensils down then lifted his eyes to hers and studied her features. "I'm taking him."

Her head jerked at his words, and she wondered if she heard him right. "You? Why? You're the boss."

"My contact thought that since I had been involved with the case, and Dante trusted me somewhat, I might be an asset to the case. Possibly get him to provide more information. Plus, since we are on borrowed time already, they didn't necessarily have time to send somebody to get him and they needed him there now so they could get everything in place as the information came in, before the drop. The only thing I know for sure right now is he is scheduled to pick up the rhodium and meet with his uncle."

Jessi's stomach dropped. Visions of what might happen flooded her mind. "But what about—"

"I've got everything covered. Kathy is going to watch the kids. Garrett is handling the station. I'm not going to be gone that long."

"So, you aren't going to be part of the actual take down. Right?"

"I doubt it. They have their team. They know and rely on each other. It's not good to throw new blood in at the last minute."

Her anxiety continued to rise. "Do you think Dante will be safe?"

Mitch took another bite. "I can't answer that. It's out of my hands.

"I know, I'm just worried. His uncle is an evil man. Dante said he was going to kill him if he didn't get the key."

"I get that you are worried about him, but Dante brought this on himself."

"True. He's trying to make it right though."

"It's a little late for that."

She let out a huff. She knew Mitch was right, but his words sounded callous. "I know, it's—"

"Can I ask you a question?"

Jessi tipped her head. "Sure."

"Why are you so worried about his safety? You brought it up earlier and I am having a bit of trouble understanding. He came within a breath of killing you. I am still surprised he didn't. You do realize he might have if your neighbors hadn't intervened, right? Whether he cooperates or not, he is still going to prison for what he did to you, what he did to Georgia, and his involvement in this case."

She could see his gray eyes darken, and the edge in his voice irritated her even though she knew he was right. "I understand. But you don't know the whole story. He was set up. You should have heard him when he talked to me. He was scared."

"He told me about the Cuban Mafia and not wanting to join his uncle, and that he felt like he had no choice. Well, long story short, he did have a choice. He just made a shitty one, and in the process, he dug himself into a deeper hole. One that included beating you within an inch of your life and kidnapping you and Georgia."

"Yes. Trust me I was there."

"So how can you defend him?"

"I'm not defending what he did." She hated how shaky her voice sounded.

"It sure sounds like you are."

"I get it. You're pissed because he took Georgia.

"It's not just about Georgia. It's about you too."

I'm simply saying I don't want him to die."

"Funny, I don't think he was saying that when he was kicking you in the ribs."

She stared at him watching his jaw tick. "What is this about?" She picked her plate up. "I didn't invite you over to argue with you."

"I'm just not understanding why you are so concerned about his wellbeing when he obviously couldn't care less about yours or my daughter's."

"He didn't hurt her."

"Not physically, and that's not the point."

"Then what is the point Mitch, because I'm not following?"

"A few days ago you were crying, telling me you were scared he was going to find you." He picked up his plate. "Then when he did find you, you suddenly forget about the fact that you were petrified of him and are all worried about him."

She could hear the sarcasm in his tone and her defenses started to rise. Anger pulsed through her. She had to make him understand. "If he wouldn't have shot Lou we would have died."

"He did it for his own personal gain."

"No, he didn't. You don't get to say that because you don't know him. You didn't talk to him. He did it because he didn't want me hurt."

"Then why did he hit you if he didn't want you hurt?"

"He was drunk."

"Not an excuse." Frustration laced his voice. "I have dealt with too many cases of abuse. There is no excuse for doing what he did to you." Jessi turned away from him and rinsed her dish off trying to calm the ache forming in her chest. She glanced at him as she took his plate. His eyes seemed so cold. Not the warm gray hues she was used to. "Do you still love him?"

The question came out of nowhere and Jessi was not prepared for it and nearly dropped his plate. "What?"

"You heard me."

"I-I—"

"I can't understand how you could continue to have feelings for someone who treated you like he did."

His comment pushed her final button. She shut the water off and glared at him. "Look who's talking."

"What do you mean?" Drying her hands, Jessi tossed the dish towel on the counter then walked past him to the living room. He followed. "We chose to keep things civil for the kids."

Spinning on him, she poked her finger in his chest. "I call bullshit. You still have feelings for her."

"She didn't nearly kill me...twice."

"Doesn't mean she didn't hurt you. I heard the pain in your voice when you talked about her." She huffed.

"Can we drop it, please? I don't want to discuss this anymore. All I'm saying is I hope he comes out of this alive."

"And if he does?"

"And if he does…nothing."

"Are you sure? Once the raid is done, are you going to want to go back to Philly?"

"I-I doubt it. Listen, I honestly have no idea what I want to do right now. I know that's not the answer you want but that's all I can give. As far as Dante, I don't know what exactly I'm feeling. He was scared and knew he messed up and was trying to make things right. I just don't wish death on him. Is that bad? It's like you hoping your ex-wife is happy."

"Sure," he said, the word saturated with sarcasm.

"What's that supposed to mean?" Her eyes burned with the anger that was boiling up inside her. The tirade he was on ripped at her heart like a wild animal. His hardened voice left no room for question and his eyes told her he was seconds from blowing up. She quickly stepped back and turned away, fear taking hold. Her arms wrapped her body and her voice quieted as she said, "Whether you believe I've been traumatized by this whole thing or not, I have. And you questioning my feelings isn't helping. I'm sorry if my feelings don't line up with how you think I should feel. The truth is, I do still have feelings for him. I care about him. We were together in a committed relationship for a long time. Those feelings don't just die overnight because he screwed up. And I realize it seems wrong, but I can't help how I feel. My emotions are all over the place right now. My whole life was flipped upside down. And honestly, I am just trying to hang on to any strand of sanity I have."

She wiped her cheek that was now wet from tears. The anger was gone from Mitch's eyes when her gaze returned to his and he reached for her. But she stepped back. She was overwhelmed as every memory from the last month seemed to hit all at once. All the pain. All the happiness. Everything was sending her into an emotional tailspin, and she was about to break. "I'm sorry Mitch. I can't."

"Jessi—"

"No. I need you to go. I'm done."

"Jessi. Please."

"Leave," she said barely above a whisper.

Mitch jerked like she had slapped him, and she could see the hurt form on his face. His jaw ticked and he reached his hand out and opened his mouth like he was going to say something, but she wrapped her arms around herself and nodded to the door. His lips pressed together, he took a step back, and walked to the door, slamming it behind him.

Chapter Eighteen

The plane ride was uneventful. Dante kept to himself, and Mitch was glad. He didn't know if he could keep his composure if Dante brought up Jessi in the conversation. The evening kept playing over and over in his head. His conversation with her couldn't have gone worse. He could hear the concern in her voice when she asked about what would happen with Dante and it dug at the thoughts that had been rattling around in his head. He didn't want her to still be in love with Dante. He didn't want her to go running back to Philadelphia after him. He couldn't stand the thought of her getting hurt again. He'd seen it happen too many times. And it hit too close to home. The scars of his childhood, although long past, still left a sharp pain in his chest. It made him realize he hadn't talked to his mom in a while.

Would there ever be a chance that Jessi would consider staying in Dalton? It didn't offer the lifestyle she was accustomed to. Still, he desperately wanted her to stay. To be with him. Choose him.

Jessi had done something to him in the short time he had known her. She helped him find happiness again. She had a way of making him open up, drop his guard, and have fun. Something even Lorrie was unable to do the entire time they had been married.

He knew she was right when she said he still had feelings for his ex-wife. It wasn't just because of the kids that they were friends. They still cared deeply about each other, but they wanted different things out of life, and it was obvious they couldn't achieve it together. As much as he hated to admit it, the divorce was the right thing for them.

He was anxious about the trip and didn't really know what he was walking into, but that was no excuse for the way he acted. He knew he had screwed up royally the minute he walked out the door and couldn't quite put a finger on why her concern for Dante made him so unhinged. But something about the man had singlehandedly caused him to possibly lose the best thing that had happened to him in a long time.

He left Jessi's frustrated at her, and himself. He wanted her to tell him she didn't love Dante, that she loved him, and when she balked at his question, it set off a wild beast inside of him. He now knew how Lorrie felt. He needed to apologize and be honest with her, but right now he needed for Dante to stay alive.

It seemed simple enough. He had to take the rhodium to his uncle and then he was done. Something told him though things are never as easy as they seem. Especially with the Mafia.

After landing, they were taken to FBI headquarters where Dante shared the information he'd previously shared with Mitch. Mitch had to admit, Dante didn't come off as a man trying to pull a fast one on law enforcement. His information was very similar to what he'd told Mitch. Even when Martin Green, Mitch's contact, peppered him with questions about his uncle and others involved in the organization, Dante didn't balk. The only time he saw any crack in Dante's resolve was when Martin asked him about his brother. He was adamant that his brother had no contact with his uncle. Mitch was conflicted about Dante. He could never forgive him for hurting Jessi, but for some idiotic reason he couldn't explain, he trusted him.

Once Dante was escorted away, Mitch was taken to a nearby hotel to sleep. But that was a joke. He was too keyed up about the day ahead and too pissed at how things ended with Jessi and him the night before. He wanted to call her to apologize but it was too early in the morning, and she was an hour behind them.

His phone chimed. Martin.

"Hello?"

"Mitch? It's Martin."

"Yeah, Martin."

"I'm sending a car for you. Can you be ready in fifteen?" Mitch inhaled deeply. It was about to get real.

"Yeah. I'll be ready."

****

A palpable buzz resonated in the office as Martin entered the room with a manila folder and tossed it on the large round table that Mitch and four other men sat at. Without any preamble, Martin began. "Giovani Angenelli made contact about an hour ago. Dante will be meeting him downtown at Redaggio's Pizza at eleven. We will have eyes on him. No wire." Martin's attention zeroed in on Mitch. "Gallagher, since Angenelli probably has a good idea of what just about everyone in this department looks like, I want you in the restaurant. You'll have comms. *So much for not getting involved.* Once the drop is made, our man should be done. The restaurant will be under surveillance, and Gallagher, you can leave in time to keep a tail on him until we pick him up." He pointed to the manila folder. "I want you to get acquainted or maybe reacquainted with the Angenelli organization. What I have on the Estovez family is also in there. I don't trust either of them, so we are going to have to be on our toes. We still have no information on the actual drop, but we will have a tail on the uncle and a tracker on the rhodium and I'm hoping our boy will have a little more information to bring back to us."

One of the men at the table dragged out the pile of photos and papers from the folder. Mitch focused on the photos as he thumbed through them and wondered how much more he would be pulled into the case. This was a whole different world than his small town, dealing with a whole different set of crimes. Well mostly.

"All right gentlemen. You know the drill." His eyes shifted to Mitch. "Gallagher. You are coming with me."

****

Sitting in the restaurant, Mitch retrieved his phone from his pocket and noticed for the millionth time that Jessi hadn't contacted him. No text. No call. When he left her last night she'd said she was done, and he couldn't help but wonder if she meant forever. He wouldn't blame her. But he couldn't do anything at the moment, and he needed to keep his head in the game.

Mitch had picked a table that was just off the corner he figured they might seek out since it was a bit isolated. His hunch paid off a few minutes later. He had the perfect position, even though he faced away from them, to hear their conversation. And everything he was hearing, Martin was hearing. Unfortunately, the conversation had been fairly benign. No discussion on the drop just mundane conversation about a construction project. Mitch wondered if it might be some coded discussion until Dante pointedly asked about the meeting that afternoon. Mitch chuckled. This guy had guts, although he was obviously unfamiliar with how crime organizations worked. His uncle was quiet for a beat then responded. "That is for a later discussion." *Later discussion?*

Mitch discretely swung his attention to their table. The plates had been cleared and it looked like the tab had been paid. The uncle rose with the duffle bag in his hand. Dante followed. Mitch picked his phone up and scrolled through his messages, waiting for their next move. "I need to show you something at the job site." Mitch cut his eyes just in time to catch a glimpse of the two of them. Dante's posture stiffened and from the expression on his uncle's face, it didn't get past him. This is not good. His uncle wrapped his arm around Dante's shoulder and escorted him out.

****

"We have eyes on the target," came the garbled voice through the radio. Mitch let out a relieved breath. To say things hadn't gone quite as expected would be a gross understatement, starting with Dante being forced to go with his uncle. Then the tracking device was rendered useless when the duffle was tossed in the trunk of the car. Plan C was to have one of their cars tail them, which worked well, until they lost the uncle's car when a train separated them.

Mitch's anxiety was through the roof. He knew there was nothing he did wrong, but still felt like he had. Martin, on the other hand, didn't miss a beat.

With one call, there were eyes in the sky. But how the hell, with the size of the city and how populated it was, were they going to find a specific car. But they did. Problem solved. Martin was barking orders from their blacked out SUV and teams were on the move.

As they traveled outside of Philly an industrial area came into view and the radio came to life. "Shots fired. Shots fired." The man behind the wheel of the SUV punched it and Mitch instinctively reached for his gun. Mitch could hear Jessi's concerned voice asking if Dante would be in danger.

In the distance, Mitch saw clouds of smoke. The SUV was heading straight for it. This didn't quite happen the way they had planned either, but in this business, a plan is just a fleeting thought that can change like the wind.

They rounded the corner of the burning building and a bullet clinked off the vehicle. Mitch instinctively ducked. "Shit." The driver threw the SUV in reverse and backed up past the burning building, stopping against a brick wall of a neighboring warehouse. All the men inside bailed out. Without thinking Mitch did too. He fell in line behind Martin with his gun drawn. Rounding the corner again, Mitch witnessed the carnage. Strewn bloodied bodies lay on the ground. Bullets zinged around them. Mitch took in the scene and his eyes locked on a body in the center of the fray. Dante. His stomach lurched. Jessi's words haunted him. "I don't want him to die." He couldn't take his eyes off him. He had no idea if he was too late, but chances were good if Dante remained there, he would be by the time the melee was over. Suddenly he was moving past Martin.

"Cover me." He crouched at the wall and waited for the hail of bullets to subside. His legs churned as he crossed the asphalt to where Dante lay. Grabbing the collar of his shirt, Mitch dragged him as bullets buzzed like bees around his head. His eyes searched for the culprit, and he watched as the assailant dropped and then another one. His eyes met Martin's and he nodded a "thanks."

Propping Dante against the wall out of the fire fight, he pressed his fingers against his neck and let out a sigh.

****

Slouching in the old worn leather chair in Martin's office, Mitch could feel the exhaustion setting in deep in his bones. Spending almost the entire day with his heart almost beating through his chest, Mitch wanted nothing more than to close his eyes just for a moment, but he was afraid he would wind up sleeping for days. They had spent hours, processing the suspects, logging evidence and finalizing the paperwork. He didn't know how they did it. This was all in a day's work for Martin and his team. He was as cool as a cucumber, it seemed, the entire time.

His phone buzzed and he retrieved it from his pocket. Four missed calls popped onto the screen and a text. Jessi.

—Mitch? Please let me know you are okay. I just saw the news. It said six people were killed in a raid at a manufacturing facility in Philly. That's what Dante was involved in. Wasn't it? —

This was something he didn't want to share through a text. He tapped her name and she immediately picked up.

"Mitch? Oh my God. Are you okay? What the hell happened?" Her questions were coming lightning fast, and it took a second for him to collect his thoughts. He still felt a bit punch drunk.

"Yes. I'm fine. It didn't go quite as well as we hoped, as you probably guessed from the news footage."

"I'm standing here watching it now. Oh my God, I'm shaking."

He could tell from the thickness of her voice that she was crying. "Nine from the Angenelli family are in custody. Eight from the Cuban Mafia Estovez family."

"And Dante?"

"He's alive, Jessi. It didn't turn out like we had planned, but he's alive."

"Obviously. I thought you said you weren't going to be a part of the operation, but I saw you in some of the news footage." He stood, shuffled his feet apart, and planted them preparing to deliver the news.

"Dante was supposed to drop the rhodium off to his uncle at a restaurant in downtown. But his uncle must have gotten suspicious because after the rhodium was delivered, instead of leaving the restaurant separately, Dante left with his uncle."

"Oh no."

"We had planned for that and had a tail set up, but we lost them for a while, and when we were able to relocate them, they were already in the process of the exchange at an old, abandoned manufacturing facility outside of town. Something went wrong with the exchange. They shot Dante and his uncle then shots were flying in all directions." A rock formed in Mitch's stomach as he recounted the incident. "By the time we had things handled, four from the Estovez family and two from the Angenelli family were dead. Luckily, we put a vest on Dante before he went to the restaurant, or it would have been three."

"So, he's okay?" The relief in her voice grated on him but he had to admit, he was relieved that he got him out alive too.

"He's going to be fine. He'll probably be bruised. They got him dead center in the chest. But I have to hand it to him, he can play possum like a champ."

"Possum?"

"Yeah. I saw that he was down, and I dragged him out of the line of fire and found out he was playing dead."

Silence filled the other end of the line long enough for Mitch to consider that the call dropped, but then Jessi spoke. "You, you risked your life to save him?"

"Well…you did say you didn't want him to die. So…" The phone went silent again except for the sound of her sniffles. He was so conflicted, wondering what she was thinking. "Jessi?"

Her tear laced voice was barely audible. "Thank you, Mitch. You're a good man."

All his life, he only wanted to be a police officer. To feel the rush of adrenaline when he did a good deed or saved someone. But at this moment, it didn't feel so good. *A good man? What was that supposed to mean?* The door opened and Martin entered the office.

"Listen, Jessi. I'm going to have to go."

"Okay. Thanks for letting me know Mitch."

"No problem." It didn't get past him that their conversation was devoid of anything other than business. She did ask if he was okay, but she would probably do that for any friend.

"Looks like over all, the operation was a success." Martin's voice tugged Mitch from his thoughts. Martin stepped behind his desk and chunked a much thicker file in the center of it. "Loss of life was low considering. Our boy got out alive. Can't say the same for his uncle and henchman. But I'm not too broken up about that."

"How many of our guys got injured? I didn't hear."

"One got a nick in his leg and another in the arm. Both were treated and released." Martin plopped down in the chair. "This was a big case, and we weren't making much headway with it. Your guy's information was vital. I appreciate everything you did. I would have rather you not go charging into a hail of bullets but I'm glad that the kid didn't die."

"I kind of promised someone back in Dalton I would do whatever I could to keep him safe."

"You must have nerves of steel to pull off a stunt like that."

"Not hardly. I don't know how you do this day in and day out. My insides are still quaking. I'd much prefer patrolling my quiet town where my exciting week would be to rescue some ducklings from a drain." Martin laughed at that.

"Well, regardless. You are welcome to work with me anytime you feel the need for big city excitement. You're a damn good cop and I do appreciate everything you did."

"Glad I could help."

Mitch was happy everything turned out okay. He was skeptical of how far Dante would actually go once he was back on his home turf and having to deal with his uncle. But he held true to his word, and because of him the raid was successful. It made Mitch's insides burn. He knew more than ever that he had to make things right with Jessi regardless of what the outcome might be.

"I guess, if you aren't inclined to transferring to our organization permanently, I need to get you back to Arkansas."

"You're offering me a job?"

"What do you think? Guys like you, with your guts

and intuition, are few and far between. I'm always looking to add men of your caliber to my team."

The comment caught him completely off guard. His thoughts flashed on Jessi. She could move back to Philly, would be back in her element. Feel more comfortable. But would he? Would he enjoy the big city life, or would he wind up resenting her because he wasn't living the life he'd envisioned? Brandon and Georgia just got settled in. He couldn't do that to them. *What the hell? I'm already including Jessi in decisions about my future, and I don't even know if she even loves me?* Suddenly everything was becoming crystal clear to what he wanted.

"Wow. I was not expecting that. I appreciate the vote of confidence. However, I think I'm going to have to decline. Dalton is my home. I'm pretty comfortable where I'm at."

"Well, the job's yours if you ever change your mind—"

"I appreciate it and I will let you know if I do."

"I will get you a flight home." Martin left the room and Mitch leaned his head back and shut his eyes, thinking about what had just taken place and what he had in store when he got home. He needed to apologize. He needed to make things right and he needed to do something to let Jessi know exactly how he felt about her. Pulling out his phone, he scrolled through his contacts. He'd planned on calling April about an idea he'd had earlier. Then things went off the rails. Now, he needed to pull out all the stops. He just wondered if he was already too late.

Chapter Nineteen

Jessi didn't quite know what to think about the radio silence Mitch had been giving her for the past couple of days. She was curled up on the sectional with a cup of hot tea, a fuzzy blanket, and her book. She had read the same page four times and still didn't know what it said. She couldn't get Mitch's angry words out of her head. He seemed wounded when he left. She hadn't texted him or called except to find out what had happened with the raid, and she wasn't going to even do that except she happened to see a news report on TV about the raid, and the reporter said several had been killed. She knew Mitch was in contact with the authorities who were in charge of the raid, although she had no idea he was in the middle of it. Relief swept over her when Mitch responded that Dante was alive. And he'd saved him. For her.

Why did it bother him so much that she didn't want to see Dante hurt? The discussion ended their dinner abruptly and left her frustrated and alone. She hadn't been able to sleep with his comments swirling in her head, especially when he asked if she still loved Dante. *What made him ask that out of the blue?*

She still cared about Dante and a part of her would probably always love him, but Mitch was right about one thing. What Dante did to her did irreparable damage to their relationship. Dante knew it too. She decided life was too short not to forgive. She knew he was in trouble and scared and it made her sad that he had messed his life up so badly, but she could never forget what he did. It didn't matter if he was drunk or drugged. If he truly loved her, he would have never put his hands on her. That night would forever be burned into her memory. Though the physical scars had healed, the mental scars would be there for a long, long time.

More than anything she wanted to tell Mitch that what she and Dante had was over. She just couldn't bring herself to do it. What if he was still mad? What if he told her it was over between them? She couldn't blame him if he did break it off. He had much more at stake than she did. Still, she wanted a relationship with him. And his kids.

With the exception of the kidnapping, she thought what they had between them was going pretty well. Then things fell apart. Why did her concern for Dante make him so upset?

She had been looking forward to this weekend hoping they would be able to spend her birthday together. Thursday's disaster dinner kind of put an end to that notion, although she did notice that Mitch cleaned his plate before everything went off-kilter. *Did he even remember it was my birthday?* She took a deep breath, threw the blanket off and shuffled to the refrigerator. It was getting late, and her stomach was growling. *What did she even eat today?* She opened the door and staring her in the face was a plate of three-day-old cannolis that were supposed to be dessert after the dinner disaster, a couple of bottles of opened wine and…nothing else unless she wanted to make a ketchup and mustard sandwich. *I guess I will be going to the store for my birthday. That sounds like loads of fun.*

****

Strolling up one aisle and then the next she didn't even really know what she wanted or needed so she just threw things in her buggy. The grocery store was the last place she really wanted to be. Where she wanted to be was with Mitch. Doing anything. They didn't have to be celebrating her birthday. She told him she didn't celebrate her birthday, so maybe he was simply honoring her wishes. Still, she was a little...lonely and bored.

Rounding the corner to head to the checkout, she caught site of a man exiting the store. It was him.

"Mitch!" She saw him jerk then he kept walking. It was obvious he heard her. She raced up to the checkout hoping she could get through before he got too far away. Her eyes stayed on his car, and she thought, for a second, she actually saw him look at her. However, by the time she was checked out, he was nowhere in sight.

—Mitch. Can we please talk? —

She threw the phone in the cupholder and headed home, hoping he would at least answer her text. Her phone buzzed and she tipped it up to see if it was him. Anson? What would he want? It's Sunday. She figured it could wait until she got home. Merging onto the highway, she glanced at her phone again as her mind went back to Mitch. Why did he ignore her? She knew he heard her.

Once she was back at the house and the groceries were put away, she checked her phone again. Nothing from Mitch but Anson's text caught her eye.

—I need you to come up here—
—Now? Why? What is going on? —
—We have a big problem—
—What is it? —

— It has to do with our last wine order. It got messed up—

—Seriously? We have to do this today? It's my birthday—

—Happy Birthday. And sorry. Yes. It needs to get straightened out before we open on Thursday because we are going to wind up having to get some more ordered and it has to have time to get here—

—Can you give me a little bit? I just got home from the grocery store—

—Can you be here by six? —

Geez. What is with him. She checked her watch. Four forty-five.

—Fine. I will be there—

She wandered into the bathroom and stared at herself in the mirror. Her hair was up in a messy ponytail on the top of her head and her face was makeup free. Ordinarily, it didn't bother her, she kind of liked to go without makeup at least on the weekends but she figured she needed to do a little something before heading over there.

She removed the band from her hair and brushed it out upside down then flipped it over. On her eyes she added a little shadow and mascara and then a smudge of blush to her cheeks. *That's all he gets.* She threw on a sleeveless, flowy, V-neck top over her skinny jeans and slid her feet into a pair of backless wedge sandals. Another check in the mirror and a fluff of her hair and she called it good.

She picked up her purse and phone checking it again for a text from Mitch. Still nothing. Her heart sank. The last thing she wanted to be doing on her birthday was working on a wine order. She was hoping to be able to spend it with a certain silver haired police officer but the chances for that were growing slimmer by the minute.

A frustrated sigh escaped her lungs as she headed up the highway. *Maybe I should call him.* She hit the button on her phone and let it ring. After the fifth ring she punched the button and slammed the phone back in the cupholder. *What the hell is going on? He could at least pick up the phone.* The sunlight was beginning to fade as she drove through town. Though she missed some aspects of living in the city, she was growing fond of the little town. It had a great vibe. There was no bumper-to-bumper traffic and things seemed to move slower. Everybody she had met seemed more relaxed and…nice.

She drove down the tree lined road to the restaurant and let out another sigh. She really didn't want to be here. *I hope this doesn't take long. I just want to be home, in my jammies, in bed with maybe some ice cream. Dammit. That's what I forgot at the store.*

As she coasted to a stop at the restaurant, she noticed several cars in the lot that she didn't recognize. Anson opened the door when she walked up. "What is going on? Whose cars?"

Anson didn't answer immediately, and she finally tipped her eyes at him. "I've got some students from the Culinary Institute here today doing a class."

"I didn't know you did that?"

"Well, I'm sure there are quite a few things you don't know about me."

"True," she said drawing the word out, curious what had gotten him in such a foul mood. It couldn't be the wine order alone. He normally was fairly even tempered, so his shortness with her was definitely out of the ordinary. Especially since he knew it was her birthday.

She followed him through the foyer and dining room still preoccupied with what had gone wrong and frustrated that she had to be there. She didn't even pay attention to where they were headed. She was simply following Anson.

When he pushed open the doors to the party room, he flipped the lights, and a huge roar of "Surprise" rang out. Jessi's knees went weak, and her hand clutched her chest trying to catch her breath. Her eyes scanned the room. There had to have been fifty people there and there were only a handful she knew. The Detwilers and Valentis stood next to each other as well as a few of the staff from the restaurant. However, that was about it.

She would have thought they had made a mistake and were waiting for someone else except there was a huge banner that said "Happy Birthday Jessi" draped over the windows above the open doors to the deck. Fresh wildflowers and lavender in hot pink vases sat on the white linen topped tables with confetti sprinkled as accents. Purple, pink, and white glittery balloons were strategically placed around the room. White Christmas lights were draped from one end of the room to the other, crisscrossing across the ceiling in between the colorful pansy lights. Tables filled with hors d'oeuvres and finger sandwiches sat up against the back wall. Everything she had mentioned to Mitch, in what she thought was a joke, was there except she didn't see him or his kids.

"How did you know?" she asked as she continued to take everything in. Anson's brows drew up in surprise.

"Oh, I didn't do this. I was just told to get you here." He chuckled.

Confused, she still tried to be excited and grateful for the party. But if Mitch didn't do this. Who did? She recognized a few faces Mitch had introduced her to, but there were so many more that she didn't. Then she heard something. It sounded like a whimper. Then a bark. The crowd parted. And sitting at one of the tables behind them was Mitch, holding a huge bouquet of pink roses and a squirming tiny cocker spaniel puppy with a huge pink bow on its collar. Georgia and Brandon were sitting with him. He set the puppy on the floor. It shook its floppy ears and then immediately trotted up to Jessi. Nothing could have kept the tears at bay. Her hand cupped her mouth. Tears cascaded down her cheeks. The lost lonely feeling she had felt moments earlier was gone. Mitch had managed to give her the best birthday present she could ever receive.

She kneeled and lifted the tiny puppy in her arms. Everyone around clapped. The puppy yipped and squirmed then her warm pink tongue brushed against Jessi's chin several times before she tried to bite it. Jessi's eyes tipped up to see Mitch and the kids approaching.

A smile spread across her face, and she quickly wiped the tears from her cheeks. "I can't believe you did this. Oh my gosh. She is adorable. She, right?" She held her out checking to confirm. "I figured with a pink bow…" She snuggled her back into her neck and Mitch put his arm around her.

Georgia hugged her legs tight. "We worked really hard. I told them you needed pink balloons."

"The balloons are perfect. This place looks amazing." Her eyes connected with Mitch's. "I have never been so surprised in my life."

Georgia reached up and petted the puppy. "I named her Bella."

Mitch chuckled. "Georgia, the puppy is Jessi's. She can name her whatever she wants to."

The puppy chewed on Jessi's finger. "I think Bella is a good name. I will definitely take it into consideration."

"So how did I do? Balloons, banners, flowers, swanky restaurant." Mitch ticked them off on his fingers as he spoke. "It's all here."

"I am speechless. I have to admit though, I don't recognize most of these people."

"Yeah." He winced. "That was kind of the tricky part. I wasn't sure, since you're new here, who you had met, except for a few people. I wanted it to be a big celebration though, so I invited my friends too. I will introduce you to everyone."

"I can't believe you did all this."

"I was pretty busy the past couple of days but trust me, I had help."

"I wondered why you didn't call."

"Well, one, you kind of kicked me out, so I thought maybe you needed a little space, and two, I was doing this and wrapping up the Philadelphia case. I'm sorry for pushing you away. I figured it would be a whole lot easier keeping it a secret if I did. Between the kids and the planning, I just knew you were going to figure it out."

"So, what were you sneaking out with at the grocery store?"

"Yeah, that would be the dog food. I just picked her up this afternoon and realized I didn't have anything to feed her." He rubbed his hand over the puppy's head. "Georgia wanted to go shopping for her, so we got her a dog bed and a leash and some bowls. Then once we got her, it dawned on me it might be a good idea to have something to put in the bowls."

"I missed you," she blurted, then averted her eyes suddenly feeling vulnerable. "I didn't know what to think. I was throwing myself a pity party thinking you forgot my birthday."

"I didn't forget. However, with all that happened in the past week, I didn't know if I could get it organized in time."

"How long have you been planning it?"

"Oh, I knew before I left, the day we talked about it, I wanted to do it, to at least lessen the pain of the memory. I just wasn't able to enlist the help of the party guru until a couple of days ago."

"Who is this party guru?"

Mitch pointed to a woman talking to a guy with headphones around his neck, aviators covering his eyes, and a backwards ballcap on his head. He was sitting behind a table that held several pieces of electronic equipment. The woman had dark brown nearly black hair fringed around her face that reached just past her shoulders. Her deep blue eyes and thick lashes made her have a modern edgy appearance. She smiled as they approached.

"Hey. Happy Birthday. I'm April." She held out her hand. Several bracelets jingled as they slid down her wrist and her hand displayed rings for just about every finger.

"Jessi," she responded and shook April's hand.

"I know. Mitch has told me all about you." She turned to the guy next to her and Jessi suddenly realized she recognized him. "This is—"

"Kaleb. Right?" He glanced up and waved with a big toothy smile, then pushed his headphones up and

"Bad Romance" thumped through the speakers. His body gyrated to the music and before they knew it, he had hopped up on the table and was shaking his hips to the sounds of hoots from the crowd. April shook her head. Kaleb slid his glasses down, winked, and flashed her another smile.

April turned back to Jessi rubbing the wrinkles between her eyes. "Heaven help the woman who gets him," April said on a sigh. Jessi laughed. "He's about to be my brother-in-law."

"Good luck with that," Jessi giggled as she watched Kaleb do his best rendition of John Travolta from *Saturday Night Fever*. Her gaze moved across the room at all the people and decorations, and finally landed back on April, and she smiled. "Thank you for this. Mitch said you put this together. It is fantastic."

"I'm glad you like it. Trust me he did a lot of the legwork. He had to since he only gave me a couple of days to put it together." Her eyes searched momentarily then she said, "Let me introduce you to Joe," and motioned for them to follow. Jessi had the puppy propped in the crook of her arm again her chest. She had fallen asleep. Mitch scanned the area for the kids, who were both grazing at the snack table. They approached a group of people Jessi didn't recognize. One woman with deep red hair held a tiny baby. April put her arm around the waist of a guy whose size made her look like a child. His light blue eyes caught her attention immediately. "This is Joe. My fiancé." He turned with a jerk and smiled, and April pointed and continued. "The crazy one over there's brother." He dropped his arm across her shoulder, and she moved her gaze. "That's Cody, his wife, Jenna, and precious baby AJ, fresh out of the oven." Jessi's head swiveled, and her eyes locked on a woman in a long rust colored sweater over a pair of skinny jeans. She was waving.

"Hey," Jessi said a bit louder than expected and the puppy flinched. Bekah, followed by Brant who was holding a sleeping Maizy, quickly made their way to her and Mitch.

"Happy Birthday," Bekah said wrapping her arms around her neck.

"Thank you for coming. This is crazy."

"Have you gotten introduced to everyone?"

"I'm trying to figure out who I've missed." April responded. "Oh. Over there. The guy with the blondish hair and beard in the cowboy hat is Jenna's brother, Ben." Jessi nodded trying to remember where she had seen him before and feeling a bit overwhelmed. April suddenly waved her arms wildly and motioned to another woman who strolled up beside her. "And this is Kaysi. She is Joe and crazy's sister. She's my partner in crime for this shindig." April elbowed Joe who lifted his fingers to his mouth and whistled. "Everybody this is Jessi."

Everyone began talking at once trying to talk to her. The pretty redheaded girl approached her holding the sleeping baby. "It's nice to finally meet you. Cody said Mitch hasn't stopped talking about you."

"Really?" Jenna's comment sent butterflies floating through her insides. She knew she had a great big crush on Mitch. She also was realistic and knew he had the kids to think about before jumping feet first into any kind of real relationship. Jessi peeked down at the sleeping baby. He had a head full of brown curly hair. "Alexander. Right?"

"Yes. We are calling him AJ. How did you know though?"

"Mitch showed me the photo your husband sent him when he was born." Her fingers brushed against his soft skin. "He's beautiful."

"So is she." Jenna nodded her head to the sleeping puppy.

"I have a feeling I am about to learn what it's like to be a new mom."

"Those middle of the night wake up calls are killer." Jenna's eyes darted to a very handsome man approaching.

"You must be Cody." Jessi stated. "Mitch has told me so much about you."

"Yes. It's great to meet you. I hear you joined the gym."

"I did. I was really impressed. You guys have a nice set up."

"Thanks. I think so. We have great people working for us and our members are our family."

"I kind of got that impression. Now, you are the owner, right?"

"Yeah, my sister Hillary and I are. I should introduce you." His eyes scanned the room. Jessi felt a pinch in her stomach. She knew she wouldn't be able to remember everybody. "She's the tall blond at the snack table with the little boy." Jessi's eyes followed his. "Remind me later and I will introduce you." He pointed to Joe. "Joe and I kind of handle membership, Hillary handles the paperwork, and we have another gentleman named Sam who handles operations, making sure equipment is working properly and stuff. Joe's brother Kaleb also helps out when he isn't in school or in

Fayetteville or flying off to God knows where."

"He's the exotic dancer over there?" Her eyes tipped up to Kaleb who was still gyrating although no longer on the table. Cody smirked and nodded.

Mitch piped up. "Cody's been gone on diaper duty."

"Yeah. I thought Hallie's diapers were nasty. Brant warned me about what newborn diapers were like, and he wasn't lying. I have a weak gag reflex and I've had to make a run to the bathroom a few times. Oh, and I've gotten christened twice now."

"Welcome to fatherhood."

"I was there for one of them." Joe raised his hand and chuckled.

Mitch leaned into Jessi and pointed to Joe. "Joe is also a carpenter. He has done a few remodeling projects for me."

Joe smiled. His bright white teeth against his tan skin made his face light up. He winked at Jessi. "Remind me to tell you the story about his little girl's room."

Mitch rolled his eyes. "Don't remind me."

Jessi smiled at him.

"Georgia had to give Joe step by step directions."

"Oh. Of course." Jessi looked up at Joe who was nodding. The puppy jerked in her arm then stretched and yawned. She stared at the little fur ball in her arms then her eyes slowly lifted to Mitch. "I'm already in love." She raised up on her toes and gave Mitch a kiss on the cheek.

"When I called April about helping me put this together, she asked me what I was getting you. I had already been thinking about getting you a puppy and when I told her the story of Layla, she told me they had eight cocker spaniel puppies surrendered at Bruins

Veterinary hospital where she works. I stopped in yesterday and when I walked up to their pen, she walked up to me and wagged her tail."

"I'm still blown away by all of this." Mitch escorted her out on the patio that overlooked the lake. A large firepit with a wide ledge around the top was lit. Several wicker backed chairs surrounded it. Tendrils of flames danced with the breeze. Mitch set his beer on the ledge and sat down. Jessi followed.

Brandon and Georgia barreled out of the doors followed by a sandy headed little boy being dragged by Georgia.

"Miss Jessi, this is Joel. He's my friend."

The little boy lifted his hand in a bashful wave.

"Hi, Joel. How are you?"

"I'm good," came his response in a cute husky voice. The tall blond, Cody had pointed to earlier, appeared.

"Joel. Why didn't you come when I called you?"

"I was with Georgia."

Her eyes connected with Jessi and Mitch. "I am so sorry."

"No need to apologize," Jessi replied.

Mitch caught Hillary's attention. "Hillary, this is Jessi Maddox."

Hillary shoved her hair behind her ear and held out her hand. "It's nice to meet you."

"You too," Jessi shot back. Her eyes went back to Joel. "He is adorable."

Hillary rolled her eyes, "And he knows it," she said as her eyes went back to Joel. "Joel, we are going to have to go. Daddy called and said the washing machine exploded and Hallie won't stop trying to ride the dog."

Jessi's eyes widened. "Oh no."

"Oh, trust me, it's par for the course with our family. Since he has our two-year-old, he hasn't been able to do much to fix the machine."

Mitch sat up. "If it would help, he can stay and play with Georgia. We can drop him by later."

"Are you sure?"

"Yeah. I'll get your address from Cody and drop him off later."

"Thank you." Her eyes zeroed in on Joel. "Be good." She leaned down and dropped a quick kiss on Joel's head and darted back through the door.

Mitch's gaze returned to Jessi. "Listen. I need—" Mitch started but was interrupted.

"We need the birthday girl to come cut her cake." April hollered from the doorway.

Jessi jumped up with the puppy still sound asleep. She passed through the open doorway in time to see Anson rolling out a three-tiered cream-colored cake draped with different colors of grapes. Over the top and sides was burgundy icing, which gave the appearance of red wine spilled on it. On the very top was a wine glass filled with red wine with lit sparkling candles surrounding it. A bottle of wine sat at the bottom. She glanced at it and a smile spread across her face as her eyes landed on Anson.

"You got my Salishan Blend." Anson shrugged his shoulders with a slight grin. His whole growly demeanor was obviously a ruse.

April pointed to Cody who started singing Happy Birthday and everyone joined in. Jessi stepped up to the cake and handed off the puppy to Mitch. It whimpered and yawned and started chewing on his finger.

"Watch out, Dad, those teeth are sharp," Brandon said as he walked up beside him.

Jessi picked up the knife then paused before making the first cut. "I want to thank everyone for coming out. Especially since most of you have no idea who I am." There was a collective laugh and she paused letting the laughter soak in. "I truly hope that we all can become close friends. And I especially want to thank Mitch for throwing this party for me, and for April, the party guru, and everyone involved, for helping him make it happen on such short notice." April took a bow.

Mitch smiled at Jessi then grimaced and hissed when the puppy took a bite out of his finger. "Ow."

"Told you her teeth were sharp."

"You aren't kidding." He stared down at his finger. "She drew blood." The puppy growled then yipped. "Yeah, no treats for you tonight young lady."

Another collective laugh filled the room and Jessi dragged the knife through the cake. April and Anson dished it up, handing the first piece to Jessi, and then poured her a glass of wine. Mitch handed the puppy off to Brandon, took his cake and wine, tipped his head back out to the patio, and started to walk away. Jessi turned to follow him and nearly plowed right into the back of the guy in the cowboy hat. *Who was he again?* He wasn't moving, just standing stock still. She sidestepped to go around him and noticed April's friend Kaysi coming in from the patio. She needed to tell her thank you also for helping. The cowboy abruptly did a one eighty and Jessi had to juggle her plate and glass not to drop them. "I'm sorry," he said trying to help her steady her plate.

"You're fine." The familiarity hit her again. "Where have I seen you before?" His uncomfortable expression told her he had no idea what she was talking about. "Have you been out to Purple Skies Winery? Or Lake Village Restaurant recently?"

"No. I haven't."

She continued to stare at him, and he kept glancing off at something or someone nearby. Then it hit her. "You were at the police station."

A deep line formed in the middle of his brow, then his eyes widened. "Oh. Yeah. I remember." He paused. "I thought your name was Margaret, or Melissa or something."

"Michelle."

He nodded.

"Long story. I was having to use an alias for a while."

"You weren't involved with that case with his daughter—"

She reluctantly nodded worried that her ties to Dante might come back to haunt her in the long run. "Unfortunately. That's all been handled though."

"So, your name is Jessi?"

"Yes." She squinted one eye, thinking. "And you're Ben. Right?"

"Yeah." He quickly pointed. "I'm the redhead over there's brother."

She followed his finger with her eyes. "Jenna?"

"Yeah."

"Great. Well, it's going to take me a little bit to get everyone sorted out but it's good to see you again. I better…" her words died when he nodded and started walking away. Through the open doors of the patio, she saw Mitch talking to Brandon, Georgia and Joel, and a smile spread across her face. He was such a good daddy.

She strolled out onto the patio, set her plate down, and motioned to Brandon to hand her the puppy. He handed her off then eyed his dad. Mitch nodded and Brandon took his sister's hand and all three kids disappeared through the doors. Jessi watched as they left, confused at the silent conversation Mitch had with Brandon. Mitch sat down and put his plate on the hearth circling the fire, then scooted Jessi's chair to face him. The solemn look that suddenly crossed his face made Jessi's breath escape. She sat down slowly.

"I know this probably isn't the best time to do this, but we need to talk."

Jessi's heart raced. The look on his face was the no nonsense cop, and all she could think about was the dinner gone wrong. Did he throw her a party just to soften the blow of breaking up with her? "Okay," she said quietly.

"I had a lot of time to think on the plane, and I need to apologize to you in a big way."

"No. It's not—"

He shook his head cutting her off. "Please. Just listen. Let me get this out." She could tell he was nervous, so she reached out and wrapped her fingers around his hand. He took a deep breath and let it out. "I was wrong for jumping on you about your feelings for Dante. It was hard for me to see that you still cared for him after what he did to you for several reasons. One being my mom went through the same thing with my dad when I was a kid."

Jessi swallowed, feeling a lump form in her throat as Mitch's expression filled with sadness.

"She took him back after the first time. And the second time was worse. But luckily, Dalton is a tight knit community with good people. Always has been. My mom's boss gave us a place to stay. My dad went to jail."

"Oh my God, Mitch. Why didn't you tell me?"

"Honestly, I haven't really told anyone. Kind of pushed it out of my mind until you came into my life. But your story was so similar to mine. My dad wasn't a bad guy when he was sober. It's just he had a hard time being sober. I think he was fighting a lot of demons and unfortunately, he took it out on my mom."

"Did he ever hurt you?"

"No. My brother and I were still pretty young when my mom took us and left. When my dad got out of jail, he packed up his stuff and left town. I didn't see him for quite a few years. Had no idea where he was. By the time he contacted me, the drinking had just about killed him. He's been gone for a while."

"And your mom?"

"Oh, she's doing great. Found her a little house on the lake and she's living her best life."

"I'm so sorry, Mitch. I didn't know."

"I know you didn't and I'm not telling you this to make you feel sorry for me. I'm telling you, so you understand why I was so upset. I left that night so angry and frustrated and confused at you and at myself. And as I replayed everything, I realized you were right about so much. Lorrie did hurt me, and I forgave her. And I still care about her." His hand grasped her thigh. "When my dad called me after all those years, yes, I was angry at what he did to my mom, but when I saw him, I saw a completely broken man and even though I hated what he did, there was something deep inside of me that still cared about him. So, I apologize for jumping on you about caring about Dante. Will you forgive me?"

The weakness of his voice devastated her. She could tell he was fighting the memories but whether it was with her or his childhood she wasn't sure. "Mitch. Of course, I forgive you. I had—"

"There was something else that made me upset though."

"What was it then?" she asked, confused.

Mitch leaned in and took her free hand in his again, rubbing the back of it with his thumb. "Jessi, you are an amazing person, and so unique, and the thought of Dante not appreciating you and seeing your value destroyed me when I thought about you possibly choosing him and leaving Dalton. But I want you to be happy, and so I have to be honest with you. Dante was the catalyst of one of the largest successful raids in Philadelphia in a long time. The information that he provided to the feds was key to their success. Your boy did exactly what he said he'd do."

"He did?"

"Yes. It still doesn't excuse what he did, but I'm sure it's going to go a long way when he's sentenced." Mitch looked away and let out a heavy breath. "I know you probably think I'm crazy and I kind of am, because you make me crazy. You make me want to take a chance at love again." His gaze dropped to their connected hands, and he quieted. Jessi wasn't sure her heart was going to survive his silence. This was one time she had no idea where the conversation was headed. "I'm crazy about you, Jessi... and I'm scared to death you are going to choose him over me and leave. They even offered me a job in Philly. And I thought about it. And, although I'm not sure the city life is a good fit for me, I might consider it if it meant I'd have you."

Nope. Heart is definitely about to explode.

"You don't know what you do to me. For the longest time, I felt like I was holding my breath, keeping everything contained, controlled. And then you came along, and I feel like I can finally breathe again. It's like Georgia said. You make me smile."

Jessi stared into Mitch's eyes, and it felt like she could see right into his soul. He was laying everything out there for her, and his eyes searched hers for her answer, but she couldn't get her mind to form words.

"I know you have only been here for a few weeks, and we haven't known each other very long. And I know you have been with Dante for a few years, and Philadelphia does offer a lot more than Dalton. I don't want to lose you Jessi, but if that's what will make you happy I—"

And there it was. The explosion. She no longer could breathe. She could feel the sobs at the back of her throat as she forced out the words. "I love you."

"I won't stand…wait. What?"

Jessi leaned forward, her hand moved to Mitch's neck, and she pulled his lips to hers, planting a soft kiss on his mouth. Backing away slightly, and tipping her eyes to his, she said, "I'm in love with you."

Mitch's eyes rounded and the corner of his mouth lifted. He tucked a piece of her hair behind her ear before leaning in for another kiss. It was slow and soft and filled with so many unspoken emotions. Tears streamed down her cheeks, but she didn't care.

"I did a lot of thinking too," she continued. "Even if things didn't blow up with Dante, it's very clear to me now that we would have never made it. We weren't committed. We lived our lives separately, together.

Maybe we cared for each other, but I don't think we were in love with each other. Love is a commitment. A partnership. You do things together. Make decisions together, and even though we lived together, it was never *our* home. We always had our separate lives."

Jessi noticed a glimmer in Mitch's eyes. "You asked me not too long ago, what was my plan when I left Philly. What did I want to happen? And in all honesty, I didn't really know what I wanted. I was scared. All I knew was I had a job and a roof over my head. That was it. Then I met you and you blew me away. You made me feel welcome and included and made my new place feel like a home. And you made me feel safe for the first time since that night. And you made me laugh again when I didn't know I could. You made me realize, that's what I wanted. I wanted you."

A smile spread across Mitch's face. "Thank God, because from the first time I saw you screaming at me to move my shit in the grocery store parking lot, I knew I wanted you to be mine."

Jessi winced. "Seriously? That wasn't one of my finest moments."

Mitch gave her a bashful smile and nodded, then continued. "It's something I've done all my life. I know when something is supposed to be mine. I tried to come up with every excuse in the book of why I couldn't have you, but every time I saw you those excuses became less and less until the only one left was whether you wanted me. I knew I had to let you decide, but I thought the puppy and the party might earn me some brownie points. Or, at least maybe some more brownies!"

Jessi snickered at the comment. "We'll see about that."

Mitch pulled her up and dug his fingers in her hair. "I love you, Jessi. Please, say you'll stay."

I love you too, Mitch—," her eyes spied Brandon and Georgia at the doors to the patio, "—and your kids. And I love this town. I can't think of any other place that feels more like home."

A word about the author…

DeDe Ramey is a Texas girl transplanted in the heart of Oklahoma. Her vivid imagination and love for people watching gave her a passion to write romance novels filled with swoon worthy heroes, smart, sassy heroines, unexpected nail-biting suspense and a good helping of steamy, heart melting romance.

She grew up in the beautiful historic town of Georgetown Texas. Her crazy life experiences with family and friends helped develop her rich colorful imagination.

She is mom to two grown kids and Nina to one grandson.

When she is not reading or writing she enjoys going to concerts, exploring the national forests and parks, or searching for adventures in new cities with her husband Keith, her very own devastatingly handsome hero of almost 40 years.